"You must ju⸻⸻⸻" Gemma said.

"Callous? No, but ⸻⸻⸻ in responded. "Patient with your nephews. Generous with your family. Defiant with me. But not callous."

"'Tis no excuse, but when I did not receive the expected proposal of marriage, I saw few options for my future. I could become a governess or wed. But I choose to stay with my nephews because they need me and I…need them."

Would Tavin make the same choice? He'd left home, but then again, there was no one there for him to love. Or who loved him. "I see."

"So I made a decision." Her lashes fluttered against her pale cheeks.

Tavin's gaze fixed on her.

"I chose to squeeze every moment of pleasure out of the Season as I could. No matter what, because this was my sole chance to experience adventure. Fun. I suppose that I pushed away any nagging of conscience, as if later, had I inconvenienced anyone, I could ask for forgiveness."

He resumed pacing over the gravel. Oh, if forgiveness were that simple. But whatever Gemma had done that needed clemency could not compare to *his* blotted past.

Susanne Dietze began writing love stories in high school, casting her friends in the starring roles. Today, she's blessed to be the author of over half a dozen historical romances. Married to a pastor and the mom of two, Susanne loves fancy-schmancy tea parties, cozy socks, and curling up on the couch with a costume drama and a plate of nachos. You can find her online at www.susannedietze.com.

Books by Susanne Dietze

Love Inspired Historical

The Reluctant Guardian

SUSANNE DIETZE

The Reluctant Guardian

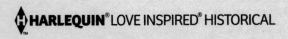

HARLEQUIN® LOVE INSPIRED® HISTORICAL

If you purchased this book without a cover you should be aware
that this book is stolen property. It was reported as "unsold and
destroyed" to the publisher, and neither the author nor the
publisher has received any payment for this "stripped book."

 LOVE INSPIRED BOOKS

Recycling programs
for this product may
not exist in your area.

ISBN-13: 978-0-373-42513-6

The Reluctant Guardian

Copyright © 2017 by Susanne Dietze

All rights reserved. Except for use in any review, the reproduction
or utilization of this work in whole or in part in any form by any
electronic, mechanical or other means, now known or hereinafter
invented, including xerography, photocopying and recording, or in
any information storage or retrieval system, is forbidden without
the written permission of the editorial office, Love Inspired Books,
195 Broadway, New York, NY 10007 U.S.A.

This is a work of fiction. Names, characters, places and incidents are
either the product of the author's imagination or are used fictitiously, and
any resemblance to actual persons, living or dead, business establishments,
events or locales is entirely coincidental.

This edition published by arrangement with Love Inspired Books.

® and TM are trademarks of Love Inspired Books, used under license.
Trademarks indicated with ® are registered in the United States Patent
and Trademark Office, the Canadian Intellectual Property Office and in
other countries.

www.Harlequin.com

Printed in U.S.A.

So if the Son sets you free, you will be free indeed.
—*John* 8:36

For Karl, my champion,
who encouraged my writing, endured historical
fashion exhibits, listened while I gabbed about my
imaginary friends and always believed this day
would come. I'm glad you're mine, honey.

Chapter One

Hampshire, England, 1817

With a furtive pat, Gemma Lyfeld blotted her nerve-damp palms on her white muslin gown. It would not do to receive a marriage proposal with moist hands. Or silly apprehensions. Besides, it was just Hugh. Her neighbor.

And she'd been expecting this moment since she was a child. Today, at long last, he'd requested privacy with her in the drawing room.

She shifted closer on the sofa to the Honorable Hugh Beauchamp and placed her clammy hands in his. It had been years since she'd sat this close to him, eye level with the crescent-moon scar on his chin he'd received when they were eight.

"I do." She bit her lip at once. *Too soon.*

Hugh's pale lashes blinked over wide blue eyes. "Pardon?"

"I do…want to hear what you have to say." She squeezed encouragement into his fingers. "No need to be shy."

He pulled back one hand and tapped her nose with a long finger. "Never with you, Gem, not after all our adventures. And you're about to have another one. A Season in London, at last."

Gemma glanced at the mantel clock. Her sister-in-law, Cristobel, had allotted them ten minutes, scarcely enough time to remark on the drizzle, much less accomplish a satisfying marriage proposal. But if conversation set a nervous Hugh at ease, some trivial talk was worth the end result.

"*Long* last. Cristobel couldn't deny me my come-out this year. I'm practically on the shelf."

"Not for long." He smiled.

A shiver of anticipation skittered up her arms like the first breeze of spring, chill but pleasant, expectant of blossoms and bees.

"Don't say you're scared, Gem."

Of what? Marriage or making her debut in society at the advanced age of four-and-twenty?

"No. I am ready." For both. Even though her insides quivered like a Christmas pudding.

"You'll love London. So many things to see and do."

"Will you introduce me to your favorite places?"

"It is my friends to whom I cannot wait to introduce you. They'll adore you, and you, them. One in particular, with whom I've grown quite close—"

The sound of boot steps in the hall swept under the door, silencing Hugh and pulling his gaze to the closed portal behind her. Gemma swung her head to stare at the oak expanse. Ten minutes could not have yet passed, but with Gemma's sister, Amy, and her husband, Lord Wyling, here to fetch her to London, the house was full of people— children and servants and Wyling's vexing associate, Mr. Knox. Any one of them could interrupt.

When the door failed to open, she turned back in time to see Hugh take a painful-looking swallow.

"Speaking of friendship." His gaze met hers. "Sometimes a gentleman has…moments in life. Do you understand my meaning?"

She nodded. *I do, I do.*

"You and I have been friends for an age."

"Forever." Her mouth was dry as vellum, but their joined hands were slick with sweat.

"There has l-long been an informal understanding between our families that you and I would w-wed. Nothing binding, but expected." He shifted. Did one knee lower a smidgen off the edge of the sofa? Gemma's breath hitched.

"Gem."

"Hugh." Her voice was just above a whisper.

"The time has come to—"

With the click of the latch and a *swoosh*, the drawing room door swung wide on its hinge. Hugh dropped her hands like they were used handkerchiefs and popped to his feet.

"Oh." With a single syllable, the baritone voice of Tavin Knox conveyed surprise and, to Gemma's frustration, amusement.

She didn't need to turn to know their houseguest grinned. No doubt that left brow of his arched, too. He had seemed unable to contain either response whenever he'd seen her with Hugh this past week.

"May I assist you, Mr. Knox?"

"I was looking for your brother. Or Lord Wyling. But I, er, perceive they're not in the room."

She spun to face him. Sure enough, Mr. Knox's eyebrow curved. So did the corners of his lips, prompting a dimple to wink in the curve of his cheek. Other ladies no doubt found the expression on his fine-looking face charming, but she was practically betrothed and had no business noticing such things, no matter how appealing.

Besides, he was no one to her. A friend of Wyling's who'd tagged along with him to Hampshire. Something about having business, the nature of which he'd not shared with the ladies. No matter how subtly she had tried to ask.

"I cannot say where Lord Wyling might be found, but my brother is out shooting. You are welcome to borrow a horse and set out after him." Preferably deep into the New Forest, taking his dimple with him.

He grinned. "Thank you. Pardon my interruption—"

"Nothing to interrupt." Hugh's serious expression from thirty seconds past vanished, replaced by his affable smile.

Gemma hopped up. "Hugh, we can walk in the garden if you—"

"Too wet for a stroll, Gem. I must be off, at any rate. I leave for London in the morning. Do stay, Mr. Knox, and keep my old neighbor company."

Old neighbor?

Mr. Knox's grin slipped.

"I'll call on you after you're settled at Amy and Wyling's."

Gemma licked her still-dry lips. For six years, she'd been confined by Cristobel in a cage of obligation. Hugh was the key to her escape. A sigh escaped her lips. Could she endure a fortnight more?

She forced a smile. "Until then, Hugh."

He bowed. "Safe travels, Gem. Mr. Knox, I hope your business is tempered with pleasure while you visit Verity House."

Mr. Knox stepped into the room so Hugh could exit. "My stay has been most productive. And entertaining, I assure you."

Entertaining, indeed. Gemma's lips compressed over clenched teeth as Hugh took his leave, her hopes trailing his pea-green coattails. And she had Mr. Knox to thank.

He couldn't help his poor timing. But she could fault him his horrid manners.

She skewered him with a scowl. "I am delighted my private affairs offered you a moment of diversion." She twirled to leave.

"Peace, Miss Lyfeld." His fingers alit just above her elbow, searing her bare skin with heat. "My words did not come out as I wished. I am not known for making good company, I'm afraid. Forgive me?"

He stood as close as Hugh had, near enough that she could smell leather and horse clinging to his black coat—and something else. The scent provoked long-forgotten memories of freedom, sending her pulse fluttering. No cologne or soap. He smelled like the forest. Wood and water.

Words didn't form, so she nodded and pulled from his light grasp, moving to the wide window, which afforded the best view in the house. Beyond the drive, where Hugh's carriage toddled away, acres of heath and copses of trees led to the New Forest. Knolls of green, including their local landmark, Verity Hill, added texture to the prospect. But Gemma didn't find the scenery picturesque today.

"Such gloom on your features. Am I truly forgiven?"

Since they had first met last week, he'd yet to look at her with such intensity, as if he truly cared what she thought. But of course he did not. What would he know—or care—of her plight, whose lone option was to go from one man's household to another, provided her sister-in-law let her go and her intended groom worked up the courage to ask?

"I cannot hold a grudge when God forgave me, can I?"

His head tipped, sending a curl of rich brown hair onto his forehead like an upside-down question mark. "I see."

Did he? No matter. "Pardon me, but I am needed elsewhere."

With a nod, she left him leaning against the mantelpiece. She ascended the main stair with unladylike haste, entering Cristobel's salon in a rush.

Two ladies, one fair-haired, the other with curls the light brown color of Gemma's, perched on Chippendale chairs, a tea tray set on the table before them. At Gemma's entrance, her sister, Amy, rose, curls bobbing against her cheeks. "Well?"

Their sister-in-law, Cristobel, grimaced. "Eight minutes, Gemma. And?"

"He did not propose." The words tasted like bile.

Amy reached for Gemma's hands. "I cannot believe it of Hugh."

"I can." Cristobel shrugged, making her blond hair bounce against her shoulders. "He's too much a coward to admit he wants out after all these years."

Gemma pulled away from her sister. "These years he's been considerate, waiting while I was in mourning for Mama and Papa. And assisting you, Cristobel." Through her nephews' infancies, Gemma had nursed them in health and illness. It had taken Amy's strong reminder of propriety— and her promise to cover all expenses—to persuade Peter and Cristobel to allow Gemma a come-out.

"Considerate? He's left you dangling for ages. For all your talk about his decency, that dandy has had *years* to come up to scratch. Instead, he's left you unavailable to other gentlemen while your youth crumbles away."

"A betrothal was discussed." Amy regained her seat.

"Between parents who were too foolish to do more than daydream about a match." Cristobel twirled a strand of hair around her finger. "Now the notion is long dead, like them."

Gemma's fingers clenched. "Six years may have passed, but there is nothing *long dead* in our grief."

"Of course not." Cristobel's eyes widened. "The way

your mama and papa perished—well, a tragedy like that would haunt the person responsible forever, not that anyone believes it's your fault, Gemma dear."

"Because it *wasn't* my fault, Cristobel." Gemma prayed her words were true. She turned to the door. "I require air."

"Take the boys with you. They need exercise," Cristobel called after her.

Amy followed her to her chamber. "You were not the cause of the fire at the dower house, Gemma. Everyone knows it."

Gemma yanked a bonnet and her cherry wool cloak from the wardrobe. She'd heard it countless times, but it never helped. "Thank you."

"Do you wish me to accompany you?"

"I prefer solitude. I know Cristobel asked me to take the boys, but they nap at this time."

"If Cristobel ever visited the nursery, she'd know that." Amy's hand rested on Gemma's arm, warming the same spot Mr. Knox had touched. Her eyes held a similar intensity, too. "You're more of a mother to Petey and Eddie than she is."

"You mustn't say that. But I shall miss the boys dreadfully while I'm in London." She pushed away the sad thought. "Cristobel is wrong, you know. Hugh will propose, and when we wed, I will live next door and I shall see the boys every day."

Amy's brows scrunched. "But do you *wish* to marry Hugh? I know it's what our fathers wanted, but do you love him?"

Gemma tied the bonnet's pink ribbon under her chin with a fierce tug. "There is friendship between us. How many women can claim such blessing?"

"Few. But I want love for you, too."

"Doing my duty and caring for our nephews—that is all I hope for."

"Perhaps God has more for you. Trust Him, Gemma."

Hot tears pricked the back of her eyes. She had set aside any such dreams long ago. Still, she nodded at her sister before she hurried outside.

She strode down the drive in seconds, at such a pace. Angry as she was with Cristobel, it was Mr. Knox whose face filled her thoughts. She swiped her cheeks with the back of her hand. Hugh's retreat was not Mr. Knox's fault. But, oh, how glad she was Tavin Knox and his amused, arched brow would not be in London to watch her wait for Hugh's proposal.

She stomped through sodden grass toward the copse of trees skirting the base of Verity Hill like an emerald-ribboned hem. Above the trees, the rise loomed green and steep before her. She hadn't stood at the top in a long time, but reaching its crest, perched higher than her surroundings, would feel defiant. Victorious, somehow.

Gemma would conquer Verity Hill, since she appeared incapable of surmounting any other obstacle in her life.

At the sound of movement behind him, Tavin lowered the spyglass and slid it under his coat. Would he never get the drawing room to himself?

Tavin spun and then let out a breath. It was only Wyling. He passed his friend the spyglass. "Aye, since the whole purpose for coming here was to stand at this window today."

"Am I supposed to see anything?"

"Soon. They're coming from the far side of the hill. Once they come 'round this side and enter the trees, I'll know it's safe for me to climb to the summit."

"Where your informant will have left you something of

an incriminating nature?" Wyling confirmed. "One would think a path called Smuggler's Road would be better concealed. Same with those who make use of it. Are they not called Gentlemen of the Night for a reason?"

"Usually." A grin pulled at Tavin's cheeks. "But here in the New Forest, smuggling occurs regardless of the hour. And you can see how the Smuggler's Road allows visibility for miles. Should a revenue agent be about on his rounds, the free traders can hide in the dense foliage of the forest."

"But that won't happen today. You led the revenue man on a false trail, correct?"

"For his own protection. He's north, leaving Smuggler's Road clear for the party hauling contraband from Christchurch." He hoped. "It's imperative this plan to learn more about how the smuggling ring works."

Nothing had worked for so long. What it would feel like to get the upper hand for a change? To at last put a stop to the smuggler known as The Sovereign—a murderer who thought so highly of himself that he called himself after the king.

While Wyling used the spyglass, Tavin's thoughts returned to Miss Lyfeld, her light brown hair framing her sad blue eyes when she spoke of being forgiven. Did she question God's forgiveness like he did? She had no reason to. Of course she was absolved. Her sins were no doubt the sort God could easily pardon. She was no thief, no liar. No murderer.

Something he could never claim.

"I upset Miss Lyfeld. Again." He fumbled with the cuff of his black coat.

"Did Gemma wish to know your whereabouts yesterday? I gather you didn't tell her."

"No, I walked in on her and Beauchamp."

"Did he do it, then?" Wyling lowered the spyglass, his expression eager. "Are they betrothed?"

"He looked like he was being strangled by his cravat, so it's possible he was about to ask. But they hadn't finished their conversation when Beauchamp left."

"You didn't leave them to it?" Wyling's brows lowered.

"I made an attempt." The words sounded feeble.

"You should have tried harder. She's waited years for Hugh to gather his courage."

"Don't give me that look. I thought he was just making moon eyes."

"Cristobel would not have allotted privacy for mere moon eyes."

"I don't have sisters. How should I know?"

"Because you're a gentleman. *Alone* means betrothal."

Tavin shook his head. Had he known that? Perhaps. But he was no gentleman anymore. These past years, he had stuffed his upbringing away with the natural efficiency he demonstrated when tucking a trouser cuff inside a boot.

Nonetheless, the trouser cuff was still there, even though it was not visible. Why had he forgotten everything he'd been taught?

"I am incapable of interacting with decent people anymore."

"That's not true." His friend clapped his shoulder. "But you have been among a different sort for too long. I hope it will not be much longer before you can stop this sort of thing."

Tavin took the spyglass, aiming it toward the New Forest, as thick with thieves as trees. Weary as he was with his life, he had a debt to repay. Perhaps if he succeeded today, he'd be able to cease being an undercover agent for the Board of Customs. He could serve King and country in another—less dangerous—capacity.

He scanned the view. No activity on the hilltop. "I'll apologize to her again later, but right now—"

He thrust the spyglass at Wyling. "This makes no sense."

"What?"

Tavin pointed to a red-cloaked figure emerging from the trees, ascending the hill at a smart pace.

"It's Gemma. Out for a walk."

"Wearing a red cloak." His plan unraveled like a skein of yarn at the paws of a cat. "I've got to stop her before—"

"What?" Wyling gripped his arm, wasting precious seconds.

"She's signaling the smugglers, whether she knows it or not. There's a woman in these parts. She mounts that hill to signal her brethren to turn back if a government man is nearby. By night she burns a lamp. By day, she dons a red cloak. Like the one Gemma is wearing."

"And the smugglers will see her." Wyling's ruddy complexion paled.

"Aye. And if they turn 'round, they'll smack into the revenue agent. If they stay the course, they'll encounter Miss Lyfeld and may not treat her kindly."

Tavin spun from Wyling's grasp, bounding downstairs and out the front door. The spongy earth sucked at his boots as he ran across the park toward the hill.

You have no reason to answer me, God, but she's an innocent. And this job is too essential to fail.

His breath came in stabbing gasps. His side ached as if he'd been dealt a blow to the ribs. But nothing would slow him. He'd worked months for this day—planned and prayed and waited.

This was justice for his sins, he supposed. He'd ruined Miss Lyfeld's marriage proposal. And now she was about to ruin his chance to end this case once and for all.

Chapter Two

"My life is not ruined." Gemma's breath grew labored as she ascended the gentle slope. "Cristobel is wrong. Hugh is too honorable to go against our families' wishes."

Saying the words aloud helped her believe them. If only Mr. Knox had not scared Hugh away... No. It was not worth playing the if-only game. Once started, she would never quit. Her list of losses was lengthy enough to fill pages of foolscap. And writing such a pitiful list accomplished nothing.

Unlike a list of blessings. She had much to be grateful for, regardless of her circumstances. All around her, the glossy green leaves of bluebells carpeted the landscape. Gusts of wind stirred yellow-flowered gorse and rustled through the budding oaks, carrying the clean fragrance of rain.

Thank Thee, Lord.

How pleasant it would be to reach the summit of the little hill and enjoy the view. Gemma marched on. Then stopped.

She was no longer alone.

A plain-dressed man hiked toward her, his gaze on the trees. Skirting the hill behind him, a loaded cart trudged across the chalky Smuggler's Road. A small party of musket-bearing men trailed in its wake, followed by a lone rider on an ink-dark horse.

Free traders.

Not that ladies spoke of such things in polite company. Nevertheless, the wealthy and poor alike avoided paying taxes and Customs duties on their tea or laces by purchasing smuggled goods, illegal though it might be. Who knew how much revenue the government had lost to smugglers? Peter and Wyling obeyed the law and shunned smuggled goods, of course. But as a child, Gemma hadn't understood the illegal nature of the smugglers' work. Years ago she and Hugh had followed Smuggler's Road, pretending they hauled exotic wares from Christchurch Harbor, with plans to sell their imaginary spoils from the sanctuary of a ditch under the trees.

It was one thing to play a criminal as a child. It was quite another to engage the illicit fellows. Gemma hastened back down her side of the hill. Perhaps she had gone unnoticed.

"Ho!" The yell dispelled the notion she had not been seen. She quickened her steps, rolling her ankle in the process and slowing her gait to a painful, awkward trot.

A hand gripped her shoulder and turned her about. He was young, this smuggler, with pocked cheeks, a slack jaw and protruding teeth. "'Oo are you?"

"No one who wants trouble."

"'Oo is it, Bill?" A shout called from above.

"Nobody, I think."

Then let go of my arm.

A shot boomed from the trees, echoing off the hill. The sound reverberated while the smugglers burst into activity. The inky horse galloped up the hill. Its rider wore a look of thunder to match the rumble of his horse's hooves.

"She's not *nobody*, you fool." He dismounted and yanked her from Bill. His free hand smacked her cheek, sending shock and pain through her jaw.

"She's a trap."

Gemma's vision sparked red. "I don't know what you mean. Unhand me."

Another shot cracked through the drizzle. "Hide before you're shot," the horseman ordered his fellows. Then he ripped her bonnet from her head. "You're too young for the Lady in Red. Too refined of speech to be a government girl. Whom do you serve?"

She wrestled against him. "I said *unhand me*."

"I'll not be generous because you are female, Jezebel. Whom do you serve?"

"No one—"

"Lies." He yanked her arm as if she were a cloth doll, pulling her toward his horse.

The world seemed to darken at the edges, but she fought against the sensation. She must stay alert. Memorize his features so she could describe him to the magistrate when she escaped.

Taller than Peter but shorter than Hugh. Brown hair, gray at the temples. Blue eyes. About forty years of age. And a fetter-strong grip she had to break.

She twisted into him. Her free hand grasped the fingers shackling her and jerked them back. Then she kicked.

Her boot found his knee. He let go and she ran.

Her rolled ankle protested each step, but she dared not slow. The sting of the smuggler's slap still prickled her cheek, and she didn't care to suffer more from his hands.

Dashing through a gap in the trees, she hurtled into the dark of the woods toward home. Perhaps if she screamed for help—

Fresh pain pressed her arm and tethered her to the spot.

A grip far tighter than the smuggler's captured her and spun her around. She prepared to kick.

Father, make my aim true.

Pain split Tavin's shin, but his Hessian boots did a fair job protecting him. He swept Miss Lyfeld's leg back with his and covered her mouth with his hand. "I'm here to help," he whispered. "But you must be quiet, or they will find us."

Her clear blue eyes narrowed when she recognized him. At her nod, his hand fell. He beckoned her deeper into the woods. "Let's go."

"What are you doing here?" Her tone was an accusation, as if this was his fault. Well, it was. In part. Still, she had no way of knowing that. Could she speak to him—even in a whisper—without sounding like a wasp about to sting?

"Later." He'd not noticed the welt blossoming across her cheek until now. Tavin's fingers itched to return the favor to the man responsible. "Are you hurt?"

"More furious than anything."

"I want to hear the details, but we must hurry."

"Aren't we safe now that we're in the trees?"

A shot cracked into the trunk of a nearby oak. Not as safe as she'd hoped.

He pulled her by the hand and ran. Dodged trees. She slid, and when he pulled her back to stand, she winced. "Did I hurt you?"

"No. My ankle twisted on the hilltop."

"I'll carry you." One arm swept around her shoulders. The other scooped behind her knees, but she stepped out of his hold.

"I won't slow us down."

His estimation of her raised a notch. "Come on, then."

Crack. Would they never stop shooting? Another crack,

as a bullet struck a tree. Then a third, hitting ground. Moldy leaves skittered up the hem of her cloak. *Of course.* He tugged her behind a thick oak and pulled on the cloak's fastener at her throat.

Her fingers fought his. "What you are doing?"

"The red draws his eye." He yanked the garment off and wadded it, inside out, into a ball. He stuffed it under his arm and gripped her hand again. To his surprise, she curled her fingers around his, pulling him to the right.

"My home is that way."

"Not yet." He jogged with her in tow for a short distance. Releasing her hand, he slid into a ditch, then lifted his arms. Before he could instruct her, she leaned into him. Her breath was hot against his cheek when he lowered her beside him. "Not much farther."

He'd spent the past few days scouting these woods, never imagining he'd be running from gunfire with Gemma. He pushed aside a clump of foliage and gestured for her to precede him through.

Smelling of decay and earth, the small clearing offered slight protection. "A moment's rest." He gestured to a fallen oak where she could sit while he thought.

"The Gypsy camp." She touched her ankle and winced. "Why did we not go straight home?"

"We cannot risk being followed." He walked the clearing's perimeter, straining to see movement through the trees. "You don't want them to know where you live and thereby learn your identity."

"But I meant them no harm."

"They may have believed that, until someone started firing a weapon."

"That was not you?"

"Do you see a musket?" He didn't even have a pistol.

"Then who shot at them?"

"It came from here in the trees. I'd fathom a guess I'm not the only person in Hampshire displeased with that particular group of smugglers."

"There are more?"

It was hard not to laugh. "Many. And it's a competitive field."

She pushed a damp curl from her cheek. Without her bonnet or cloak, she appeared vulnerable and young, but not as young as he'd first thought. Her cheeks had lost some of the fullness of girlhood. She may be about to embark on her come-out, but she was no chit fresh from the schoolroom. "This makes no sense."

It did to Tavin, but he'd not explain now.

A rustle. Tavin spun, his hand reaching behind his back for his knife—

Through a parting in the leaves, a dun-colored body sauntered several yards' distant. Tavin's shoulders relaxed.

"A pony." He could hear the smile in her tone. "They run wild in the forest."

"And it wants naught to do with us." Tavin watched the creature. Its ears twitched, but it didn't exhibit signs of alarm as it disappeared around a group of trees. That boded well for him, and Miss Lyfeld, too. He gestured for her to rise. "I've not heard a shot in a while. We'll take a roundabout way and return to the house."

"Where you will explain all of this to me?"

Her tone brooked no argument. Nor did the set of her jaw.

Better to change the subject than agree. "You said the man meant to take you with him. How did you break away?"

"I would not be a good aunt to two boys if I paid no mind to their tricks."

Despite himself, he laughed. His smile fell when he reached the far side of the clearing. The pond he'd planned to skirt had swollen from last night's torrent, blocking their path. "We could have walked around it yesterday."

"You don't mean we're going through it."

"I see no better option. We aren't visible, with the trees circling us. And I'm certain the pond isn't deep. Must I carry you?" He meant his words to be gallant, but they sounded frustrated. Of course. Everything he said came out wrong with Miss Lyfeld.

She squared her shoulders, shot him a glare and marched into the pond ahead of him.

Gemma might as well have trudged barefoot through snow. Spring-chilled water soaked her to the knees and flooded her kid boots, which found little purchase on the slimy stones underfoot. Not that she would complain. This was not the first time she'd crossed a pond.

"Take care with your steps," he warned, "but make haste."

"Make haste," she mimicked, muttering under her breath, "but don't slip—"

Faster than a blink, her twisted ankle rolled. Her foot slid out from under her.

Mr. Knox grasped her arm, pulling her upright. She expected to be chastised, but his eyes were soft and warm, like her morning chocolate.

Then he slipped, pulling her into the frigid water.

Gemma's hands and rear smacked the stony bottom. Her backside stung, but she waved off Mr. Knox's outstretched hand and stood on her own power. Shivering as the wind's chill fingers stroked her soaked garments, she hastened toward the edge of the pool, thoughts of a hot cup of tea and thick blanket urging her forward. At least her front side was dry.

He extended his hand. "May I—"

"No." She would do this.

Her wet gown tangled around her legs and she slipped again, this time landing on her elbows and belly. Frigid water drenched her bodice and lapped her chin as tendrils of slimy water plants tickled her neck.

Mr. Knox hauled her into his arms, as a lamb to its shepherd. With a sharp catch, her breath stuck in her throat, and her face warmed despite her soggy state. She'd never been this close to a gentleman before. She'd always imagined Hugh's future embrace, slow to unfold, tentative, with a proper distance between them.

Mr. Knox's arms felt nothing like her imaginings. He held her so close she could hear his heart thudding against her cheek, and his arms were solid and blessedly warm around her. Her insides flipped and rearranged themselves, and all she wanted was to turn her head toward his warmth and wish he could carry her all the way home—

What nonsense was this? She didn't even like Tavin Knox. Did she?

He didn't like her, either. But then he set her down on the bank, leaving her skin cold and her heart thumping, and his hand rose as if he'd touch her face.

"Hold still." His fingers brushed damp tendrils of hair from her chin. More intimacies she'd never permitted a gentleman. Her pulse pattered in her ears as he leaned closer.

"You've a leech on your neck."

All tender sentiment vanished. Her fingers flew to her collar. "Get it off."

"Patience." He glanced about, reminding Gemma of a dog sniffing the air for a fox. "Come into the trees."

He led her into the cover of the oaks. She lifted her chin and he set to work with a touch far gentler than she expected. His fingers pressed her skin, first under her ear, then lower, where her pulse throbbed in a frenetic beat. Gemma forced her breath into evenness, concentrating on the calming sounds of the forest—the rustle of wind in the trees, the *chit-chit* of a nuthatch.

Still, she couldn't ignore the fact that she hosted a leech. While wearing a sodden gown, allowing a man she didn't like—or maybe did—to touch her neck.

Or that she'd been slapped by a stranger. Who then had shot at her.

"There." Mr. Knox flicked a brown blur from his fingers. "Just think, you'd normally pay a physician for the privilege of losing your blood."

For a moment his eyes met hers, then another shot cleaved the quiet.

A smuggler, or the man on the inky horse? Mr. Knox had her by the hand again. "Let's go."

They hurried, twigs scratching her arms and snapping in her hair. The trees thinned and they hastened over the path and then the slick grass behind the house.

They hurried through a French door into the ground-floor library of Verity House. Amy and her husband, Lord Wyling, hurried toward her, their faces etched with fear.

Amy's arms reached out. "Darling. Let's get you dry, shall we?"

"Amy, there were smugglers on the hill and then—Mr. Knox, where are you going?"

He brushed past toward the hall door, Wyling at his heels. "My business cannot wait, madam."

"It must." She stomped after him. "You know why this happened, don't you? You aren't the least shocked. Who chased us and why?"

The eyes that had gazed on her with warmth earlier now stared, dull as coal dust. "I don't know him, but he would have interrogated you and perhaps killed you because you wore this." Her cloak was still under his arm, and he dropped the sodden mess onto a chair. "Burn it."

This was maddening. Mr. Knox, Wyling, Amy—not one of them showing the least amount of astonishment at today's extraordinary events. Concern, yes, but they knew much more than she did. He'd said they'd speak later. Well, that time was now. "I demand to know what's about, Mr. Knox. And I'm keeping my cloak."

"Burn it," he ordered, his hand on the doorknob. "Because that man will be thirsty to silence whoever wears it."

Chapter Three

After leaving Miss Lyfeld in the house, Tavin and Wyling dashed up Verity Hill in the mad hope Tavin's informant, Bill Simple, had dropped the promised clue before everything went wrong.

They'd found naught but Gemma's discarded bonnet and a separate green ribbon, the hue of a budding oak leaf, wedged half under a stone.

It might be debris, carried atop the hill by the wind.

Or mayhap it was the promised clue to help Tavin comprehend the Sovereign's plan. Nothing else made by human hands lay atop Verity Hill, although he and Wyling had spent more than an hour searching. No note, no sample of smuggled goods. Just a cheap ribbon lodged under a rock, its ends cut by a jagged edge.

Rubbish or clue?

What he wouldn't give for silence to ponder things. Or to still be outside, where it was cool. Instead, he was now incarcerated in the Lyfelds' overwarm drawing room, subjected to an incessant barrage of moans.

Eyes shut, Cristobel Lyfeld lounged on the sofa where Gemma—he'd given up trying to call her Miss Lyfeld in his head—had held hands with Hugh Beauchamp hours ago. "What will the neighbors say when they learn Gemma was mistaken for a smuggler? We will be pariahs."

"No one will know." Gemma perched beside her sister-in-law, blotting a compress on her brow as if she tended a feverish child.

This was ludicrous. His superior at the Custom House must be informed. In person. Tavin didn't dare entrust a message—even a coded one—to a servant. "I must return to London with all haste. If I might—"

"I am faint! Oh!" Cristobel groaned, no closer to fainting than he was, and everyone in the drawing room seemed to know it. Wyling looked out the window, Peter studied his boots and Amy handed Gemma a cup of tea with a resigned air. Gemma alone ministered to Cristobel, murmuring words of comfort as she lifted the cup to Cristobel's lips. She may have poor taste in suitors, but Gemma proved herself a capable, calm sort of female.

Pity she could not assist his work. Many of his hired men didn't possess her patience.

Since their return from the forest, she'd washed and changed into a fresh white gown. A gauze scarf about her neck hid any trace of the leech's bloodletting. "Mr. Knox, I am yet unsatisfied with your explanation."

Of course she was. "I have told you all I can."

She set down the teacup and hobbled toward him, favoring her untwisted foot. The scarf didn't quite cover the kiss of the leech, after all, for the crimson Y-shaped mark was bright against her skin.

"All you've told us is that you work for the government and in my red cloak I looked like a certain lady smuggler."

"Those are both true."

"But you aren't telling us everything. I insist to know what this is about, Mr. Knox. You owe me that."

"Gemma." Cristobel roused from the sofa. "Mr. Knox will think you a hoyden, speaking so boldly."

But Gemma was right. Tavin had told her almost nothing, and if he was in her place, he'd be vexed, too. He rubbed his temple.

"Smuggling activity has increased in the area of late, with fatalities, so the government sent an investigator. Mr. Thomason. My friend." Tavin swallowed past the sudden ache of pain brought by speaking Thomason's name. "He was tasked with disbanding the ring led by a man who calls himself the Sovereign. But Thomason was killed."

Not just killed. Left as a message, tied to a tree, a sovereign coin on his tongue. The Sovereign must think himself clever, leaving the coins as a signature.

Gemma's eyes were soft. "I am sorry for your loss."

Tavin nodded his thanks. "You can understand why it is so vital to me to stop the Sovereign, but he's never been identified or thwarted. Until today. By you."

Gemma flinched. Cristobel moaned.

Peter stood, and said, "When Wyling brought you to me, you said I'd be serving the Crown, allowing you to conduct your business here. You never said it would put my family in danger."

"The danger existed long before I arrived." Tavin stepped to the center of the room. "It met your sister on the bounds of your own property."

"You knew, Peter?" Gemma strode past him, hands fisting. "You all knew? Yet no one thought to tell me. Even you, Amy?"

"We couldn't, dear." Amy bit her lip.

Overhead, the patter of small but heavy footsteps drummed like a tambour, rat-a-tatting across the nursery floor. Masters Petey and Eddie had escaped their inept nursery maid yet again. The Lyfeld boys were more of a handful than a sack of cats.

A memory flashed through Tavin's brain, decades old, of him and his brother, Hamish, causing a ruckus by introducing a toad to their nurse's pocket—

A ragged gasp tore from Gemma's throat. Her gaze, fixed on the ceiling where the boys' footsteps echoed, were wide. "The children. What if they'd been outdoors? They might have been shot. Or taken."

Gemma cared more for the bairns thunking about above stairs than did their own mother. Tavin's throat ached. "They were not. They are safe."

She swiped her eyes. "If those children had been touched—"

"They weren't. All I expected today was the drop of a clue—"

"Something else *was* expected, too." Hugh Beauchamp's proposal. Her voice was clear and cutting as glass, slicing into a part of his conscience he didn't know felt pain anymore. "I would say that everything that's happened to me today is *your* fault, Mr. Knox."

The snapping of logs in the fireplace—a noise that always set Gemma's nerves to fraying—was the lone sound in the drawing room while everyone's surprised stares fixed on her.

Oh, dear. She shouldn't have spoken like that. Mama had taught her better. "Forgive me."

Mr. Knox's brow quirked. Was he amused or aggrieved? "It is I who requires forgiveness, yet again, Miss Lyfeld."

"I cannot blame you for today's…events." Her slapped jaw ached. Her ankle throbbed. Noise from Petey and Eddie's exuberant play pounded against the ceiling, assaulting her temples but providing a means of escape. "Excuse me while I see to those boisterous boys."

"You cannot go, Gemma." Cristobel clutched the arms of the settee, her fingers like talons gripping the painted silk.

"I cannot see to the boys?" Was there more she didn't know?

"You cannot go to London. Smugglers, weapons, the boys. I am in far too delicate a state to do without you now. You must forgo your come-out."

Gemma's next breath shook. She should have expected such news, for she'd heard it annually these past six years. The familiar pangs of conflict twisted within her. Every year when Cristobel postponed Gemma's come-out, Gemma experienced a sense of relief, for she would be able to tend to the boys.

But there was also a feeling of loss. She yearned to experience the world. To leave this house and Cristobel's domineering thumb.

Perhaps keeping her from London was God's protection. She might well grow greedy in the capital. Yearn to visit more of the world. She would meet handsome gentlemen and might like one too much. She was promised to Hugh, even though she did not love him. Staying home prevented her from falling into temptation.

The hair on her nape prickled, causing her to look up. Mr. Knox stared at her, his brow still quirked, as if he could read her thoughts.

Ridiculous. He knew nothing of her. She turned away. "Mayhap it is for the—"

"It is not." Amy stood. "Peter will be Baron Lindsay someday. It is expected that his sisters be presented at Court. Peter?"

"I cannot manage alone," Cristobel interjected. "Those boys are too much to be borne."

"We have a nursemaid," Peter murmured.

"I shall take the children with me." Gemma should have asked Amy and Wyling first. Her gaze begged them. "Will that ease your burden, Cristobel?"

Mr. Knox watched her, his face etched with—what?—disbelief. No matter. This didn't concern him a whit.

"We would welcome them." Amy laced her arm through her husband's. "Think how the boys would enjoy London."

Wyling, bless him, nodded. "We've plenty of room."

Stomping and shrieks continued to sound from above. Gemma itched to join them. And tell them to quiet down, of course. After she embraced them.

Cristobel sighed. "For the Season. Then you must return home."

Joy rose in Gemma's chest. Amy sent her a triumphant grin. Wyling smiled. Peter stared at the rug. Mr. Knox, however, glowered. "I suggest we leave tomorrow, then."

"We?"

His arms folded over his strong chest. "I will escort you. As long as you remain in Hampshire, you should not dismiss the danger of crossing paths again with the Sovereign."

London filled Tavin's eyes and ears and nose, familiar in its looming buildings, loud traffic and the sharp smell of the Thames. Home. Yet this didn't feel like a homecoming.

He envied Wyling, who dismounted his horse outside his town house on Berkeley Square and assisted the women and children from the coach. Two long days' travel had taken its toll on Tavin's body and his nerves. He would not be off his own bay, Raghnall, for a while yet, and their rest would be brief. Come dawn, he and Raghnall would be back on the road to Hampshire.

"But I wish to ride Mr. Knox's horse again." Petey Lyfeld's freckled features were burnished with eagerness as the six-year-old gazed up at Tavin. "Why did you name your horse Ronald?"

Tavin laughed. "Rao-nall." He spelled Raghnall's name as he patted the gelding's broad neck. "It is an old word that means *wisdom and power.*" A tiny reminder of the Gaelic tongue that had infused his childhood.

"A fitting name for a fine bit of blood and bone." Petey sounded like his father. "I should like to ride again with you, sir."

"Me, too." Eddie, Petey's ginger-haired four-year-old brother, pushed forward.

"Another day, perhaps." Gemma inserted herself between the boys. Despite the hours of wearying travel and the boys' precociousness, her voice was gentle. "We are at Uncle Wyling's."

"And I must take my leave."

The boys' faces fell. A pang of conscience speared Tavin's gut, but he wasn't obligated to give horsey rides to children. What had possessed him to take them up with him, in turns, after they'd left the posting inn today, anyway?

Ever the gracious hostess, Amy inclined her head toward the house. "Will you not at least partake of a cold collation?"

The boys jumped. "Please," Petey begged. "Say you will."

"I cannot." Tavin hoped his smile was apologetic enough to placate the children.

"I want to ride Raghnall more." Eddie stuck a finger in his mouth. Petey still hopped.

Despite his best intentions, Tavin puffed out an impatient sigh. With every passing minute, his investigation cooled like bread going stale on a windowsill.

Gemma's lips pinched. "Mr. Knox must be on his way. He is a busy gentleman."

"Like Papa." Eddie's face turned grave.

Tavin almost relented and let the boys take another short ride about the square on Raghnall's back. Almost.

"Say farewell." Gemma took her nephews' hands.

"Good day, sir." Petey bowed and nudged Eddie, who bent at the waist.

Tavin inclined his head. "Good day, gentlemen."

At Gemma's signal, the meek, sparrow-boned nursery maid took them inside the house, but Gemma paused at the stair. "Thank you for your kindness to the boys."

"They are sweet souls. Besides, everything *is* my fault." The words escaped before he thought them through. But when had he ever spoken correctly around her?

Her brows rose. "At last we view things in the same light. Good day, Mr. Knox."

Such a dismissal should sting; instead, he grinned as he turned Raghnall toward Billingsgate.

He could well imagine Gemma's delight at never having to see him again, but he didn't share her antipathy. He hadn't taken such delight in a sparring match in years.

Granted, he didn't engage in many verbal clashes. His exchanges were mostly physical. His crooked nose and aching left shoulder attested to that.

So did his work. The Custom House came into view, a place he knew too well. No matter the season, some things never changed: the whiteness of the ionic exterior, the clamor of men and waterbirds, and the smell of decay sweeping in from the Thames. This afternoon, a stiff wind swirled cool air under his coat, prompting him to hurry inside. He left Raghnall and a shiny coin with a lad.

Weak shafts of sunlight streamed through the great room's nine arched windows. Tavin hurried through, passing the "long room" and its crowds occupied with the tedious business of paying duties. After several turns, he entered a cramped antechamber, furnished with a simple desk and two chairs, testimony that there was little need to accommodate more than one guest—or anyone of significance—in this office. Yet few knew how vital this office's work was to the Crown.

A blond fellow in a vibrant blue waistcoat rose from behind the desk. With his fair looks and dandified clothing, he reminded Tavin of Gemma's beau, Beauchamp. His stomach clenched.

Perhaps he should have eaten some of Amy's cold collation, after all.

He inclined his head. "Good afternoon, Sommers."

"Mr. Knox. I hope you have *good* news."

"Garner's in a foul mood, I take it? He'll not appreciate my call, then."

"Pity. I'd hoped this day might improve." Sommers rapped on an interior door, entered and returned after a moment, nodding.

Tavin crossed the threshold and shut the door behind him. The closed-up smells of wax and ink harkened a strong sense of familiarity, as did the drab furnishings.

Horatio Garner straightened a sheaf of papers and glanced up. Flickering candlelight from an unadorned candelabrum intensified the shadows under his blue eyes and gave prominence to the gray streaks in his mouse-brown hair.

"You lack the air of a gentleman who bears glad tidings." No preamble, no greeting. Typical.

"Our antagonist's name and face remain a mystery. As yet." A grim determination settled into his bones. He'd solve this riddle if it took decades.

"Then why are you here?" Garner indicated a chair with a brusque gesture. His dark moods were notorious, but Tavin had never taken them to heart. According to snippets of conversation, Tavin understood that the custom agent had lost his family some time ago and had naught but work to keep him company at night.

The similarity between himself and his superior soured his stomach. *No. I have Thee, Lord.*

Tavin sat in the wobbly chair before the desk. "Four days past, the Sovereign moved contraband from Christchurch into the New Forest. My contact, a fellow by the name of Bill, promised to leave something for me on the crest of Verity Hill, a clue to the nature of the Sovereign's business."

That got Garner's full attention. "What was it?"

"He was interrupted." Tavin sat back in his chair. The green ribbon was probably no more than a snippet from a village girl's bonnet. He'd not waste Garner's time until he knew otherwise. "There was a complication. A lady."

He recounted the events, omitting details irrelevant to the case. How Gemma's eyes had blazed with fury when he'd walked in on her and Beauchamp. How she had kept pace with him despite her fear and the pain of her twisted ankle. How she had felt in his arms—soft, sweet, even sopping wet.

"This Miss Lyfeld." Garner scribbled her name on a scrap of foolscap. "She saw the Sovereign?"

"I've no proof the man was the Sovereign, but I believe so. She said his speech was educated, his horse fine. Light eyes, medium build, graying brown hair, like a thousand men in England. I'd have liked to see him myself, but I had to choose whether to identify him or save her."

"So you chose the girl." Garner smirked. "Are you besotted?"

Tavin snorted. He'd behaved like a lovesick pup once, and look where that got him—exiled from home in Scotland and working here. "Absolutely not. But I think Thomason would have understood my choice. Besides the fact that I lacked a weapon—"

"That's never stopped you before," Garner muttered.

"—I had to remove Miss Lyfeld from danger."

"You sacrificed the greater good to save the life of one."

And so the conversation renews again. "With all due respect, each life is—"

"Of value to its creator, I know. At least, according to your faith." Garner's mouth twisted. "Miss Lyfeld remembered no other unique characteristics about the Sovereign?"

Tavin shook his head. "A pity, but no. I've no doubt he'd hurt her if he learned her identity, though. I'm relieved she's safely away from Hampshire, here in London."

Garner's eyes narrowed. "You underestimate him time and again. I deem it wise for you to remain here, close to Miss Lyfeld, should our foe search for her. She might require your protection."

Icy dread pumped through Tavin's veins. "It's doubtful he can identify her at all."

"But you will be at hand, should she remember something of vital importance about his appearance. Or if the Sovereign is correct and she is, indeed, some sort of spy." Garner tapped his fingers against his desk.

Preposterous. "She's no more spy than I am a chimney sweep."

Garner's gaze lowered to his papers as if dismissing Tavin. "It cannot hurt to be certain. Just stay near her."

Play nursemaid to a come-out? "Are you punishing me?"

Garner laughed. "'Tis unlike you to question orders."

"She doesn't merit my protection or my investigation."

Tavin's fists clenched. "She's a country miss on the verge of a betrothal, and no more."

"Monitor the situation. You may cease and return to Hampshire if she remembers nothing and no ill befalls her, or if she behaves with suspicion, or if she becomes affianced and her betrothed dismisses you. But until then, stay close. You're the perfect man for the task. With your entrée to the upper crust, no one will look twice at you."

"*Everyone* will look twice at me." He stood. "They know who I am and what my mother did."

"History as ancient as dust."

"If I am seen among the ton, my grandmother will believe— Never mind." Tavin rubbed his suddenly aching forehead. "I'll follow Miss Lyfeld to ensure no harm befalls her, but I'll not escort her about town like a moon-eyed pup."

"As you wish."

What Tavin wished was to mount Raghnall and ride to Hampshire.

A wave of foreboding roiled in his gut. He could not fulfill anyone's expectations. Not his family's, not God's and certainly not his own. He should be in Hampshire, putting an end to the Sovereign and his murderous spree.

Hugh Beauchamp had better propose to Gemma Lyfeld by the end of the week or Tavin might have to do it on his behalf.

Chapter Four

At the creak of the library door flinging open behind her, Gemma startled and dropped the book from her hand. Despite being safely away from Hampshire for a full week now, her nerves felt raw, exposed. She spun to the doorway.

"Oh, 'tis you." She slumped against Wyling's desk.

"A pleasure to see you, too, sister." Amy grinned. In her yellow-trimmed dress, she looked reminiscent of sunshine and puffy clouds, a pleasant contrast to the overcast skies outside.

Gemma bit her lip. Amy had always been the prettier sister. The more beloved sister, perhaps. As a child, Amy had never trudged through the mud with her and Hugh, never required reminding she was a lady. Now that they were grown, Amy held the favor of a dutiful, titled husband and the respect of her family and peers. Including Gemma, who couldn't blame anyone for preferring Amy. Her sister was kind, gentle and wise. And a woman of strong faith, too. Without the model of Amy's forgiveness after their parents' deaths, Gemma's faith might well have disintegrated along with the ash from the fire that had killed her parents.

She scooped her book from the floor and smiled. "Forgive my unfortunate greeting. I was caught unawares."

"Woolgathering about Hugh?"

Discussing Hugh was far easier than speaking about that Sovereign fellow. The throb in her ankle had nearly dissipated, but her thoughts of that day still ached. Hoping for distraction, she'd come here, her favorite room in the town house. Its soothing green palette and shelves of books invited her to curl into a plush, padded chair and lose herself for hours.

And wait for Hugh. "We expected him a sennight ago. I hope he's not ill."

"I'm certain he's giving you time for shopping and your court presentation. Do you miss him so much? Perhaps you do love him."

Gemma blinked. Did love feel like annoyance? "Are you certain he hasn't dropped by while we were out?"

"He'd have left his card." Amy patted Gemma's arm. "I'm certain he has good reason."

Or perhaps Cristobel was right. Did Hugh have no intention of honoring his obligation? Her stomach soured. *God, if Hugh begs off, where will that leave me? Serving Cristobel for the rest of my days?*

And what if God wanted that, for her to live as Cristobel's companion? Would she obey Him with joy or bitterness?

Gemma pushed the question aside. God understood how important it was to honor her parents and wed Hugh. And once they had married, she'd be close enough to see Petey and Eddie every day. It was best for everyone.

"In the meantime, I promised I'd find a book to read to the boys when they wake from their naps. Something with, as Petey demands, 'a-venture.' This title is promising. It has the word *journey* in it. Maybe it's about a sailor, although a book on knights would have been preferable."

"It must wait, I fear." Amy's mouth set in a grim line. "Mr. Knox has been closeted with Wyling these past forty minutes. Now he asks for you."

A jolt shot up her spine. "What happened? Has that villain harmed Peter or Cristobel?"

"I don't think so, else Wyling would have told me."

At her words, the door opened and Tavin Knox entered the room, dressed in his usual black coat, boots and pantaloons. Although plain in style and color, his clothing was well tailored, revealing the breadth of his shoulders and lean waist to perfection. When he folded his arms over his broad chest, Gemma recalled what it had felt like to be held there, just over his heart.

Such notions would *not* do. She clutched the leather-bound volume to her chest.

Wyling followed Tavin, who offered a hasty nod of greeting. "You won't like what I'm to say, Miss Lyfeld."

"Good day to you, too, Mr. Knox."

His dimple flashed. "Where *are* my manners?"

His sarcasm grated like clothing over a wound. "Where they always are, I expect."

Amy tugged her to the silk settee and bade her to sit. "Enough, both of you."

"Forgive me, ma'am." Tavin's smile grew. "Shall we start again? Good day."

Despite herself, she smiled back.

His stance spread, reminding her of the portrait she'd seen of Admiral Lord Nelson. Confident, unmovable despite the churning waves beneath him. "While I expected to continue my search for the Sovereign, my superior has issued new orders for me."

Disappointing, considering the sooner the Sovereign

was caught the sooner she'd sleep through the night. "Is someone else investigating the Sovereign, then?"

"Not...exactly." Tavin speared her with his stare. "As a precautionary measure, I have been ordered to watch you."

Her jaw loosened, fell. "Like an animal in the menagerie?"

"Yes. That is to say, should you remember any more details which would help us in our investigation—"

"I have told you everything."

"—or should some danger befall you, I shall be close by to protect you and apprehend the Sovereign or his henchmen."

She gripped the book to her chest, wincing when it dug into her ribs. "He is coming here? To London? To me?"

He shifted his weight from one boot to the other. "My superior, Garner, wishes to ensure your safety in the unlikely event the Sovereign has identified you and comes to London."

She searched her relatives' faces for protests, help, sympathy, something. But Amy's smile was forbearing, and Wyling just shrugged.

"I cannot name the man. I am no threat to him."

"But he is a threat to you. Potentially." He expelled a long breath. "The Sovereign cannot be underestimated. I told you my friend Thomason was killed by the Sovereign, but I did not elaborate because it is unfit for feminine ears."

How maddening. "If there is something to be said, please do so."

He glanced at Wyling and stared into her eyes. "Several months ago, the revenue agent assigned to your part of Hampshire noted a change in the local smugglers' habits. Five local men murdered...in the same singular fashion."

"Why did I not hear of five murders until now? Not from Peter, nor in the village."

"You are a woman. And the men were not wellborn. It is little surprise you never heard of it." He shook his head. "Thomason must have discovered something, for he was murdered in the same manner as the others."

What manner? Gemma's hand pressed her churning stomach. Perhaps she did not wish to know. "And I may meet the same fate?"

"Doubtful. I spent the week watching you—"

"You have spied on me?" The book smacked the table.

"'Tis for your own benefit," Amy insisted.

"You knew?" Again? They had told her nothing and, worse, had allowed someone to observe her? What else had he done? Pawed through her drawers with his enormous hands? Gemma's teeth clenched, reverberating pain through her jaw.

"We just learned it, Gem." Wyling shook his head.

Tavin held up his hands. "They didn't know. And I didn't *spy*." He said the word like she'd no idea of the true definition of the word. "I watched the house. Nothing more. I had hoped to convince my superior that you were in no danger so he would alter his orders for me. Unfortunately, he wishes me to continue on awhile longer."

"Spying on me?"

"Guarding you," he corrected. "Which will be easier to do if you are aware."

"I do not require a guardian. Tell your superior I decline."

"Whether you or I wish it, I will still be tasked with watching you." He looked no more pleased than she.

"I cannot believe this Sovereign would follow you here, but I trust Knox." Wyling's voice was firm but kind. "If I had to entrust you—or Amy or Petey or Eddie—to another, it would be him. So I say, yes. You must tolerate it, both of you."

She'd grown adept at tolerance these past six years. But this seemed ludicrous.

Tavin's gaze seemed to burn into her, so intense it brought to mind how he'd looked at her in the drawing room back home, smelling of wood and water, right before she'd stomped off to climb Verity Hill.

And started this whole mess. So she nodded. Amy's shoulders sagged in relief, and a pang of remorse shot through Gemma for making things difficult for her family.

"I'll follow from a distance. If necessary, I shall attend the same events." Did his cheeks pink? "A few rules will make this easier on both of us. Tell me where you're going and when. And no going off alone or hiding from me."

"In other words, you're my new governess." She sighed.

"A discreet, invisible one."

Wyling chortled, Gemma squeezed Amy's arm and then rose. "If that is all, I should get to the nursery."

"Good day, Miss Lyfeld." Tavin's brow quirked. She nodded back and hastened to the nursery. Despite whines of protest from their harried nursemaid, Nellie, her nephews bounced on their beds. As he jumped, Petey tossed toy soldiers into the cradle in the far corner—still desolately empty despite Amy and Wyling's desire for children. Eddie jigged on his cot in imitation of his brother, his finger in his mouth, cackling in delight.

"What terror is this?" Gemma dropped the book on a lacquered table with a reverberating smack. "My nephews do not screech and hop like jungle creatures. Cease at once."

"So sorry, miss—down, boys!" Nellie's voice sounded panicked.

"Sowwy, Aunt Gem." Eddie's bouncing slowed.

Petey thunked to his bottom, creaking the bed frame. "Sorry."

"Express your apologies to Nellie, and we may move forward." She retrieved the book while the boys embraced Nellie. Opening to the first chapter, her hopes sank to her red leather shoes. She scanned a few pages and set the book down with a sigh of disappointment.

"This book will not do." A book of sermons, the writings would certainly edify, but they would not provide the adventurous fiction she had promised the boys. "Nellie, get the boys' coats. Let's venture to Hatchards."

"For books?" Petey's eyes grew wide as his coat buttons.

"I've yet to find a book which quite meets our needs." Until Wyling and Amy were blessed with children of their own, their library would no doubt remain lacking in suitable material for young ones.

She tugged on Eddie's coat and fastened the brass buttons. What had Tavin said? Tell him where she was going and not to go out alone?

Well. She was not alone in the least. She was accompanied by a nursemaid and two small children. She tried to inform Tavin, but the butler, Stott, was emphatic Mr. Knox and his lordship were in the library and not to be disturbed, so she did not feel the slightest trepidation leaving the house after jotting him a short note with word of her whereabouts.

The sun broke through the clouds in gleaming shafts as Gemma, her nephews and Nellie walked the well-kept square down Berkeley Street to Piccadilly, past the grand gardens of Lansdowne House and Devonshire House. Crested carriages pulled by fine horses traversed in both directions, while well-dressed persons sauntered by at a sedate pace. A gentleman tipped his beaver hat and wished her good day, and Gemma returned his greeting with enthusiasm.

New faces. New experiences. Freedom. London was wonderful.

A crisp breeze ruffled her hem and fluttered the ribbons of her poke bonnet, carrying the pleasant smells of scythed grass and wood smoke, twined with the tangy odor she had come to associate with London. Perhaps its source was the Thames, but the smell made her nose wrinkle. A small price to pay, however, for the delights of the city.

Piccadilly bustled with traffic. Her little party crossed the busy street and within moments, the gleaming wood facade of the booksellers came into view.

"Miss Lyfeld." The baritone behind her held no trace of amusement. Or patience.

Oh, dear.

The boys spun around and began to bounce. "Mr. Knox!"

"You are on an outing?" Irony dripped from his words.

"We're off to the booksellers." Petey hopped on his toes. "Aunt Gem says she'll read us something with an a-venture in it."

"Like a knight jousting." Eddie spoke around his finger. Gemma gently pulled it from his mouth and took his wet hand in hers.

Tavin's lips twitched. "Serious business, indeed. May I accompany you?"

"It is unnecessary." Gemma spoke before the boys begged Mr. Knox to *please do.*

"May we go inside now?" Petey hopped.

"Manners, my love." Gemma released their hands. "Nellie, would you to take the children in? I shall join you in a moment."

Gemma watched until they disappeared into the depths

of the bookstore. When she turned back, Tavin leveled her with a frown.

"Ignoring my rules already, Miss Lyfeld?"

"Hardly. I am not alone. Nellie is here, as are the boys."

"Feeble protection, honestly."

"I left word for you. What else could I do? You were not to be disturbed, according to Stott."

"Disturb me. Always." He leaned closer and, oh, there was that wood smell again. "From now on, take me or Wyling with you."

Lovely wood smell or not, this was absurd. "'Tis most impractical."

"We must all bear the inconvenience for now." He gestured to the door. "Now that we understand one another, do you care to look at books?"

"Not particularly. I'd rather throw one at something."

"I shall find a shield for myself, then."

Did everything she say and do amuse him? She gripped her reticule and turned. Catching sight of another familiar face, a grin pulled at her cheeks. Hugh, on Piccadilly of all places, smiling down at her. Now, God willing, everything would be well.

A young lady clung to his arm.

Yellow curls peeped from under a silk bonnet embellished with snow-white feathers, framing a schoolroom-fresh face. A bow under the bosom of her white pelisse accentuated her generous curves, inviting the eye to linger most improperly on her ample décolletage.

Gemma fingered the linen fichu at her neck.

Hugh's shining face radiated excitement. "Gem, pleasant journey and all that? So good to see you. And you as well, Mr. Knox."

"Mr. Beauchamp." A genuine smile spread over Mr. Knox's lips, as if he were relieved.

"How delightful to see you." Gemma's glance flicked at his companion.

Hugh turned to the girl on his arm. "Where are my manners? Abysmal of me. May I present Mr. Knox, and this lady before you is, of course, my Gem—Miss Lyfeld."

Something inside Gemma fluttered at his possessive words.

His smile grew wider, if possible. "Gem, Mr. Knox, may I present Miss Patrice Scarcliff? Pet, I call her."

Pet? What sort of name was that for—

"My fiancée." Hugh beamed. "I had planned to tell you about our betrothal back in Hampshire, but the opportune moment did not present itself."

Gemma's lungs stopped functioning. So did her mouth.

"Felicitations." Tavin's congratulations ripped her back to the moment, to Piccadilly, to her nephews waiting inside.

"Felicitations," she repeated, staring at the sweet-faced Pet.

She couldn't look away from the lady's pretty face. Because for a hundred shiny gold sovereign coins, she couldn't have forced herself to smile at Hugh.

Chapter Five

At dawn the next morning, the wind whistled cold and shrill around Tavin's ears, drowning out the sounds of everything but the pounding of Raghnall's hooves on the fog-soaked turf. The faster he pushed the gelding over the verdant slopes of Richmond Park, the more distance Tavin placed between himself and his troubles.

Especially the frustrating female with light brown hair, who no doubt slept snug in her bed in Wyling's town house.

Tavin dug his heels into the blood bay's flanks, enjoying the sensation of being pulled backward for the briefest moment when the horse increased its pace. No impediments blocked their way. Situated a dozen miles from London, Richmond Park was deserted at this hour. The sun had yet to penetrate the dull blue-gray of clouded dawn. Galloping like this had a way of clearing his head. At this speed, his frustrations vanished. He heard nothing, felt nothing but his own thudding heartbeat and the whip of the wind. At least, until today.

The Sovereign would continue his operation in Hampshire, but Garner would keep Tavin with Gemma. There'd be no wedding in her future. No Beauchamp to take Gemma off his hands.

He'd wring the dandy's neck if he could find it under the yards of linen Beauchamp called a neck cloth. Tavin may have forgotten a great deal about females and rules and expectations, but even he knew when a gentleman crossed a line.

The betrothal may not have been documented, but hadn't there been some verbal understanding? For years? He needed only to close his eyes to see Gemma's eyes, lifeless with shock, when that dandified Beauchamp had announced his betrothal to the infant at his side.

Hugh Beauchamp had ruined everything. Both for Gemma and for Tavin.

God help us. He should have prayed it already. Should have given thanks for his blessings: the rich mahogany of Raghnall's coat, the sweet fragrance of wet grass, merry birdcalls, Raghnall's nicker when Tavin turned him back to London. Reminders, each one, that God's mercies were new every morning.

And they were especially sweet, considering he might have missed them all if, six years ago, he'd received the punishment he deserved and moldered in a stark, stinking prison. Instead, he'd received the chance to repay his debt.

It was natural, perhaps, that such thoughts directed him to the Custom House. Despite the early hour, Garner sat behind the desk in his chilly chamber, papers in hand.

"Something happened?" Garner's brow rose. "The girl recalled something more about the Sovereign's appearance?"

"Nothing like that." Tavin recounted Gemma's all-too-ordinary life and the tale of Hugh's betrothal. As expected, Garner shook his head.

"Could she be an agent, working for an unknown group?"

"Hardly, unless she passes codes at the linen drapers."

His tone bordered on insubordinate, but he couldn't stop himself. "She's a country miss. All she cares about is her family."

Garner's gaze pierced him, its effect almost like pressure on Tavin's chest. "Everyone cares about something with such intensity they rarely speak of it, because it has the power to break them. Even her. She holds a secret. It would be wise to befriend her and uncover it."

Tavin's brow furrowed. The request was a violation, unnecessary and uncouth. He wouldn't do it. He would watch her, protect her, take a knife for her, if necessary. But he wouldn't become her friend in order to gain leverage against her. There was no need.

But Garner wouldn't hear it. Tavin forced a smirk. "I shall end up reporting on her passion for Gunter's ices."

"Something will have hurt her. Or she dreams of something. When you learn what, you'll know who she really is. Harmless little come-out, as you say, or something more dangerous."

Harmless, no. But dangerous? Only to Tavin, it seemed. The woman had a strange effect on him—on his circumstances and to something inside of him he'd rather not think about. At least not here, under Garner's too-watchful eye.

He shifted on the hard chair. Truth be told, he'd rather *never* think of it. "Are you certain? Because if I could just go back to Hampshire—"

Garner waved away the request like a dust mote. "She's heartbroken over that Beauchamp fellow. Vulnerable. You'll see a new side to her. Take advantage of it."

Tavin stood. "You'd best prepare for a tedious report. No doubt I'll be kept waiting in the library while she mopes and wails in self-pity."

* * *

There was a wail, after all. The sound from somewhere upstairs reached Tavin the minute Wyling's hook-nosed butler, Stott, showed him into the Chinese-styled drawing room. Then the cry trilled into laughter.

The boys, of course. But another laugh joined in, giddy and excited. It had to be Amy's, because Gemma wouldn't be—

Cackling like the children. She was still laughing when she came into the room, alone. No sign of swelling appeared around her eyes, which sparkled with mirth; nor were there red blotches on her heart-shaped face. She pressed her lips together, stifling further giggles. "Welcome, Mr. Knox. What a surprise."

Yet he was the shocked one. Hadn't she loved Beauchamp? Planned their wedding for years, written his name in her diary and sighed when he walked into the room?

He bowed. "Am I interrupting?"

"Oh, no. The boys were ready for a snack. Wyling and Amy are out, but I expect them home soon. Won't you take a seat?"

He hesitated. He'd not sat alone with a female in a room since—beyond recall. But he nodded. She sat away from the fire as if she were overwarm. He dropped to a plush armchair between her and the fireplace. "I have but one question. What are your plans?"

"Plans?" Her gaze met his. And his breath hitched.

She was pretty. He had thought her pleasant from the moment they'd met, but this was different. Pink lips, wide-eyed, of slender form. What was wrong with Beauchamp, choosing another over her? The man was a dolt.

She blinked. What had they been talking about?

"I shall ring for tea." She sprang up, sending the summery scent of lavender wafting through the air. "Just the thing to warm your bones. It must be chill out, indeed."

After instructing the footman to bring refreshments, she resumed her seat. "My plans, you said? For the day, or the remainder of the Season, since Hugh has made plans of his own?"

His shock must have shown on his face, for she laughed again. "I cannot say what the rest of the Season holds, but tomorrow, I take the boys to the circus."

He leaned forward, about to speak, when the tea things arrived. He declined sugar, accepted the delicate cup and set it, untasted, on the table beside him. "You may not be in mourning over Beauchamp, but the circus? If Garner's correct and you are in danger, public settings are foolish places to be."

"Astley's Amphitheatre is not dangerous except to the trick riders and acrobats."

"Really, Gemma. Can you not sit home and embroider something like other females?" He'd used her Christian name. He should not have, and yet he couldn't help himself. Might as well get her permission, since he'd be sure to do it again. "May I call you Gemma? Perhaps you might call me by my given name, too."

Her cheeks flushed. "I am not certain that is proper."

"Little between us is."

"Very well, then. Tavin."

His name sounded sweet—if shy—on her lips, and it brought a strange rush of pleasure to his chest. "Was that so difficult?"

"I shall keep the answer to that a secret." She smiled, but no trace of levity reached her eyes. "I am sorry to be the cause of so much trouble. You do not need to come to the circus, you know. Wyling will attend."

"You are not trouble." Although protecting her at a place

like Astley's would prove more difficult than at a supper party. "This is my occupation."

"You want to catch the Sovereign desperately."

There was no use denying it. "Yes."

"Will you tell me why? Beyond his crimes, something drives you."

A shaft of panic surged up his spine, cold as ice. Could he tell her? Explain his past, or how he might be free once he completed this particular job? "It is a complicated matter."

She folded her hands on her lap and peered at him. "I shall be honest with you, despite your ability to return the favor. I will not curl up and embroider away my Season. He will never find me here, and I'll not cower in fear that he might. We will enjoy every minute of our time in London, the children and I. We shall visit with old friends and see the Tower and the menagerie. We shall sail on the Thames and watch balloons ascend."

"This is about the boys?"

"Everything is about the boys."

Tavin couldn't break the contact of their locked gazes. Garner had been correct, after all. In light of Hugh's defection, she'd revealed her heart. Tavin hadn't even had to wheedle it from her. What had Garner said? She would be harmless? Dangerous? She was neither.

What she truly cared about, the thing that could break her, was the fate of her nephews. She was fierce when it came to those sticky, hopping children. Something his mother had never been for him and his brother, Hamish.

"But if you'd married Beauchamp?" That didn't make sense.

"I'd have lived next door and seen them daily. As it stands now, well, the result is the same. Despite Amy and Wyling's invitation to take me with them to Portugal for

Wyling's diplomatic task, I will never leave Hampshire, because the boys are there." She smiled. "This is my one chance to experience London. Am I understood?"

With a pang in his chest, he nodded. Her one chance, before she went home to sit on the shelf, an old maid, an ape leader, any of those derogatory terms indicating she was dependent, undesired, past marriageable age. Tavin understood now. He admired the lack of self-pity in her tone and words. Respected the glint of determination in her eyes.

But he didn't like it.

He drained his tea, the delicate bohea as unappetizing as ditch water after this conversation. "It would be my pleasure to escort you to Astley's on the morrow."

"We shall be ready for you."

He snorted. He had a feeling neither of them would be ready for what lay ahead of them.

Fire. All around her. So hot. Gemma turned, searching for escape, but flames surged up the walls and curtains, blocking her escape. She gasped to scream, but smoke filled her chest, and her call died in her clogged throat.

Mama. Papa. God help me.

Brighter than noonday sun, the flames grew closer, curling over the library furniture. Then, at her feet, prickles. She would be next to burn. But the flames licked damp, cold. She jerked—

She sat up in bed, the coverlet twisted around one leg and buried under her body. Moist with sweat, her night rail clung to her. The mauve light of dawn crept around the curtains' seams. The house was still and quiet, unlike her thundering heart.

Gemma flopped against the pillows. *Lord. Help me.*

God was there. It was the one thing she knew. No matter what she had done, the Lord promised to never leave or forsake her. She had to keep repeating what she knew was true.

I am forgiven by God. I am forgiven.

But she couldn't repeat one thing she didn't know. Would Mama and Papa still be alive if she had gone to bed that night when they had asked?

The nightmare shrouded her all day, dampening the prospect of a lighthearted day at the circus with the boys. She prepared early, changing into a muslin walking gown, and wandered to the drawing room where Amy perched on the settee with a stack of letters and a delighted smile.

"Gem, come see." Amy waved a piece of vellum like a fan.

"Something from Cristobel?" At last.

"I fear not, but good news, nonetheless. Vouchers for Almack's. We have been deemed worthy to receive entrance to that estimable bastion of respectability," Amy joked. "There will be enough eligible men there to make you forget Hugh."

Gemma's eyes rolled. "I can never forget Hugh. He's our neighbor."

"He doesn't have to be. Your neighbor, that is. Not if you leave Verity House." Amy pulled Gemma to sit beside her. "You did not love him, so you'll soon heal from his, er…"

"Jilt."

"He didn't jilt you. Well, in principle, I suppose, but now that we harbor no expectations, I shall insist to Peter that I have need of you." Assurance shone from Amy's eyes. "After the Season, you'll come with Wyling and me to Portugal. He'll be delighted I'll have your company while he's occupied in diplomatic matters. What say you?"

Portugal sounded exotic, colorful and distant as the moon. If only it could truly be. Gemma dropped the Almack's vouchers onto the table. "What of the boys?"

Amy's shoulders slumped. "They are not your sons, Gem."

"But I love them as if they are."

"I know." Amy shook her head. "And losing you would be difficult for them. We shall continue to pray on the matter. And, for today, we shall enjoy the circus."

Very well. "I'm unsure which will prove more entertaining—the pantomimes and riders in the ring, or Tavin, wishing he were anywhere else?"

Amy stifled her laugh when the butler, Stott, entered with a silver tray. "Perhaps that's him now."

But the silver salver bore a calling card for one Frances Fennelwick, not Tavin Knox.

"Do show her in." Gemma rose in anticipation.

Dressed like the summer sky in a blue gown, blonde Frances made a fetching sight. Gemma welcomed the dainty miss and introduced her to Amy. "How good of you to call with such haste."

"After receiving your letter informing me you'd arrived in town, 'twas all I could do not to rush and bid you welcome." Frances grinned.

The vouchers still lay on the table, and Amy's cheeks pinked. "Pardon the mess. We just now received vouchers for Almack's. Will you be in attendance next Wednesday, Miss Fennelwick?"

"Oh, no. I attended twice my come-out year." She inclined her head at a sympathetic angle. "I am sorry to bear such ill tidings, but the place is a dreadful bore. It may be a bastion of exclusivity, but I prefer to remain home with a book."

"But the status of having vouchers is important, is it not?"

Frances selected a biscuit. "I suppose Almack's is as good a place as any to meet a gentleman. But I am a bluestocking. It is a badge I wear with pride, not the scorn others attach to it. I do not need a husband, so I am freed from playing by the stifling rules imposed upon marriage-minded females."

"I do not require a husband, either." As much as Gemma longed for adventure, a family of her own and freedom from Cristobel, she loved Petey and Eddie. They were enough for her. "I would simply like to experience all of London that I can."

Again Stott entered the room with the salver. At Amy's nod, he left and returned, Tavin at his heels, clad in another formfitting black coat, his gaze intense. Gemma's breath caught—how foolish—and she couldn't tear her gaze from his until the weight of another pair of eyes drew her gaze away.

Frances's lips turned up in a smirk. Heat flooded Gemma's cheeks.

She'd told Frances she didn't want a husband, but it was obvious Frances didn't believe her now.

Sitting still was harder than it should have been, considering a decent percentage of Tavin's career was spent waiting, immobile. But standing. Even now, he would have preferred to stand outside the box at Astley's Amphitheatre, keeping watch from the hall. But the boys had begged and it would have seemed odd to say no, so he took his seat in the box with Gemma and her family.

"Am-a-zing!" Petey cried as a trick rider galloped past.

Eddie looked up at Tavin. "That horse is as fine as Raghnall!"

Was he? Tavin hadn't been watching. Not the riders or the pantomimes or acrobats who made the boys clap and laugh. Nor did he watch Gemma, although from the corners of his eyes he could see how she doted on her nephews, reading the program aloud to them and patting their arms. Love for the boys glowed on her features, adding an extra dimension to her beauty.

Not that he should think of *that*. He focused on the crowd, searching for a lone man peering at Gemma a second too long. Even though it was a waste. No one hunted Gemma.

Then Tavin saw the family in a box across the ring. His chest filled with dread. His aunt, the Duchess of Kelworth, was still beautiful, regal in bearing. A worthy duchess. Her husband, his *mither's* brother, hadn't joined her today, just the silvery-haired girls. While their eyes were wide as they watched the trick riders, they didn't clap like Gemma's nephews.

Beautiful girls, his cousins. Helena, the eldest, was near old enough for marriage now. How she'd changed from the little girl who'd begged him to push her higher on the swings. Would he have recognized her or her younger sisters if they had not been seated with their mother?

He stared too long. The duchess lifted her gaze. Heat rose up his chest as her gaze encompassed his party. Then she returned her focus to the ring, as if she didn't know him.

Tavin's fists clenched. His legs twitched. He needed to move. Needed to do something, be anywhere but here. His aunt was a gossip. No doubt she'd tattle to her friends he was in town and at the circus, of all places.

Worse, her whispers would reach his grandmother.

Chapter Six

Tavin paced his grandmother's gold-and-crimson Aubusson rug, no doubt wearing holes into the wool. By his best estimation, he'd waited thirty minutes to be received, twenty minutes past his point of patience.

His occupation demanded waiting, true. Hiding, observing and loitering in cold, in damp, in darkness, all for a case.

But waiting for a woman? That was another matter.

Perhaps he should sit down, but he'd never trusted the dainty-legged, feminine furniture in this room, all painted silk chairs and narrow pink lounges. He'd be seated when all other options were exhausted.

With the click of the latch, the door opened, revealing Groves, the ancient, snub-nosed butler. Striding past the servant in a rustle of plum-colored fabric, the tiny Dowager Duchess of Kelworth bustled into the room. Her lace cap framed her wrinkled cheeks, giving her a maternal appearance, but Tavin wasn't fooled.

"How nice of you to condescend to visit your grandmother."

"Forgive my overlong absence, Your Grace." He bent to kiss the pale, rose-scented wrist of the woman he'd never called *Grandmother*. He wouldn't have dared address her as anything but *Your Grace* or *ma'am*. Neither, come to think of it, had his mother.

The dowager settled into a Chippendale chair by the hearth. "Tea, dear boy?"

"How thoughtful." He perched on the fragile-looking sofa where she had bade him to be seated, near enough to note the additional strands of gray peeking out from under her cap. "You are well?"

"I am never unwell. I wouldn't wish to give my enemies the satisfaction."

"Indeed not."

"Nor did I admit to surprise when Caroline mentioned seeing you, at a circus, with *children*—"

The clatter of cups and silver sounded from the door. The dowager poured fragrant bohea and served buttered bread, which he took despite not wanting it.

"I was with Lord Wyling." He hoped the explanation was enough. "The boys are his wife's nephews."

"Still no heir for him? 'Tis the fault of his wife, for certain. She is but what, a baron's country relation? What a waste."

His fingers rapped the arms of his chair. "The Countess of Wyling is a worthy wife to my closest friend."

Her expression didn't alter from bland courtesy. "How is your tea? It was our custom to enjoy tea every school holiday, do you recall?"

As if he could forget. Back then, he'd thought those years would be the worst of his life. He'd been a fool. "You taught me many things during those afternoons."

Like how to pretend he didn't have a Scottish father.

Tavin's father might have been too lowborn to wed a duke's daughter, but he was no pauper. Their home in Perthshire was large and fine, the land abundant with healthy herds of Highland cattle and black-nosed sheep. It was a glorious, rich place where Tavin—although yearning for more attention from his parents—was happy.

And he was Scottish. He had known nothing else, known naught of his English family, until the dowager duchess had appeared like a violent storm, rushing him south as if on a flood. She'd insisted he receive a proper education at Eton—a gift she had not provided his elder brother, Hamish, who was heir to Scottish land, not fitting for her cause.

His grandmother sighed, as if wistful. "I saw more of you in your school days, despite our residence in the same city now. One might be inclined to take offense."

"I have been traveling on business, Your Grace."

She waved her hand. "Men and their business. But you are here now. For how long?"

Until Garner freed him from playing nursemaid. "Indeterminate at this time."

"Then you must come for supper and tell me how your dear brother fares."

The rich taste of his buttered bread soured on his tongue, and he swallowed it down with a painful jerk. "I would be honored, but you know I cannot provide any information on Hamish."

She sipped her tea. "'Tis a pity when relations disagree. Even when they are in error, as your mother was. But let us not speak of that. I sense you are not here out of familial duty. Is it something as vulgar as money, then?"

He choked on his tea. "No, Your Grace. I would ask a favor, if I may."

"Why should you not? My connections are estimable." Her expression held no trace of self-deprecating mirth or apology. She stated facts, 'twas all.

Why was he less afraid of criminals than the woman before him?

"I require entrance to Almack's." And he must have the approval of a patroness to procure a voucher.

Ah, she reacted at last, her brow furrowing like a tilled field. "I may be aged, grandson, but my hearing has not yet gone the way of panniers and powdered wigs. Or so I thought. You said *Almack's*?"

He'd prefer to be cuffed by a beefy-armed smuggler than don high-heeled, beribboned shoes and do the pretty at Almack's. "I did."

Glee sparkled like jet in her gray eyes. "Almack's? The most tedious of places for a gentleman of your age?"

"I do not *wish* to go—"

"No man does. But you *will* go. This is delicious."

"You misunderstand, ma'am." A headache manifested, pounding directly between his eyes.

"Pah. Why else would you subject yourself to the marriage mart if it wasn't for a female? Am I wrong?"

The pounding in his head intensified. Could he not just lie? "It is not what you think."

"Of course it is. You are seven-and-twenty, and finally a lady has caught your eye. But Almack's, darling? Isn't this like diving headfirst into a shallow pond?"

"Please, Your Grace?"

"Will you not tell me the lady's identity? If she is to marry into this family I must ensure she is suitable."

He stared at the plaster ceiling. "I am not marrying anyone."

"Yet." She cackled. "Very well. I shall compose a missive to Lady Cowper the minute you leave. She will not deny my request." She lifted her shoulders like an excited young girl. Or an imp, bent on mischief. "Your young lady must be remarkable, indeed, to lure you into the hallowed halls of Almack's. I would have thought such a place would be your worst nightmare."

Tavin shut his eyes. "You have no idea."

Her knees quivering under her gown of snowy gauze, Gemma nodded farewell to the Almack's patronesses assembled on the raised dais. When Countess Lieven, patroness responsible for Gemma's vouchers, tipped her dark-curled head and bestowed a hint of a smile on Gemma, Gemma returned the gesture. The countess did not disapprove of her—an achievement not unnoticed by Amy, who grinned.

Gemma turned, her spirits glowing brighter than the gaslit lusters illuminating the great room. The worst was over and the fun could begin. At least for her.

Poor Tavin. Not that he looked ill this evening. He cut a fine figure in his black coat and the required knee breeches. His muscular calves clearly had not required padding any more than his broad shoulders. The man was as handsome in elegant dress as morning clothes.

But his jaw clenched. His fingers fisted and flexed. He adjusted his cuffs and fingered the simple gold stickpin fastened at his neck cloth, all while scanning the room— for what, the Sovereign? Or perhaps freedom from acting as her *nursemaid.* She scowled.

He made a similar grimace at his beribboned shoes.

Was he not the relation of some nobleman? Surely he had been to London and appeared at court. Danced with ladies and made polite conversation. He should know how to behave here.

Or perhaps he had never entered Almack's before and felt the weight of its exclusivity, which could intimidate anyone. It certainly did Gemma. She had heard about the patronesses who ruled over the proceedings like begowned feudal lords. Their expectations and standards were of the highest caliber. Indeed, if it were not for Wyling's diplomatic relationship with Countess Lieven's husband, Gemma might not have received the vouchers.

These few ladies held the power to grant or deny entrance to anyone, for any reason. Poor family connections, Amy explained, or ill manners. Even jealousy.

It was best for all concerned to please the patronesses. One wouldn't wish to be denied entrance. Or permission to dance once inside. Or to be on the unfortunate end of their gossiping tongues, since the patronesses held the power to decimate a young woman's reputation. Gossip and speculation ran through London like pungent water down the Thames. It was a fact she had best not forget.

Help me be mindful and to cause no scandal, God.

Yet she almost did, spying Hugh across the room. His beloved Miss Scarcliff—Pet—stood at his side, a shimmering pearl in her creamy gown and headdress. Her ensemble was the first stare of fashion, and Gemma resisted the urge to touch the lace trim covering her breastbone on her own, far simpler gown. Hugh smiled as Pet took to the floor with a stout gentleman, and then, oh, dear, he approached Gemma.

Amy murmured to Wyling at his approach. Tavin grunted.

She knew how he felt. Speaking to Hugh—while monitoring her tone, word choice and facial expressions—was not going to be easy. Or pleasant.

"Gemma." By contrast, Hugh sounded as if Christmas had arrived seven months early. "How delightful to see you." He exchanged greetings with everyone, seemingly oblivious to the distance in their manner, perhaps because his smile-crinkled eyes focused on Gemma all the while. "I hope you might do me the honor of a dance. If you are not otherwise engaged, of course." His gaze flittered to Tavin, accompanied by an indulgent smile.

Tavin's head snapped back as if he'd been struck. "No."

Gemma was too amused to be insulted by his discomfiture. It felt pleasant—if perhaps not righteous—to be the one laughing at their odd relationship for a change.

Since this might be her only chance to have privacy with Hugh, she placed her hand on his outstretched arm. "I would be honored, Hugh."

Passing by the set containing Miss Scarcliff and her stout partner, Hugh led her to the far corner of the floor to square off for a cotillion with three other couples. While they waited for the music to begin, Hugh inclined his head toward her. "You look well."

So did he. His tall, lean form was well suited for the obligatory finery. "Thank you."

"Do say you forgive me." Under the light chatter of the other couples, he spoke just loud enough for her to hear. He looked so sad, and he didn't tear his gaze from her for a half second. Anyone watching—and someone most certainly did watch—could not miss his intensity.

Tender emotion lapped over her, washing away the offense of his rejection. He wanted to explain, she could see that now. He knew he had hurt her. And he appeared grieved, too.

Perhaps Miss Scarcliff had tricked him into an engagement. He hadn't wished to break with Gemma, but something terrible had occurred, something wicked, which trapped him into a betrothal to a scheming debutante. Little else could explain his actions. "Oh, Hugh."

"I was a cad, surprising you on the street like that." Their hands touched for the dance, and her fingers twitched to grip his. Would it draw too much attention if they quit the floor? If only she could hear his side of the events and help her oldest friend through this terrible circumstance.

The patterns of the dance separated them, then drew them together. "I thought you were angry, but then I thought, not my Gem."

How well he knew her. As a rule, she was usually hurt, then angry.

"*My* Gemma was not angry with me at all. She only wished I'd remembered my manners. I shouldn't have told you my news in public. Nor should I have intruded on your outing with your beau."

She stumbled and drew sharp glances. That was what plagued him? Interrupting her outing with her... *"Beau?"*

"I never guessed you and Mr. Knox—well, you may be a summer bride yet." He wiggled his brows.

Her foot landed square on his. Accidentally, of course. Had the act been purposeful, she might have ground down harder with her heel.

He winced. "Have a care, Gem. Wouldn't want to get a reputation as a poor dancer."

To think she had imagined him trapped by a scheming Miss Scarcliff. Cristobel had been right about Hugh all along.

Earlier she'd desired to quit the dance with him. Now she just wanted to quit him. Impossible, of course. Much as she would prefer to jerk her chin toward the ceiling and leave him on the floor of Almack's, she could not. Instead, she fantasized about ripping the diamond stickpin from his neck cloth and snapping it in twain with her bare hands.

Focusing on the pin's gleam kept her gaze from his face, at least, while she followed the patterns of the dance. Together. Apart. Hands meeting. Good thing she wore gloves. Otherwise, he would balk at the iciness of her touch.

"Is something wrong?" His eyebrows rose to his hairline.

Other than his manners? "What makes you think such a thing?"

"Your silence. But I suppose you are concentrating on the steps since Knox watches us."

If Hugh knew Tavin was *paid* to watch her, he might not sound so smug.

It was their turn to execute a move in the center. While she circled Hugh, Tavin strolled past in her line of sight. His bored expression didn't change when their gazes locked.

"Mr. Knox isn't *my anything*, Hugh. He's a friend of the family."

"If you say so." He looked at her as if, were they alone, he might tap her nose.

The strains of violins sounded their final, lingering notes, and she curtsied while Hugh bowed. He offered his arm and led her to Amy, who waited under a gilt mirror beside a young fellow with high shirt points, an unexpressive face and sandy-blond hair curled over his ears. Where was Tavin? Amy's eyes sparkled. "Gemma, may I introduce Mr. Scarcliff, Hugh's future brother-in-law?"

Mr. Scarcliff inclined his head, forcing his shirt points into his cheeks. Did the fashion cause him pain? His bland expression didn't alter, so he was either uninjured or accustomed to the sensation. "When Hugh speaks of you, it is with utmost affection."

Not enough affection to fulfill his obligation, apparently. "How kind."

A small smile cracked Mr. Scarcliff's mask, to pleasant effect. While not possessing the classic good looks of his sister, he was not unhandsome. And he was not married, either—a fact that Amy seemed to have noticed. She lifted her brows in silent communication at Gemma.

"Shall we look for Pet, Gerry?" Hugh jerked his head to the door.

"In a moment." Mr. Scarcliff paused. "Miss Lyfeld, would you drive with me through Hyde Park? Thursday, at the fashionable hour?"

Gemma glanced at Amy, who nodded. "Thursday would be pleasant."

"My anticipation is great." He didn't look it when he bowed. Then he departed with Hugh, who turned to wiggle his brows at her.

Gemma sighed. Where was Tavin to lend a scowl when one needed him?

"There you are, darling." Wyling strode up, Tavin at his elbow. "The premises are secure to Knox's satisfaction. It's past eleven o'clock, so no one else will gain entrance tonight. Now that duty is done, may I persuade you to be so vulgar as to dance with your own husband?"

So that was where Tavin had been.

"I do not mind if the world knows we live in one another's pockets, my dear." Amy took Wyling's arm as the strains of a waltz began. Gemma and Tavin stood side by side, watching them go.

Tavin glanced at her. "I do not dance. Ever."

Gemma almost laughed at the gravity on his face. "I see."

"But I do walk." He held out his arm. "Do you care for a turn about the room?"

His forearm was solid under her hand, and a thrill of flame licked up her arm. Why must this vexing man inspire such a response in her? Her nerves must be overset from her talk with Hugh.

"Beauchamp blathered about you taking a drive with Scarcliff." Tavin led her past a bank of twittering dowagers. "You are not stewing in the juices of heartbreak, I see."

"It is none of your concern."

"Where you go, and with whom, is my government-directed concern."

Amy and Wyling waltzed past, laughing. Would she ever find that sort of happiness? "My choice to accept an invitation is no indication of my affection. It is a drive, no more."

He paused with her beside a potted plant, his gaze scanning the crowd. "Scarcliff is the brother of Beauchamp's affianced. I warn you, inspiring jealousy among friends—or brothers—is a dangerous game to play."

The thrill of flame on her arm sparked to fire in her abdomen. "Hugh wasn't jealous. He was amused. Mr. Scarcliff asked, and I consented because that is what one does when one comes out into society. 'Tis just a drive, and Amy thought him proper enough."

He made a sharp, snuffing sound.

Gemma lifted a shoulder. "If he's at Almack's, he must claim excellent connections."

"Yet *I* am at Almack's. What does that tell you?"

It was a joke, but when his gaze met hers, her smile fell. He didn't look away. Neither did she. She breathed in his earth-and-air scent, feeling nothing of her body but the spot where her hand rested on his arm.

The music ended on a flourish, breaking the connection. What had she been thinking, staring at him like that? She forced a smile. "How did someone like you come by vouchers tonight? Is one of the patronesses a member of His Majesty's service?"

If he was aware of the mortifying effect his eyes had on her, he showed no signs as he resumed their stroll. "No, I came by vouchers the traditional way. I threw myself prostrate before my grandmother's whims."

She had never thought of spies having grandparents. Was the woman engaged in subterfuge, too? "How did she accomplish it?"

"She is the Dowager Duchess of Kelworth."

Her surprise must have shown on her face, because he laughed heartily enough to draw curious glances. "Does my illustrious pedigree endear me to you?"

"Hardly. And no matter that you are the grandson of a duke, you are not coming on the drive with Mr. Scarcliff."

"I'll be there." His tone brooked no argument.

"How? Disguised in Scarcliff livery?"

He returned her teasing smile. "Alas, I'm too old to pass for a tiger." The image of muscular, frowning Tavin clinging to the back of a carriage made Gemma laugh. "I shall be nearby, but I leave it to you to discover precisely where."

"Your presence is not necessary," she said for probably the tenth time.

"You and I are a twosome for now, like it or not."

She didn't like it, and she wasn't certain if it eased or worsened things that he didn't like it, either.

Chapter Seven

Gemma's stomach thrummed like a humming beehive when Gerald Scarcliff offered his hand to assist her into his glossy black phaeton. The conveyance may have been fashionably sleek, but its high seat gave it a dangerous aspect. Mr. Scarcliff's matched grays shook their massive heads as if they were anxious to gallop to Brighton and back.

Gemma's courage slipped somewhere in the vicinity of her slippers and she gave herself a shake. She had wanted adventure, had she not? Then why was she being such a ninny-heart?

Mr. Scarcliff's arm was steady when he handed her up, but she couldn't help comparing it to Tavin's. Less solid. And his bergamot cologne was comforting, like her Papa's smell. Nothing like Tavin's woodsy scent. Was his smell the sort of thing that came in a bottle, or was it just a part of him?

She bit her lip. This would never do. She smiled at Mr. Scarcliff and clung to the handle of her taffeta parasol as if it would anchor her to the carriage.

It was quite a parasol. The lace trim complemented the flounced hem of her white carriage gown, visible under the shorter hem of her celestial-blue pelisse. Amy said the

color brought out her eyes and Gerald Scarcliff was sure
to be appreciative.

Perhaps he was, but aside from his stiff smile, his face
registered the same lack of enthusiasm he'd displayed at
Almack's.

No matter. She was on an adventure on a fine, cloudless
day. She required no chaperone for the drive, but Tavin
was somewhere nearby, or so he had promised. Was he
loitering on the green of the square or waiting by the entrance of Hyde Park? Did he still think her cruel enough
to make Hugh jealous, or did he wonder if she had devel-
oped a tendresse for Gerald Scarcliff?

She didn't, but he would just have to keep guessing.
Gemma smiled at Mr. Scarcliff. Sky-high phaeton, wild
horses and all, she would enjoy the drive.

"Ready?" He fingered the ribbons.

"I am." With a lurch, they quit Berkeley Square and
trotted toward Hyde Park, veering too sharp around a gig
at the Piccadilly intersection. Mr. Scarcliff's face brightened as he increased the horses' speed, only to grimace
and yank the reins the moment a wagon blocked their way.
Gemma braced her feet and clung tighter to her parasol.

"Pity I can't give the horses their heads in this traffic."
He frowned at her. "Are you frightened?"

"No." She wouldn't allow herself to be.

"I suspected not. Hugh said you are not in the least
missish."

Except when it came to careless driving. Oh, and that
Sovereign in Hampshire who by now had forgotten her.
"Hugh and I thought ourselves quite brave as children.
Your family must be pleased about your sister's betrothal."

"Indeed." He slackened his grip on the ribbons. *Not
again.* Gemma braced against the seat as they sped into
another turn. Pity Tavin was not, in fact, clinging to the

back of the carriage. He'd hold on to her should the phaeton tip over.

"Hugh is a decent fellow." Mr. Scarcliff returned his full attention to the road. "Quite taken with Pet, too. Can't ask for better."

"No." A shaft of pain pricked her, like a bee sting to her heart. The ache wouldn't kill her, but it was bothersome all the same. "She must be a special young lady."

He yanked on the ribbons, pulling the poor horses to a standstill. They'd entered the park, and half of the beau monde seemed to have done the same. She saw acquaintances, matrons from Almack's, but not Tavin. Where was he?

Something of a twosome, he'd called them. But it was not as if she were in any real danger. They both knew it.

Her grip on her parasol relaxed as they continued at a sedate pace. This was not so bad, with Mr. Scarcliff unable to speed or direct the horses in anything but a straight line. Being up so high afforded the ability to view a great deal—the soft green of new leaves unfurling on the trees, the couples on horseback, and the come-outs in carriages with beaux. "This is lovely."

"Too crowded, though."

A fellow with light brown hair and a cross expression appeared to hail Mr. Scarcliff. Gemma squinted. "Do you know that man?"

"Eh? Oh, that's Dillard. Don't mind him. He's not the sort one introduces to a lady. Gaming sort."

Gemma wondered how he knew such a thing, but Mr. Scarcliff's expression brightened. "Hugh's glad you're in town. You're like his sister, and he won't ask, but he hopes you'll help Pet adjust to Hampshire and all that."

Was that why Mr. Scarcliff had invited her on a ride? To request she assist the girl Hugh had jilted her for? That was bold. Yet Pet would be her neighbor for the rest of her life, so she shuttered the nag of irritation elicited by his request.

"But of course." She hoped her smile matched her words. "Is she overwhelmed, this being her first Season?"

"Hardly. She's bored. Routs, musicales, balls, the same faces, same stories. She wouldn't have bothered with Almack's again if our mother hadn't insisted. Pet and I would like to do something different."

Did Pet need an adventure, too?

Gemma chose her words carefully, tasted them in her mouth before she spoke them. "You spoke of Pet's adjustment to Hampshire. Our society is pleasant, but small. It is not like London."

"I doubt they'll spend much time there. Neither are the countrified sort, content with dining with neighbors and nights by the fire."

Hugh's long absences lent validity to Mr. Scarcliff's statement, but she had credited his extensive trips to business. Had she been blind not to realize that had she married Hugh, she might well have been removed from Petey and Eddie, after all?

A cool breeze caressed her jaw and fluttered her bonnet ribbons. With it came an unexpected sense of peace. She would never know what her life might have looked like if she'd married Hugh. But perhaps God had seen fit to protect her, because, unlike Pet, she could not stay in London. Her future lay in Hampshire, watching her nephews grow up.

But for now, she was here, among throngs of people and possibilities, and she did not want a one to slip through her gloves. She had something in common with Pet.

"What would you and Miss Scarcliff like to do?" Mayhap Gemma would learn about new experiences she could try. A shiver of anticipation lifted the hairs on her nape.

"Vauxhall Gardens, for one."

She had heard of it. It was not too scandalous a locale, but Amy had frowned when she'd described its walking paths and the dark corners where a beau could pull his lady into the shadows for a kiss.

Gemma put a hand to her mouth. She had never been kissed—another sign she'd missed of Hugh's disinterest—but Vauxhall Gardens was almost synonymous with temptation.

What would it feel like? No one kissed her but her family. Amy's lips were dry on her cheeks, and Petey and Eddie's mouths were wet and smelled of milk.

But a man's lips, touching hers in a stolen moment on a dark pathway...

Her hand returned to her lap. There were adventures, and then there were *adventures*. Some were best not taken. Pet could go down the path of scandal if she wished, but Gemma would not face temptation at Vauxhall Gardens, especially not with—

Tavin! Dressed black as a beetle, astride his red horse, he sauntered through the park toward her. His gaze took in everything and everyone but her, it seemed, as he wove his horse through the traffic, drawing alongside Gerald's high-perch phaeton and past it, as if he did not know her at all. Her mouth popped open.

It was all well and good to insist on watching someone, but the act was impossible when he faced the other direction. A small puff of exasperation passed her lips.

"One more thing," Mr. Scarcliff continued. "A trifle, really. Pet would love to attend a masque."

Now that sounded feasible. And memorable. "Where?"

"Hugh and I attended a public masque several months ago, before the engagement. Pet was so jealous she's

begged Mama ever since, but Mama will only allow it if
we're invited to a private masque."

Mama and Papa used to laugh about the masquerades
they attended, with everyone dressed in costume or dominoes. Once, Papa pretended not to know Mama's identity
yet pursued her with relentless devotion. *Ah, how I miss
you both.*

It wouldn't do to grieve now, here, so she forced a smile.
"Mayhap you will be invited to a masque."

"The most exclusive masque is held by the Comtesse du
Vertaile. An invitation is more difficult to come by than
vouchers to Almack's."

"I am not acquainted with the comtesse."

"Truly?" Mr. Scarcliff peered at her again, slackening
his grip on the horses. "Hugh said you know Miss Fennelwick. The comtesse is her relation. An elder cousin of
her father's, I believe."

"I was not aware of the connection." Unlike Cristobel,
Gemma did not make a habit of memorizing the contents
of *Debrett's Peerage*.

"I have seen her from afar, but I have yet to make her
acquaintance."

Did Mr. Scarcliff have a tendresse for Frances Fennelwick?
Who would have thought such a thing? Perhaps Gemma
should have felt slighted, but instead her spirits were buoyed
at the thought of potential romance. It was not as if she were
attracted to him. Not in the least. "Would you like an introduction?"

His features brightened, as if a candle took flame behind the careful mask of ennui he cultivated. "I would,
Miss Lyfeld."

"You must come to our at-home next week, then. Three
o'clock."

A black-clad figure on horseback rode past, two yards

to her right, this time traversing in the same direction as she and Mr. Scarcliff, out of the park, toward home. His eyes never alighted on her, though surely he could feel her stare through the wool of his black coat.

After all his talk, all his insistence he would protect her, he didn't even notice her! She huffed out a snort, and at Mr. Scarcliff's quizzical glance, she cleared her throat.

Oh, dear. She had paid more attention to her guardian than her escort once again.

"I look forward to it. Perhaps then we may make plans to ride together."

"That would be lovely."

It only occurred to her later, when she peered out the drawing room window onto Berkeley Square, that she had agreed to ride astride a horse, something she had not done in so long she could scarce remember how.

But Amy had ordered her a becoming rust-hued riding habit, just in case. And wasn't this what her London Season was all about? Adventure. She would accept every invitation she received with relish and gratitude.

As she was about to release the drape, something caught her eye. Tavin rode past the house, his gaze straight ahead. Poor man, guarding her for no real reason. Although he probably returned her pity, since she'd been jilted and her lone male caller preferred Frances. She released the drape. It did not matter. Tavin and his pity would be gone soon from her life, anyway, and she would have naught but her memories of her single London Season.

She lifted her beaded reticule from the gilt Chinese table and withdrew one of the ten sovereign coins from inside. Glimmering gold in the candlelight, it rested on her palm, heavy and cold. *Georgius III Dei Gratia 1817* surrounded the profile of her king.

With a sigh, she slipped the sovereign into the taped

pocket of her gown and cinched the other nine tight in the reticule. It would not be long before her caller should arrive, and she had best be ready for a brief but instructive appointment with him.

It was not as if she could meet him here again, not if she did not wish anyone—not Amy, nor Wyling, and certainly not Tavin—to ever know the nature of her business.

Two hours later, Tavin tossed a coin to a boy in an ill-fitting coat standing outside the coffeehouse. "Another awaits if you stand by my horse."

"Aye, sir." The boy took Raghnall's reins and bit the coin. The gap between his front teeth reminded Tavin of Hamish as a child, his teeth too big for his freckled face, back before Hamish abandoned Tavin to his own devices and stole from him when Tavin was not looking.

A shaft of ancient agony pierced his gut. He'd forgiven, but that was all. There would be no reconciliation.

The pleasant smell of coffee met him at the door. Wyling sat with a pot of the brew at a table in the center of the sparsely filled chamber. As always, the earl had left the chair facing the door for Tavin. "Sit. Tell me how you fared in the park." His ginger brows wiggled.

Tavin uttered a mock groan. "Scarcliff will never be a member of the Four-In-Hand Club the way he drives. No attack by the Sovereign, either."

"Amy is out with the boys, but Gemma gave me her word she will not leave the house until I return."

Tavin pictured her, an embroidery hoop in her hands and a scowl on her face. "Did she complain?"

"Not at all. She was weary from the castle."

Tavin swallowed too fast, burning the back of his throat. "Castle?"

"Gem and Amy transported the nursery into a castle

using bedsheets for fortress walls. Chairs and tables are turned on their sides—it's a delightful mess of knights and medieval mischief. But a noisy one."

"I shouldn't wonder." Tavin set down his cup. "I've an errand whilst your sister-in-law is occupied. Care to come?"

Wyling dropped his cup and hopped to his feet. "Even a grown man requires adventure now and again."

"You might regret it when you see where we're going."

"Never." Yet Wyling's eyes took on a wary edge when they stopped on the gritty street some distance from Mayfair. The sour smell of the Thames was sharper here, the buildings grimier and the passersby dressed in drab clothing. Tavin and Wyling handed their horses and coins to a boy in a too-short coat outside a noisy tavern.

"Your usual haunt?" Wyling's irony was quiet.

"Better than some I frequent." Tavin shouldered his way inside the threshold and scanned the room. The men at the tables wiped their jaws with hands far more callused than those of the dandies at the gentlemen's clubs. This was hardly a smuggler's den. But the tavern's occupants held secrets aplenty.

Spying a vacant table in the corner, Tavin led Wyling to it and took the stool facing the room. He could see everything from this vantage, every furtive glance and twitchy finger, but he didn't view the one he sought. Wyling spread his hands over the coarse table, acting as if he visited such places every day.

A hollow-cheeked woman stopped at their table, carrying tankards. "Dobbins is out back, waitin' for ye."

"My thanks, ma'am." Tavin pressed a coin into her weathered hand as he rose. Then he led Wyling onto the street and into a fetid alley. "Don't step on that."

"A warning I shall heed." Wyling skirted the pile of filth.

"This shan't take but a moment." Tavin paused, listened. A cough rumbled—the signal—and Tavin slunk behind a heap of refuse, Wyling stomping noisily behind him.

"Dobbins."

A man of great girth and height leaned against the tavern's rear exit, arms folded over his ample midsection. His lazy smile faded when he caught sight of Wyling. "You brought a friend."

"He *is* a friend, Dob. No trouble. Right, Wyling?"

Wyling's nod was casual, as if he savored the story of action and intrigue he'd later share with his wife. Tavin smirked and then leaned toward Dobbins.

"What do you know about the New Forest?"

Dobbins rubbed his neck. "I heard 'bout Thomason. He was a good 'un for a custom man, he was. You and he were two of a kind, eager for a fight."

"Was that what got him killed? He walked in when he should have walked away?"

"I couldn't say, but I've heard tell 'bout that area. More activity than usual."

Tavin stuffed his hands in his pockets. His fingers encountered the green ribbon he'd found on Verity Hill. Refuse or clue? Would Dobbins know? How could he even ask such a thing? *Pardon, Dobbins, but do any smugglers you know like ribbons? Pretty green ones to wear on their bonnets?* Ludicrous.

The ribbon had to be garbage. Yet it had been pinched under a rock. And the image of a bonnet ribbon brought something else to mind, something amorphous.

"Dob! Yer help, if ye please!" The voice of the hollow-cheeked woman called from inside the tavern.

"Fair warning from me wife." Dobbins grinned. "Anything else?"

"Just one more thing." Tavin pulled out a coin. "Heard of any female spies?"

"O' course. Some assume a woman's too feebleminded or weak. They ain't been leg-shackled to me Meg, now, have they?" Dobbins's elbow jabbed Tavin's rib, a sensation more annoying than painful, although there might be a bruise tomorrow.

"Anyone specific?"

Dobbins scratched his head. "Just the womenfolk of the free traders. Wives, sisters, them like that."

Them like that. Like the Lady in Red who would climb Verity Hill to warn her smuggling brothers of the revenue agent's presence, the one Gemma had resembled when she'd donned her red cloak. The Lady in Red had an interest in smuggling, true, but not in a government capacity. "So there are no female agents on my side, or another's?"

"How many sides can there be?" Dobbins's arms folded. "There's them and there's you. Smugglers and lawmen. No in-between, 'cept those of us who cater to the preferences of both."

In cases of tea or liquor, perhaps. But some other sort of trouble brewed in the hiding places of Hampshire. The green ribbon clenched in his fingers probably had nothing to do with it, but he couldn't toss it just yet.

Chapter Eight

When Frances scrunched up her nose, she looked like a schoolgirl at their Bath seminary again. Gemma linked her arm through her friend's as they strolled through Hyde Park, Petey and Eddie racing ahead with Nellie, Wyling's footman trailing behind, and Tavin *somewhere*. The poor agent must be bored out of his wits.

"Does the idea hold any appeal?" Gemma leaned into her friend.

"I do not know Gerald Scarcliff, except by sight."

"Hence his request for an introduction tomorrow at our at-home. He must be taken with you."

"He does not know me well enough. He must have liked my looks," she said, without a trace of boastfulness. "Are you certain you do not wish him as your suitor?"

"Quite."

"Then Papa and I shall call on you tomorrow at the appointed hour. And if I am not repulsed, I will agree to ride."

Gemma's laugh was interrupted by a yowl. Petey flew into her arms, his grin revealing an empty spot where his front tooth had been this morning.

"It fell out!" He opened his hand, and there it was, like a pink-tinged pearl.

"Well done." Frances nodded.

"Indeed." Gemma cupped his cheek.

"May we write Mama of it?" Petey's gaze pleaded.

"Of course." Gemma touched his head. *Father, please soften Cristobel's heart, that she might respond to her son.*

Her gaze lifted. Tavin sat astride Raghnall a few yards distant, his brow furrowed. With concern for Petey?

So he *was* paying attention to her, after all. She smiled wider to let him know all was well. He responded with a tiny nod, and she expected him to turn the horse or at least look away. But he didn't. Not for the span of several breaths.

Her heart fluttered in her chest. She recognized the desire sprouting in her chest, wanting him to turn back. Join them. Admire Petey's new smile. Which was utterly ridiculous. She was nothing to Tavin but an unsavory task.

And he was nothing to her, despite the strange current pulling her gaze toward him.

Tavin couldn't help but watch Gemma the rest of the afternoon. She drew his attention like the point of a compass to true north, and he had to struggle to fix his focus on other things, like his task. His surroundings. Potential threats. Even, later that evening, the hole in Petey's smile where a tooth used to be.

And the next day, during the at-home when Frances Fennelwick called five minutes after the Scarcliffs. Tavin had fought to keep his gaze on things other than Gemma.

But now that the guests had departed and he sat in the drawing room with the Gemma and Amy, Tavin was free to watch Gemma while she divided stacks of vellum invitations with brisk efficiency. As she peered at the calendar and cross-checked events, the tip of her tongue snaked between her lips, a sign of intense concentration.

His chuckle tugged her gaze from her task. "Poor fellow. You needn't stay."

"I'm not bored." Not when in her presence. "Just surprised. I never would have fathomed the similarities between our occupations. Hours of meticulous planning. Gathering intelligence. Poring over schedules and maps. Who would have guessed work for the Custom House so strongly resembled meeting one's social obligations?"

"What fustian." She giggled. "A lady's work is far more tedious than what you do."

His laugh was hearty and loud, something that hadn't happened since—he couldn't remember when. "And dangerous."

They were both unable to stop laughing at the absurdity of it all.

Amy patted her arm to call her back to the job at hand. "What would you have us do the eighth, Gemma? Shall we accept the invitation to Haverby's rout or the drum at Mrs. Grant-Wither's? We cannot do both."

"Whichever is easier for Tavin."

He blinked. This was the first time she'd sought his advice.

"Both are the same." His choice would be the Haverby event, but not because of the ease protecting her. Mrs. Grant-Wither's wastrel son would not welcome Tavin into his home. Not that it would matter. He'd not been invited. He'd have to watch outside at either event.

"I do not wish you to be uncomfortable."

"I would be far more uncomfortable inside than out on the street, thank you."

Amy laughed, but Gemma did not catch the joke. How could she? She knew nothing of him or what had happened years ago. And it was best if it stayed that way. He stood and stretched his legs, ending up propped against the mantelpiece.

"Then I say the rout." Amy thunked the two invitations into two separate piles, a smaller one of acceptances and a towering one of regrets. "What a successful day. Miss Fennelwick's introduction to Mr. Scarcliff went well."

Tavin snorted at the understatement. Scarcliff acted like a lovesick pup at Miss Fennelwick's feet—obnoxiously so. At least Gemma did not seem to mind. She had focused on Beauchamp's fiancée, behaving kindly considering she'd been jilted for the girl.

Amy twiddled her pen. "I overheard you and Frances discussing some sort of party for which we should expect an invitation?"

Gemma's lips curved up in a sly smile, and something about the look made Tavin's stomach sank. "A masque."

"No." The camaraderie they'd just shared evaporated like steam.

Gemma sighed. "Not *that* sort of masque. In a few weeks, Frances's relation, the Comtesse du Vertaile, will host the most exclusive, grandest affair of the Season."

Amy's brows rose to the brim of her cap. "The comtesse is selective of her guests."

"She is also fond of Frances, who wishes us to attend. We will be invited."

Tavin's arms folded. "And you shall decline."

Her mouth opened to protest. Fortunately, Wyling entered the room. He could talk some sense into the chit.

Amy smiled at her husband. "Gemma expects we'll be invited to the Comtesse du Vertaile's masque."

"All of us. Even you, Tavin." Gemma fiddled with some ribbon on her white gown.

"What say you, Knox?" Wyling folded his arms, an

amused expression on his face. He already knew the answer by watching Tavin pace a path into the rug.

Tavin understood why she stared at him, wide-eyed as a fawn. She wanted to grasp all the fun in London she could. A masque held excitement. The chance to feel liberated, to be someone she was not by hiding under a mask for a little while.

But masques provided excellent cover for all manner of unquestioned exchanges, from the flirtatious to the illicit. Gemma might not be in real danger, but she could be pawed by a masked man. The idea set his teeth clenching.

"I find the idea unwise." A gross understatement. "Quiet activities are better suited to her needs."

Gemma shot him a look of exasperation. "This is as tiresome for you as it is for me, but you cannot forbid me."

Tiresome. It was not precisely tiresome anymore. But it was frustrating, to be sure. "I can ask you to be wise." Tavin ran a hand through his hair. "Choose your activities with care, at least until my superior is convinced of your safety."

"I am in no danger. The Sovereign did not follow me."

He believed she was right. Nevertheless, they had no choice. "I think you misjudge how grievous an individual he is."

Amy stood. "Awhile longer, Gem."

"If I must ask Tavin's permission for my every move, so be it." She jutted her chin at him. "Hugh will call tomorrow to escort the boys and me to the Tower Menagerie. If we promise not to stick our fingers inside the cages, will your superior allow it? Or should the children and I instead challenge Hugh to a game of spillikins?"

Irksome female. "The menagerie is acceptable."

But why she would want to go anywhere with Beauchamp mystified him. The jackanapes had chosen another female, yet Gemma accommodated him into her ridiculously tedious schedule.

His jaw clenched. He'd never understand women.

The next afternoon, Gemma settled against the plush squabs of Hugh's luxurious landau, her smile fixed on her nephews, but her attention lay across Hyde Park. On one of the gravel paths, a man in a black coat trotted on a reddish horse.

Tavin kept enough distance that Hugh had not recognized him; nor had her nephews. To any of the few people enjoying the park before the fashionable hour, he seemed another gentleman exercising his horse.

No doubt he'd rather be galloping away from her. The prospect of watching them roll through the park after wandering through the Tower probably bored him. The crown jewels and the menagerie were certainly not of interest to a calloused government agent.

Hugh hadn't seemed to mind the outing, however. Neither had Nellie, who rode beside John Coachman in the driver's bench. Nellie's presence today was necessary, not so much to mind the children but to act as a feeble sort of chaperone.

Against scandal, of course. Not danger. For that she had Tavin, who at the first sign of trouble from a smuggler miles away would have—what? Thrown her over his shoulder only to drop her into a leech-filled lake?

Eddie patted her leg, drawing her to the present. "That big bear in the menagerie, Old Martin, was not fearsome at all, not like in books. He looked sickly."

"Green in the gills," Petey agreed.

"Poor bear." Hugh nodded. "The whole place was rather depressing."

"What does that mean?" Eddie's face screwed up in confusion.

Gemma touched his bony knee. "It means we all—bear included—might be happier if the animals had more room to roam about. To climb and run."

"Would he run after me?" Eddie's eyes widened.

"He'd still be caged," Petey scolded.

Gemma sighed. She was the only one in the carriage pursued. Not by the Sovereign, of course, who no doubt carried on his wretched business without giving another thought to the red-cloaked girl on the hill. No, Tavin trailed her in the same way shadows cling to their hosts, close and dark. She had seen him three times today, including now, across the park. Once, he'd ridden past as they sampled lemon ices at Gunter's. The other time, he'd lurked at a distance at the Tower, shrouded in shade.

"Speaking of running." Hugh's grin split his features, giving him the carefree air he'd borne as a child. "The park is not at all crowded. Would the boys like to get out?"

"Huzzah!" Petey cried.

The carriage stopped and they descended to stretch their legs. The boys bolted, chasing each other around trees.

"I am a mauling leopard!" Petey cried.

Eddie shrieked in mock horror.

"Shall we walk? Staying in sight, of course." Hugh offered his arm.

She took his arm, but Eddie spun and ran back to her. Already? Had Petey hurt his tender feelings? Gemma readied her arms to receive the child, but he barreled into Hugh.

"I like you, Mr. Bee-chum."

Hugh patted Eddie's tiny hat. "I like you, too, young Lyfeld."

Eddie pushed off and chased after his older brother. "Ho, I'm a bear!"

Gemma's teeth caught the inside of her cheek. This was what she'd planned for her future. They would have been a little family, taking in the sights of London while Peter and Cristobel saw to their own desires back home.

She grieved the loss of that life. Not for the loss of Hugh—whose invitation for today's activity was difficult to refuse since he had offered it in the presence of the children—but for the family she might have had with the boys. She puffed out a sad breath.

"What is it?" Hugh nudged her.

"Cristobel has not written to the boys yet. Perhaps she will acknowledge Petey's lost tooth, although she has not responded to our previous letters."

"Pity. They are fine boys." Then Hugh's head swiveled, reminding her of the way Tavin scanned his environs. "There." He indicated a small group of trees and pulled her under the low-lying branches. She could just make out the boys through the leaves.

"Hugh?" What was he thinking?

He spun her about and leaned her against the thickest, shadiest tree. With his arm over her head, he braced himself against the trunk, too close to be proper. Fear skittered up her arms. Was this what it felt like to be at Vauxhall Gardens, pulled into the darkness by a suitor? No wonder Amy disapproved of it.

"This is inappropriate." The air was thick, scented with Hugh's cologne.

"I do not know how else to speak to you alone. I must revisit that last rainy day in Hampshire. Remember it?"

She would never forget. "The day you came to sever our ties?"

His head jerked back, as if she had slapped at him. "How could you think that? I'd never lose you, Gem." He lowered his arm and took her hands.

"You are betrothed to another."

He squeezed her fingers. "Don't miss the point. You're no longer bound to me by some antiquated agreement our fathers made. We deserve better than the life they contemplated for us, but I had the courage to do something about it. I made a way for you to be happy."

She felt anything but happy, staring at their entwined hands. He had a far different understanding of their relationship than she. She may not love Hugh, but his rejection still stung.

"Now you can wed whom you wish." He nudged her.

She glanced at the boys, her only future. "We should go back to the carriage."

"As you wish." But he didn't release her. "Do you mind that Gerry calls on Miss Fennelwick?"

His abrupt change in subject was far preferable to the one that preceded it. She shook her head. "Not in the least. We would not suit."

"Was Mr. Knox jealous by your drive with Gerry?"

She choked. "He is no suitor."

"I've seen how he stares at you. A decent-looking fellow, I suppose, if not intimidating with those hefty arms. Like he spends too much time sparring at Gentleman Jackson's."

Staring. Arms built for pummeling. That was Tavin. "He has no intentions toward me, I assure you."

"We should all dine together. Amy, Wyling, Pet and Gerry, Miss Fennelwick. We shall even invite Mr. Knox for you—"

"He is Wyling's *friend*." She emphasized the word.

"Not to sound mercenary, but you could do worse than

the Duke of Kelworth's nephew. Money and connections. That has to count for something. I have both in Pet—and affection." He pulled a hand free and tapped Gemma's nose.

At the stroke, disgust roiled in her stomach. Hugh shouldn't touch her like that, shouldn't even hold her hands. It was not honoring to her or Pet.

She pulled her hands free. "Perhaps we should call the boys. They will be ready for a rest—"

He took her arm just above the elbow. "You'll thank me for tossing our agreement someday, Gem. It's not as if you harbored any feelings for me."

But she might have. She had misread all of those nose taps and wiggling brows for affection. If her emotions had been inclined, she might still be waiting for his love. She might have been trembling with hope here under the tree.

Hugh was right about one thing. Marriage should be more than an arrangement where one party didn't want to be involved.

Relief washed over her and she tugged free. His fingers slipped from her spencer in what she hoped would be their final touch. If God ever granted her a husband—when the boys were grown—she would not want one who took other women behind trees, no matter his reason.

Tavin forced himself to stay on his horse, despite every last muscle urging him to dismount and push his way into the trees. What was the woman thinking, pushing the bounds of propriety with that jackanapes Beauchamp?

Still, Tavin had no call to intervene. He was here to guard her from the Sovereign, not from Beauchamp, who dangled hope before her like a prize.

Gemma's feelings were not Tavin's concern. If he allowed himself to think otherwise, he'd fail. At protecting her, protecting his plans.

He had a job to do, a God to repay. He had no heart to concern himself over. Or to give. Not to Gemma or anyone.

He'd best not forget it.

Chapter Nine

Gemma had a difficult time forgetting Hugh's boldness last week. Dragging her behind a tree! Inappropriate, not to mention embarrassing. What Tavin must have thought or maybe still did think, considering Hugh watched them now with a ridiculous grin.

Perhaps Hugh considered himself a matchmaker, ensuring both were invited to his future mother-in-law's for tonight's dinner party. If only Hugh knew Tavin would have been here, anyway, invitation or not. Only as an unseen observer.

She mashed her lips and focused on the task at hand, finding a duet in the messy stack of sheet music. Mrs. Scarcliff had asked her and Frances to perform a duet for the other twenty-odd guests, a simple request. Gemma sat at the pianoforte bench, hunting a suitable piece while Frances settled her father into a chair by the fire in the green-and-gold drawing room. The others, like Hugh, chatted in small groups but, unlike Hugh, ignored her. His gleeful gaze unnerved her.

It did not help matters that Tavin stood beside her, so close she could tip her head back a few inches and rest against his black embroidered waistcoat.

She'd lain against his chest once before, that day he scooped her out of the lake. She'd been fool enough to think he might fancy her. And then he'd just pulled a leech from her neck.

She ruffled the sheet music. Tavin did not fancy her; nor were they friends. But he gave a far different impression to Hugh and everyone else, lurking over her like this.

She turned back to him. "There is no need for you to assist me. I doubt the pianoforte has orders from the Sovereign to attack me."

"Ah, but one should never underestimate one's foe. The sheet music might slice your delicate fingers."

Fighting a smile, Gemma returned to the stack. "Wouldn't you rather chat with the gentlemen?"

"I would rather be in Hampshire." He bent over, his chest mere inches from her cheek. "What about this one?"

"The title may refer to two people, a shepherd mourning his lost love, but that does not make it a duet. Clearly, you do not play pianoforte."

"My hands find better use cuffing scoundrels."

She spun around to him. "I hope no one eavesdrops."

"Not a soul pays the least interest to us except Beauchamp, whom I might remind you is betrothed."

"I do not require your reminder."

"I was not certain, the way you two snuck into the trees."

Embarrassment heated her skin from her fingers to her neck. She'd wondered if he would bring up the topic and had been relieved when he hadn't mentioned it all week. Until now. "I do not like what you infer."

"I infer nothing. Only that I could not see you for a time."

"Nothing happened."

"That doesn't matter. If I cannot see you, I cannot fully

protect you. Don't you know I am protecting you now? Look around." She followed his gaze around the chamber. "The staff's shoes are cheap and squeak against the floor, but the noise assures me the servants are who they claim to be. I've noted everyone's activities, from Wyling and old Scarcliff talking corn laws, to Miss Fennelwick settling her father so he can enjoy the duet that does not seem to be forthcoming anytime soon. One might think Mrs. Scarcliff does not truly own any duets and she attempts to keep you from her prospective son-in-law."

Impressive. But he was wrong on one count. "She has naught to fear from me."

"Not from you. Him."

He was wrong there, too. "Not that it is your concern, but when we were hidden from you, Hugh and I spoke of his betrothal. He did not wish the children to overhear."

He snorted.

She glared up at him with narrowed eyes. "Why are you here?"

"To help you find music." His brow quirked.

"Do not be thickheaded. Why are you here, tonight?"

"Because I was invited to dine. And I am to watch you."

"You do not *watch* me. You watch everyone else."

He laughed. "Does that pain you?"

"Like the prick of a hairpin. Annoying but soon forgotten." She squared the music into a neat pile, patting the sides with too much vigor.

"I regret the inconvenience. But you were the one who intruded on my case—"

"Had I been informed of the reason for your visit to my house, I would not have intruded. If only to avoid your so-called protection."

"My protection cannot be that intolerable. I'm a decent sort." He grinned, and her frustration melted. Why did his smiles—the full ones that crinkled his eyes—have that effect on her?

"I am shocked you did not taste my food at dinner to ensure I was not poisoned. I should have held out my fork of turbot in oyster sauce to you." The teasing words slipped out before she realized how flirtatious they sounded.

Would he balk? Instead, his mouth twitched. "Is that an invitation to share your cup? Next time, before the whole company, I shall do it."

"Scandalous."

"Coward."

Heat flooded her neck, cheeks, arms. He wouldn't *really* offer his cup. Would he?

He didn't look away; nor did his smile slip. *He's flirting with me, too.* She caught her lower lip between her teeth, breathing in Tavin's woodsy smell while her heart galloped against her ribs. *Say something clever.* She leaned forward—

Crash!

Strong fingers circled Gemma's upper arm, pulling her from the pianoforte and spinning behind Tavin. One of his arms reached back to form a protective crescent about her. She could see naught but his shoulder blades. Had the Sovereign found her…here?

Laughter erupted. She peeked around Tavin's solid form. The group of young people stared down at the floor. Gerald Scarcliff righted a chair and Hugh pulled a fellow to his feet.

"Deep into his cups," a matron muttered.

The flushing fellow offered the room a gallant bow before resuming his seat. Tavin's arm dropped and he stepped away from Gemma.

The whole thing had lasted seconds. Drawn by the commotion of the tipsy cousin, not a soul in the room had taken notice of what Tavin did. Thankfully. How to explain it?

Gemma's limbs trembled as she resumed her seat. Not from the crashing chair or Tavin's response. It was the speed of his protection. The noise had startled him, and he'd acted. He'd protected her without thought of the cost to himself.

She'd been such a fool, resenting his presence. He took it far more seriously than she—serious enough to fight for her. To die. How could she resent him or even flirt with him, ever, after this?

Frances sauntered to the pianoforte, an elegant vision in a simple gown of blue silk. "Have you found us something to play?"

"Ladies." Tavin bowed, sending an errant lock curling over his forehead, and strode away, taking a seat beside Frances's elderly papa. She watched after him. What would he have done had she been in true danger? Perhaps he carried a weapon on his person. Or maybe he used his colossal fists.

Gemma swallowed, then remembered Frances awaited an answer. "I cannot find a duet."

"How curious." Frances perched beside her, smelling of violets. "Shall we look again, if only to appear as if we tried?"

Gemma nodded and flipped through the sheet music, her vision too blurred with emotion to take in a single note. Frances giggled. "If we do not find a duet, it will be for the best, you know. My musical efforts will not impress anyone."

"So you wish to impress someone in particular?" Gemma grasped at the diversion.

Frances scrunched her nose. "If you imply Mr. Scarcliff, do not draft the banns for us. It is not at all like your situation with Mr. Knox."

She was as bad as Hugh. "There is nothing there."

Frances thumbed through the stack. "Do not fib. I see the way he watches you from the corners of his eyes."

He watched her from the corners of his eyes? Gemma peeked.

He was turned toward Frances's father, revealing his profile. Strong jaw, slightly crooked nose, dark hair curling over his forehead, a wide smile on his full lips. My, the man generally seemed miserable in Gemma's company.

"Fascinating." The deep timbre of his voice sounded relaxed as he spoke to Mr. Fennelwick. "So those shards may have been Roman implements?"

"Indeed." Frances's father, a slender gentleman with a white shock of hair, rubbed his hands together.

"I kept them in a box when I was a lad." Tavin formed a triangle with his fingers. "My favorite was about this long, broken at the top, but heavy."

"That could well have been a spear point. Where did you find it?"

Gemma craned her head, eager to learn where he'd grown up.

"Near the northern border."

"Hadrian's Wall, no doubt." At Tavin's nod, Mr. Fennelwick beamed. "So many artifacts surround the environs of the wall. Who knows what lies just under the soil? Pots, coins, more of your spear points. Oh, for a shovel and a strong back, and I would uncover all I could."

When Tavin smiled, he seemed younger. For a moment, Gemma could imagine him as a boy, playful as her nephews, before he grew and chose to live as a spy. Frances was wrong—he didn't watch her from the corners of his eyes. But Gemma was happy she had looked up at him, anyway. Imagining him as a cheerful child lightened her spirit. How she'd like to see him carefree again.

I do not claim to know what Tavin needs, Lord. But I suspect the little boy who found the spear points is still inside of him somewhere. Help him to rediscover the sense of peace and joy that he must have had then.

Just then, his eyes moved. Not his face, not the tilt of his head, not his bearing. Just his eyes, quick as a cat darting under a bush, glancing at her from the corners.

A thrill shot from her core and down her limbs. How to liken the sensation? Anticipatory, like something lovely was coming soon, like the heady scent of orange blossom heralds the promise of fruit.

She lowered her gaze to her lap. Tavin might be handsome and he might have glanced at her, but she'd do well to remember why he'd done it. He was being paid to ensure she wasn't attacked while she sat at a pianoforte.

Still, she felt a joy she couldn't squelch. And to be honest, she didn't wish to.

Frances nudged her. "Play something alone. I recall how our old music teacher, Mrs. Drund, praised your skills. Do you remember her?"

"She entrenched that sonatina into my bones." Gemma had loved the way her fingers had flown over the keys and the feeling of freedom music provided. Cristobel had grown so weary of the tune, however, she'd forbidden it.

"Play it for us," Frances urged. "I so enjoy vigorous music."

Could she? It had been so long. Then Tavin peeked at her from the corners of his eyes.

"I shall try."

Frances stood and clapped. "Gemma is to play for us."

Tavin's brow quirked. In return, she sent him a dazzling smile. Let him—and the others—wonder what it meant.

The guests settled into chairs. Gemma's fingers found home, and she began.

While her fingers traced the keys, up and back, up and back, her mind wandered. She was no longer in a London town house, dressed in pearl-colored silk, her hair bedecked with ribbons and lace. She was young, donned in the serviceable gray of her school dress, playing for her favorite teacher. Happy days.

Her fingertips hit the final keys. Despite the years, she'd done it, and fairly well, too.

Applause filled the room. Pet's smile seemed forced, but Hugh, Frances, Amy and Wyling all beamed. Tavin's smile was less wide, but it was there, and his dark gaze held hers for a span of several heartbeats.

A tall figure moved between them, drawing Gemma's gaze upward. "Well done, Miss Lyfeld." Gerald Scarcliff bowed.

Frances clapped. "You exaggerated your lack of practice. I scarcely noted any mistakes."

Gerald smiled. "I hoped we all might ride in the park. I mentioned it to you, Miss Lyfeld, some time ago."

"I remember." But she had yet to practice on a horse.

"Would you ladies care to join me Monday next? Just a trot through Hyde Park?"

Frances's eyes glowed bright. "I should enjoy it. What say you, Gemma?"

"Very well." She had best don her riding habit, climb astride a horse and practice.

"When we go, we might discuss your relation's masque," Gerald said. "I received my invitation from the comtesse."

"As did Gemma. What a delight we shall all have."

Gemma's eyes met Tavin's. From the thunderous look on his face, he'd clearly heard. She braced herself for a lecture when he pulled her aside.

"I thought I made my views on your attending a masque quite clear."

"Your *no* was most emphatic." But this was not Tavin's last chance for adventure. It was hers. She would take hold of it with both hands. "Nevertheless, I do not require your permission. I do not wish to cause you difficulty. Truly. But I am in no danger. Except from falling off a horse."

A quizzical look replaced his glower, and she explained Gerald Scarcliff's invitation to ride. "I fear I have not ridden in years."

"I'll teach you, then."

Her lips popped apart. She'd intended to ask a groom. Maybe Wyling. "A generous offer, but I wouldn't wish to impose on you."

"'Tis no imposition. I'll call in the morning. Early."

And despite her frustrations with him and their circumstances, something liquefied in her bones at the thought of spending time with him. Not near him, but with him.

Then she realized that if she went riding, his devotion to his task of protecting her would have made him follow after her, anyway. She turned away so he wouldn't read the disappointment in her eyes.

Chapter Ten

"Hold tight." Tavin took Gemma's left hand in a perfunctory gesture and placed it on his right shoulder. "But not so firmly you strangle me."

"I shall restrain myself." Her light brown eyebrows rose as she took the reins and crutch in her right hand. "At least until after you teach me to ride this *beast*."

Tavin exhaled. Gemma's borrowed mount, Kay, was as harmless as she was overfed. But the gray mare was the perfect choice for Gemma, considering she had not ridden in years.

"Do not toss me over Kay's other side, now." Her breath, scented with tea and honey, warmed his cheek and lifted the hairs at his nape. *Fool!* No doubt he smelled of breakfast, too. The pudgy mare certainly smelled of hers, among other less pleasant things.

Best to get Gemma out of his hands, in every way possible, before he embarrassed himself as he had done at the Scarcliffs'. Jumping up to protect her at the crash of a chair? Idiotic.

He could hardly look Gemma in the eye even now without wanting to kick himself. Good thing he could teach her to ride without making eye contact. He knelt, took her left boot in his hands and hoisted her aloft.

She gasped when she landed on the sidesaddle. "This was not so terrible."

"Do you refer to my assistance or the height of the horse?" He placed her boot—half the size of his—in the stirrup with a none-too-gentle tug.

"The horse, of course. It is a long way up."

"Kay is a mighty dragon." He patted the mare's ample flank. "If she manages to take twenty steps, I shall be astonished."

Gemma patted the mare's neck. "Do not mind mean Tavin, Kay. You are perfectly frightful to me."

Tavin scanned the empty park while Gemma situated herself on the saddle. Here and there, shafts of sunlight penetrated the pale gray clouds overhead, promising another fine day. While the hour was not as early as he preferred, Rotten Row remained virtually deserted. Only a few others took advantage of the decent weather, the occasional lone rider and nursemaids and their charges. A pair of romping toddlers reminded him of Petey and Eddie.

"How do the children enjoy London?"

"Very well." Tendrils of her light brown hair escaped her jaunty hat. "We hope to visit Montagu House to see the Elgin Marbles in a few weeks. If that is acceptable, of course."

By the gentle way she tacked on the last words, it was clear she was trying to initiate a truce. Perhaps he'd gone too far, challenging her about Beauchamp, but her private rendezvous with the cad made his work more difficult. For certain, his annoyance had naught to do with her foolish desire to keep time with such a dandified bounder.

If she offered a truce, he'd take it. "More than acceptable. But I thought children weren't permitted inside." He swung himself onto Raghnall's back.

"Wyling secured permission. You may accompany us if you wish. Rather than following behind us, that is. Unless you're released from duty by then. And if you do not mind being with the boys." Her cheeks pinked.

"I do not mind. They remind me of myself and my brother." In their mischief and in terms of their lack of attention by their parents.

"Splendid." She fussed with her habit. The reddish-orange of a bullfinch's breast, the hue went well with her coloring. It also looked too much like her red cloak for his tastes.

"You seem to favor red clothes."

"This is not red. It's vermilion." Her lips pulled into a teasing smile. "Do you fear the Sovereign will hunt the realm for a lady in red? Because I am not the only female with crimson in my wardrobe."

He bit back a grin. "Shall we ride?"

"I am ready."

"Hold the reins like this." He bent and slipped the reins between her third and fourth fingers. "Excellent. Now we walk in a straight line."

Raghnall led the way, clearly comprehending he served as an example. Kay walked alongside.

"Success." Gemma laughed, but her smile dimmed when her gaze met his. "There must be a thousand other things you'd rather be doing."

"Not in London." His words were clipped, and he bit the inside of his cheek. Blood and regret tinged his tongue. This was not her fault, after all. And his attitude had grown tiresome, even to himself.

Her lips quirked. "So what would you be doing in Hampshire? Skulking? Picking locks?"

He laughed. "I am adept at both. I could teach you to pick locks. All one requires is a set of sturdy pins."

"And practice."

"And practice." He smiled. "And truly, today I am happy to be with you, practicing for your ride with your friends, what with Wyling under the weather."

"Amy, as well. Even toast disagreed with her constitution. Poor dears. Perhaps I should not have left the house."

"Fresh air does us good. Are the boys ill?"

"Quite the opposite. Petey lost another tooth. He now wiggles all the other loose teeth, hoping to repeat the experience." Her brows knit together. "I am sorry. I should not bore you."

"It does not bore me. They are good children. Their parents must be proud."

Her mouth turned down at the corners. "We await word from Peter and Cristobel. Any word. We have written several times. I hope they have not taken ill."

"You would have heard from the staff if that were so. I am certain your brother and sister-in-law are occupied with other matters. My parents were much the same."

Her sharp gaze speared him. "Were they?"

He had said too much. He bent toward her again and gently took her left hand. "We will tell Kay to turn now. Lower this hand and tug the rein gently to the right."

Kay responded to Gemma's urging. They practiced turning and advanced to trotting before deciding they had put Kay through enough paces today. Up ahead, the Wyling carriage waited to collect Gemma, and he'd send Kay with the lad in Wyling livery. But for one minute more, while the horses walked toward the gate, he'd take advantage of their privacy.

"I wish to discuss the comtesse's masque."

She glanced at him, her expression wary as if she

expected him to storm on again about the subject. He wouldn't. Arguing solved nothing—but talking might. If she understood why he felt the way he did, perhaps her views would alter.

"Again, I ask you to reconsider the wisdom of attending an event so fraught with risk."

She puffed out an exasperated breath, sounding like her horse. "I shall be disguised, you know."

"I cannot protect you if you look like everyone else, shrouded under a domino."

"Then I shall not wear a domino. You will be able to recognize me, I promise." Her eyes were pleading. "I do not wish to make your task more difficult, but we both know your assignment is a waste of time. I am in no danger."

Tavin looked away, seeing the park as if for the first time. It had grown more crowded, but he'd not noticed. Just like at the Scarcliffs', when he'd been so captivated by Gemma that he'd ignored everything else in the room and the smallest thud startled him into action.

If he'd kept his gaze on his surroundings—where it should have been—he'd not be caught by surprise. But today, just as at the Scarcliffs', he wouldn't have seen danger coming if a mob had surrounded them with flaming torches. He'd been too focused on Gemma.

I am slack at this job, Lord. Thank You that she was not attacked—

But she would never be attacked by the Sovereign. Almost a month had passed, and there had been no repercussions. No peril. Gemma was not in any danger whatsoever.

He dismounted, slipped her tiny boot from the stirrup and lifted her down. Enfolded in his arms, she looked up at him, her pink lips parted.

A longing filled his core and spread in dizzying waves to his fingers and toes. He wanted to kiss her. There was no use denying it. But even a once-gentleman like him knew better than to kiss her. They were in public. And the minute Garner released him from this chore, he'd return to where he belonged. Hunting prey and attempting to repay his debt to God.

His hands dropped from her red-clad waist as if she were flame itself.

Gemma swayed when Tavin's hands fell. The way he'd looked down at her, his gaze on her lips, she'd thought he might kiss her. And even though she didn't understand how she felt about him, even though they were in public, the idea of it made her toes tingle.

Oh, but she would have allowed it. Welcomed it.

How foolish she was. And mistaken about his intentions. His fingers were back on Raghnall's reins even as he bowed; clearly he could not escape her fast enough. "Until later, then?"

She nodded, not trusting herself to speak, and hurried inside the house.

Amy was still ill, and Wyling nursed a megrim headache. She spent a quiet day with the boys and retired early, a pleasant change after so many busy evenings.

In the morning, the absence of fire—in her dreams, as well as in the grate across the room—pulled Gemma from the depths of sleep, beckoning her awake with the awareness that she had slept through the night.

She stretched like a contented cat. Lilac-hued light illumined her still-cold bedchamber, speaking to the early hour. Even the nursery above her was hushed. Gemma pulled the coverlet more tightly about her and drew up her legs for warmth.

Her favorite trick to return to sleep was to recall her last dream. Sometimes, she would fall back into it. What had she been dreaming? It had been happy, a scene in a vast green meadow. Ah yes, the deep red of a horse's flank, the wind in her ears, the fragrance of cedar and pine, a hand taking hers to help her from her horse, twinkling brown eyes—

Oh! She'd dreamed of Tavin. Except in her dream, he'd been about to kiss her.

She flopped to her other side, curled into a ball and pulled the hem of her night rail down to cover her toes. It was not as if she had a tendresse for Tavin. Oh, he was handsome and he made her laugh. Sometimes. But she was no schoolroom miss. Handsome and amusing did not make a man marriageable.

Marriageable? Where had that come from? She buried her head under the pillow.

Although—if she were to look at him that way... He was the grandson of a duke and nephew to the current duke. He was *somebody*, to society's judgment. Even Peter and Cristobel would approve of his connections, although one's standing in society wasn't of particular importance to Gemma. Not that she should be thinking of him as a beau. He was her guardian.

What made him pursue such a dangerous occupation, when he was a gentleman?

Her toes weren't warming; nor was she the least bit sleepy anymore. But she nestled in bed for warmth, mulling the mysteries of Tavin, until she heard noises of stirring in the house. Without ringing for her maid, Mary, she donned a long-sleeved gown of white lawn, grasped her Kashmir shawl and went down to breakfast. The mouthwatering scent of bacon met her in the hall outside the morning room, and her stomach grumbled in anticipation.

The pale green room was occupied. With a snap, Wyling

lowered a newspaper and rose to greet her. "Good morning. Sleep well?"

"I did." Despite her disturbing dream. "How is your headache?"

"A distant memory." He joined her at the sideboard. "Amy is still abed, however. Perhaps by tomorrow, she'll be as hale as I."

"I pray so." Gemma took the seat to his right and nibbled a roll while he tucked into his shirred eggs. "I hope I did not tire her last night by reading to her."

"On the contrary, it cheered her immensely. She was also pleased you'd done so well with her little mare."

"Anyone would do well with Kay. She is a gentle creature."

"Indeed she is." At Amy's weak voice, Wyling stood and Gemma popped around in her seat. Amy entered, pale but smiling.

"Darling, should you be up?" Wyling frowned.

"The scent of bacon is more appetizing than I would have expected. Perhaps I am coming around. Forgive me for falling ill during your come-out, Gemma." Amy took a tentative bite.

"What silliness." Gemma's head shook. "Do not concern yourself with anything other than regaining your health. We have naught on our calendar for the day, you know. You may sleep the hours away."

"But what of you?" Amy eyed her over her teacup. "Wyling will take the boys to view horseflesh. What will you do?"

"Sit by your side. Another quiet day will do me good."

Wyling drained his coffee. "I thought you might have plans to ride with Knox."

Her cheeks heated as she recalled her dream. "Not today."

"You should be well practiced for your ride with Frances and Mr. Scarcliff now." Amy smiled. "Although I still say the outing could prove awkward. If I'd suspected Mr. Scarcliff had eyes on Frances rather than you, I would have discouraged him. Are you disappointed, dear?"

"Not at all." It was true. "His motives were twofold, I believe. Frances and my watchful eye over his sister, since we shall be neighbors in Hampshire."

Amy's eyebrows pulled low over her eyes. "I've said it before, and I'll say it again. Come with us to Portugal."

"I have prayed, but my mind has not changed. I cannot leave the boys."

Amy's fork settled on her plate with a soft chink. "I know Peter and Cristobel ignore them. The staff they hire to care for them is inept, and without you serving as aunt, governess and tutor, the boys would be wild as wolves. But Petey will go to school in a few short years, and Eddie will follow. Then what?"

"I shall be there for their holidays." But the thought ached.

"And betwixt those? You will be Cristobel's companion for life, if you allow it. Miserable, abused and weary."

Even Wyling's kind gaze bespoke pity. "We want you to be happy. And we love Petey and Eddie, too. We—you, Amy and I—will invite them to stay with us once we return from Portugal, and I am confident Peter and Cristobel will allow it. Those boys will live with all of us."

Hot tears pricked the backs of her eyes. How blessed she was to have the love of two rowdy boys, a kindhearted sister and a brother-in-law who opened his purse and home to provide for them all? *Thank You, Father. But they do not understand. I am needed by Petey and Eddie now.*

"Maybe once you return from Portugal. But nothing needs to be decided today." Gemma set down her serviette and stood. A ride on Kay was sounding better by the second.

Her family nodded, and she left them to their breakfast. Swiping the damp in her eyes with the butt of her hand, she hurried toward the stairs, but two men stood in the foyer: Stott, the butler, and Tavin, whose black coat was speckled with raindrops. He caught sight of her and smiled, bowing his greeting.

After their awkward parting yesterday, she'd not been certain how he'd act toward her. Or how she'd behave with him. She'd been about to let him kiss her, after all. At least he couldn't read her thoughts about him.

Pity they hadn't planned to go riding today. It seemed her thoughts clarified when she was on horseback, and right now, her brain was a tangled mess of thoughts and questions about the boys...and Tavin.

Her hand went to her throat. "Are you free for a time once your business with Wyling is concluded?"

"I have no business with Wyling. I am here for you." His brow quirked. "May I assist you?"

"You might indeed." She peeked at the butler. "Thank you, Stott."

He nodded and started to withdraw, but a footman entered the foyer with a salver in hand. "A message for you, Miss Lyfeld."

She recognized the spidery writing at once—it belonged to the solicitor she'd hired to help her prepare for her future, but had not told her family about. "Should I receive any more correspondence from this address, send it to my chamber, please."

"I shall have it sent upstairs at once." He bowed and hurried away, followed by Stott.

"Do you wish me to wait while you read it?" Tavin tipped his head. "It might be from your brother."

She shook her head. "It is not. It is…business." The words sounded ridiculous in her ears. What *business* did a maiden have? "Do you care to ride with me?"

Surprise flickered over his features. "You do not mind the rain?"

"I welcome it." The damp no doubt would keep others away from Hyde Park. It would be quiet and green, more like home in the New Forest.

He grinned, revealing his white, even teeth. "I shall inform Wyling, and wait until you are ready."

Chapter Eleven

The joy Tavin had taken in this morning's ride with Gemma dissipated the minute he entered Garner's office. Something about the place felt oppressive today. Off.

Garner's lips turned down. "The Sovereign's claimed another victim in the New Forest."

Tavin's head jerked back. "Who was it?"

Garner consulted the page at his elbow. "A fellow by the name of Bill Simple."

Gap-toothed, pockmarked Bill Simple. Tied to a tree, murdered and left with a sovereign coin on his tongue, the same as his friend Thomason had been. Tavin's bones melted to aspic.

"He was my informant. The one who was to leave me the clue atop Verity Hill. And it got him killed." Tavin's vision darkened around the edges. *Another death for my sins. God, when will you forgive me?*

The green snippet of ribbon he'd found on Verity Hill and kept in his pocket shifted against Tavin's hand. Automatically, he took it into his fingers, the way a small child worked a favored blanket. Would the fragment of green fray under his fidgeting? Was it refuse or clue? Rubbish, or a final gift from Bill Simple?

The question couldn't be answered in London.

"Let me return to Hampshire, sir. Naught has befallen Miss Lyfeld, nor has she recalled anything." And the only clue he had was the green ribbon, but if he showed it to Garner, he'd be laughed from the office. "She's a normal come-out, concerned with her family and her routine plans. Not that the Comtesse du Vertaile's masque tomorrow is routine—"

"But you are certain she is no spy?" Garner squinted. "You are not—because she's hidden something from you, hasn't she? Letters she won't read in your presence? Or perhaps she's snuck away from you."

Tavin threw his hands in the air. Beauchamp had pulled Gemma into the trees—she hadn't sneaked from him. But there was that letter this morning. Perhaps just one letter of many he'd no clue about. His laugh was mirthless. He was shackled to Gemma for a while longer, as surely as if they were chained at the ankle.

But a part of him—a part he didn't completely understand—relaxed at the notion he'd stay here with Gemma. Just for a while longer. Except—

"Is someone investigating the murder of Bill Simple?" Tavin couldn't bear the thought of Bill's death receiving no inquiry.

"The local revenue man paired with the magistrate." With a deep sigh, Garner leaned back in his chair. "Do you ever wonder if the smugglers have it aright? Most of the time, they harm no one. People are hungry, Knox." Garner tapped the newspaper. "Have you read this? More parliamentary bickering over the Prince Regent's social calendar. Nary a word of people starving in the counties. Some would say rebellion is imminent."

"Such rumors are the talk of a few radicals, no more."

"Since the Prince Regent's carriage was attacked on the opening day of Parliament, there has been more than *talk*." Garner's gaze was cold. "The tricolor of France is worn here on English soil."

Tavin shook his head at the mention of the symbol of the revolution in France. "Thistlewood, you mean? His attempt to take the Tower of London was an isolated incident—"

"Isolated? What of the Blanketeers of Manchester?" Garner tossed the newspaper aside. "Men cannot express themselves without fear of arrest."

"Men cannot discuss *sedition*." Tavin shoved his hands in his coat pockets again.

"There would be no need to discuss it if Parliament did its job."

"There are good men in Parliament, like the Earl of Wyling. He's diligent—"

"When he is not dancing with his wife."

"He is *always* working. Even at social gatherings." Tavin stood. "The hunt for the Sovereign has drained us both. I am ready for it to end as much as you are."

"You refer to your occupation or playing nursemaid to Miss Lyfeld?"

Tavin shrugged. A short ago, he would have agreed to the latter without hesitation. But, now, he didn't know how he felt. And if he did, he certainly wouldn't have explained it to Garner.

Prepared to receive his second scold of the day, Tavin squared his shoulders and strode into the Dowager Duchess of Kelworth's rosy drawing room.

He bowed at the waist, sat where she bade him to and waited for her to begin.

"Tea?" His grandmother gestured with her ring-laden fingers.

"Please, Your Grace."

Busy with the silver urn, she presented a picture of domestic bliss—a nurturing grandmother, sweet as pudding.

"I received a missive from Hamish yesterday," she said, shattering the illusion. No matter how innocent her words, the declaration was barbed. "He, Flora and the children are well."

"Good." He may not speak to his brother, but he did not wish Hamish harm. Neither did he wish to talk about Hamish. Just the mention of his name curled Tavin's fingers into fists, endangering the handle of his grandmother's Wedgwood teacup.

Not that it had been Hamish's fault in the beginning. Hamish hadn't known about Tavin's long-standing infatuation with Flora McInnis, or adolescent Tavin's grandiose plan to escape England at first opportunity and set up housekeeping in Scotland with the bonny lass. How Tavin would live happily-ever-after. Until he returned home and found Hamish had married Flora himself.

Hamish had blamed Tavin for shunning his Scottish heritage and embracing England, when all Tavin had ever wanted to do was come home. He had accused Tavin of thinking himself better than Hamish, Flora, Scotland and everyone they'd ever known, down to the village dogs.

Her Grace tutted. "When will you forgive Hamish? Let bygones be just that."

As his grandmother had not done, choosing to all but disown his mother for eloping with his father?

"Our family is complicated."

"Your mother made it so."

Tavin startled at the direct mention of his mother. His

grandmother generally ignored the human link between them. Discomfort stirred in his chest, not just for his mother but for his grandmother, too. The scandal must have been great thirty years ago when his mother had fled with a handsome but unsuitable Scotsman. His proud, ducal grandparents must have suffered shame and embarrassment.

"My mother cared for you." His voice was quiet.

"She was a fool." She set down her teacup with a *clink*. "Do not forget it was *I* who made something of you. I was the one who saved you from that farm where you were born. No one now would guess you once spoke like your Highland nursemaid." She added a lump of sugar to her tea. "Much has been given to you, and therefore, much is now required of you."

Tavin grimaced at the twist of Scripture.

"It is past time you made amends with Hamish. Visit, and then you will see he is to be pitied, not envied. He's naught compared to you—thick-tongued, married to that red-haired harpy with a house full of bairns."

The dowager did not have reconciliation in mind. Rather, she wanted Tavin to rub his so-called superiority in his brother's face.

"I do not pity him. He is fulfilled." For years, Tavin would have traded places with Hamish in a moment. The land, the bairns, Flora...

"I did not show him the kindness I showed you."

"No, Your Grace."

It had not taken long to learn his grandmother's kindness was reclamation of property rather than investment in a grandchild. The dowager had hoped Tavin would grow up indebted to her, rejecting his father and loathing his mother. To break Cassandra Knox as his grandmother had not been able to do.

Pity his *mither* hadn't noticed or cared what Tavin did. Like Peter and Cristobel Lyfeld, Tavin's parents had ignored their two boys.

He swallowed hard, aware that his grandmother watched his every twitch.

"I have forgiven my family." *Even you, Your Grace, for using me instead of loving me.* What was it the Lord said about judging the man with a speck in his eye, when a log filled his own? Tavin well knew he was not free from sin. He had no cause to hold grudges.

"But you have not forgotten anything, have you?" She quirked a graying brow.

"No." The tea tasted flat on his tongue. "It is better for me and Hamish to be apart."

She waved her hand. "I did not request your visit to discuss family matters."

Now this was uncommon. But the dowager loved theatrics as much as his *mither* had. She would make him wait before she spoke. She gestured to the tray. "More seedcake?"

"Thank you, no, Your Grace."

She sampled hers, nodded her approval and then looked at him. "My friends are gossipmongers, but they are *reliable* gossipmongers. Perhaps you have heard the latest tidbit? It involves a love match between a come-out and a gentleman."

"Alas, no one ever tittle-tattles with me."

"Mayhap they are struck mute by your imperious expression. But you shall want to hear this bit of gammon. It involves a member of my family."

"Has Cousin Helena found a beau?"

"She's not yet made her bows to society. I mean, you, of course." She sipped her tea, a look of relish crinkling her eyes. "And a certain Miss Lyfeld. You went to Almack's for her, didn't you?"

Denial wouldn't assuage her thirst. Neither would the truth, so he settled on skirting the issue. "I went to Almack's for myself."

She made a noise like a sneezing cat. "What about a supper party? And a balloon ascension? And a breakfast on the Thames? You were with her, according to my sources."

Her sources would make excellent spies. "We were invited to the same events."

"That does not explain you riding with her most mornings. Or is there another black-coated gentleman astride a blood bay escorting about a red-habited chit?"

"Vermilion," he muttered. His grandmother may not believe his protestations, but he'd not allow her to believe he'd soon be caught in the parson's mousetrap. "I offered her riding instruction. That is all."

"Has Lord Wyling no grooms to see to the matter?" She blinked, all innocence.

"A groom escorts us. As have Wyling and his wife. There is nothing between us but friendship." But was that true? He guarded her—he was not her friend. Yet the past few days, rain or brilliant dawn, Gemma awaited him after breaking her fast, donned in her red riding habit. Every morning, he cupped his hands for her boot and hoisted her into the saddle. They rode and talked of everything but the Sovereign, Beauchamp and the masque. And afterward, when he assisted her from Kay's back, he held her in his arms for the briefest of moments.

Each day, 'twas harder to let her go.

That was not quite friendship, either.

"This has been most enlightening, my boy." The dowager rang a bell to summon her butler, thereby dismissing

Tavin, but she grinned. "Enjoy the comtesse's masque. The both of you."

Tavin's stomach submerged to his boots as he bowed and left her. Her Grace would make a far better spy than he did.

Chapter Twelve

Behind her silk mask, Gemma felt free to gape at the magnificent foyer of the Comtesse du Vertaile's grand home, as well as at the other guests, all bedecked in cloak-like dominoes or creative disguises. Betwixt the candle-light flickering off gilt decor and the elaborate costumes, tonight was like a fantasy. If Tavin did not ruin the evening with his incessant scowling—visible despite the shroud of his domino cloak—Gemma would have the most extraordinary night of her life.

A man dressed as Henry VIII strolled past, a milkmaid on his arm. She spun to Tavin. "The boys will love hearing of this. See how fine everyone looks."

"I am looking, to be sure." Tavin's tone prickled like a briary bush. "But it is you who bears watching, madam."

A sharp retort formed on her tongue, but she bit it back—as well as the inside of her cheek—rather than risk the Comtesse du Vertaile overhearing her. A tall, stately woman wearing a gold gown and laurel-festooned turban, the comtesse offered a welcoming smile as she greeted Gemma's party to the ballroom.

"Welcome." Her lack of French accent did not surprise Gemma. Honore Haversash had been an English come-out when she'd married the Comte du Vertaile, who perished during the Terror in France after sending his wife and his wealth back to England.

"Comtesse." The hood of his black domino not quite covering his ginger hair, Wyling bowed low. Amy, resplendent in her shepherdess costume, curtsied. Tavin and Gemma followed suit.

After the requisite presentations, the comtesse examined Gemma from the top of her scarf-shrouded head to the turned-up toes of her slippers. "My young Frances speaks well of you."

The compliment sounded almost like a warning.

"She is an exceptional lady, Comtesse." Gemma smiled. The comtesse need not fear she would ever hurt dear Frances.

"And you, Mr. Knox. I knew your grandmother in our salad days. I have thought of her and her numerous tragedies often. Losing her husband, and before that, her daughter." Her head tipped. "How fares Her Grace?"

Tragedies? Gemma bit her lip.

Tavin's eyes narrowed behind his mask. "Well, Comtesse."

"I am gratified to hear it. Enjoy yourselves." The comtesse turned her attention to the party behind theirs, and Gemma followed Wyling and Amy into the ballroom.

Tavin muttered something.

"I beg your pardon, sir?"

"Nothing. Just do not court trouble in your unreasonable ensemble."

"Unreasonable?" Crafted in the Egyptian style, her pearl-strewn gown harkened to a country she would never visit, but for one night she could pretend she was someone else, someone exotic. "I am in costume."

"You are donned in *red*." His tone intimated that she was a cabbage-headed fool.

Gemma's hand flew to her left shoulder, where a pearl pin secured the vibrant train over her gown of white sarcenet and flowing lace headdress. "It is not *red*. It is rose, far too delicate a shade to be *red*. And you should not complain of my choice. I shall be easier for you to watch than if I wore a black domino."

Amy held up her beribboned shepherdess crook. "Will you spend your time bickering, Gemma, or will you enjoy the masque?"

Wyling speared Tavin with a scowl. "Gemma is not in peril because she wears red, er, I mean, rose. Try to enjoy the party, why don't you?"

"I don't like parties," Tavin muttered.

A stooped, gray-haired gentleman approached, arm in arm with a grinning, blond woman in a feathered headdress. The gentleman wore a toga-like costume, and the lady's eyes twinkled behind a green-feathered mask.

"Mr. Fennelwick. Frances." Gemma nodded her greeting. "How wonderful you look."

"You are supposed to ask, 'Do you know me?' Not guess my identity." Frances shook her head. "That is how things are done at masquerades."

"Very well, then." Gemma grinned. "Do you know me?"

Mr. Fennelwick chortled. "I believe we are all revealed by now. My, what a becoming Egyptian costume, Miss Lyfeld. Red becomes you."

Tavin nodded, the set of his jaw communicating that it was not the praise of Gemma's looks he agreed with. Rather, he was vindicated at his knowledge of hue.

As Amy, Wyling and Mr. Fennelwick conversed in the comtesse's grand house, Tavin moved away, allowing

Gemma to come alongside Frances. "Thank you for arranging our invitation with your kinswoman."

"She was delighted to include my friends. Is the masque to your liking thus far?"

Gemma glanced about. Bedecked in shades of blue and gold, the comtesse's ballroom glittered in the soft illumination of dozens of candles. Crystal vases of roses lent splashes of color and an enticing fragrance to the room, and the strains of violins carried from behind a gilt screen. And everywhere milled the costumed guests—members of the haut ton, no threat to Gemma whatsoever. Why did Tavin insist on causing such a fuss?

"It is wonderful." Gemma sighed.

"At least no one will lose his inhibitions, despite the anonymity of their costumes." Frances leaned closer. "Because of what she endured through the Terror, the comtesse values honor above all else. She perceives misbehavior as a personal insult to her hospitality."

"She has naught to fear from me."

Frances jutted her chin toward the far wall. Although he was disguised by a black domino, it was not difficult to recognize Tavin. No one else had such powerful shoulders; nor would anyone else stand apart, alone, watching the party.

"He must feel a deep affection for you to attend a gathering he so clearly dislikes. Is he your suitor *yet*?" Frances's matter-of-fact tone carried the gravity of a solicitor's.

Gemma tried to laugh, but it sounded feeble. "He is no such thing."

"So you say. Yet you have been riding with him every morning this week, twice to Richmond Park, a dozen miles away. I hope he will not mind that you have made plans with me for tomorrow. Or will he be joining us on our walk through Kew Gardens?"

"He will not." At least, not where Frances could see him. "He may come if you wish."

Two could play at this game. "What of Mr. Scarcliff? He has danced attendance on you."

"He has, although our latest outing was a disappointment. We visited the Elgin Marbles."

"We are to attend the exhibit with the children next week. Is something amiss with the displays?"

"No, I refer to Mr. Scarcliff. I tried to instruct him on the ancient Greeks as we viewed the relics from the Parthenon, but he did not seem interested in the knowledge. He may be handsome, but I cannot spend my life educating a husband. It is too exhausting."

Gemma's cheeks pained from smiling so wide. "Poor Mr. Scarcliff."

"I shall have to attend the display again so I might enjoy it better." She stiffened.

"Is that he, drawing near? So many gentlemen wear black dominoes."

"Let us retain a bit of mystery, then." When the gentleman reached them and bowed, Gemma grinned. It was time for her to cast herself aside and assume the persona of an Egyptian princess.

"Do you know me?" The gentleman's voice was unfamiliar, and a dash of pleasure rushed to the tip of her pointy-toed slippers. The fun had begun!

She giggled with Frances and dipped her head in her best impersonation of an Egyptian maiden. "I know you not, sir. Do you know me?"

"Do you know me?" A fellow in a jester costume leaned close to Tavin, reeking of wine.

"I hope not." Tavin stepped aside. When would this wretched evening end?

Perspiration trickled behind his collar and snaked down his spine. These affairs were all the same. Too many bodies in a cramped space, too few open windows, too many candles. Tavin would shed the miserable, hot cloak the instant Gemma agreed to quit this ridiculous masque.

Which, from her laughter, didn't seem likely to occur anytime soon.

A pity, because aside from the stifling air, he'd heard snippets of talk that would no doubt reach his grandmother come morning. *Knox. Kelworth. Elopement.* His mother's scandal, revitalized by his "sudden interest" in the social whirl and his attention in Gemma. No wonder Her Grace was in a froth.

God, this situation is a tangle. May it end quickly, for Gemma's sake as well as mine.

The red fabric of Gemma's costume fluttered in his peripheral vision, and he followed at a discreet distance. He'd done well tonight, following his own rules for the acquisition of information.

Do not directly watch the subject. Observe the environs of the subject. Note who follows, who fidgets, who stays close.

Tavin snorted. For his taste, too many stayed close to Gemma, providing Tavin several masked individuals to monitor.

Most were not of interest to him, as far as protecting her went. Wyling had been pulled into a political discussion some time ago. Amy occupied a chair beside a bored-looking Miss Fennelwick and her dozing father. Gerald Scarcliff had stayed close to Miss Fennelwick for a brief while but now huddled with a group of bucks Tavin knew to be too rich and bored for their own goods. Beauchamp and his betrothed also sought out Gemma—Beauchamp's excessively white teeth and trilling laugh gave away his identity—but it was the others who made Tavin anxious.

Men in dark dominoes, drawn to the woman in red like wasps to honeysuckle.

Little did those fools know she was no sticky-sweet bloom. She might smell of lavender and honey, but she was barbed as any rose.

Tavin's grunt elicited a smile from a woman in a low-cut gown and black mask. "Do you know me?" Her voice was a purr.

"Doubtful." Perhaps if he scowled, no one would ask him that inane question again.

Gemma glided toward a new group. Despite his earlier protestations, she did create a fetching picture. The red—*rose*—scarf brought out the pink in her cheeks and the gold tones in her hair.

Admit it, some part of his brain ordered. *You are drawn to her.*

And he wasn't alone. Other men sought her, spoke to her or worked up the courage to do so. A lean gentleman followed after her, his fingers fidgeting against the seam of his domino. When Gemma stepped right, the man followed suit. It was enough to rouse Tavin's suspicions, but he forced his fingers to uncurl. Undoubtedly, the slim-shouldered gentleman was taken with Gemma's joyous laugh.

Just like Tavin was. It was difficult not to watch her, she so enjoyed herself.

The man stepped forward. And in the palm of his hand, a circle of gold, twisting through his fingers. Gold like a coin. A sovereign coin.

Or a button, or anything gilt the fellow fingered out of habit. It meant nothing, and even if it were a coin, innumerable sovereigns circulated the realm.

But a sick sensation speared Tavin's gut and tightened

the muscles in his arms and legs. He'd learned to never ignore it.

Sovereign's man, or the Sovereign himself, but someone stalked Gemma.

He rushed forward, smacking into a woman. Her enormous feathery headdress blocked his vision. He stepped to the side.

Gemma was gone.

No red fluttering. No slim-shouldered gentleman. No time to waste.

Weaving through the revelers, he forced himself to breathe, to remember the rules he'd set for himself. *Never panic. Use your senses.* He'd caught many a quarry through patience and perseverance. But he'd never had a person under his protection before.

He burst through the door where the comtesse had welcomed them scant hours earlier, pausing in the deserted hall. Four doors led from it. The first, a library, stood empty. The second was full of men talking. The next two doors were closed. He twisted the handle of one, interrupting what looked to be an argument between two women. He shut the door.

Where was Gemma? She couldn't have slipped onto the terrace or gone to the staircase without him seeing her red costume. Tavin sucked in a hard, shaky breath. How had he missed her?

Then he heard it. A man's voice, from the final closed door. Tavin pressed against the wood, the better to hear.

"No, thank you." The words were muted, but they were Gemma's. Firm but calm.

"Lady in Red, it has been difficult to get you alone."

Lady in Red. The appellation of the woman in Hampshire who climbed Verity Hill to signal her smuggling brethren, the female Gemma resembled in her cherry-red cloak—

"Unhand me."

He'd heard enough. Tavin dashed inside. A man in a black domino faced the far wall, his cloaked arms outspread like raven's wings. But the cloak was not enough to obscure the woman pinned between the folds: the bit of red, the light brown hair curled over her brow.

Tavin gripped the man's shoulders. Yanked. Fastened the man to the wall, cuffed his wrists in his left hand and pressed his right forearm against the villain's throat.

"Who are you?" Tavin's forearm jutted harder into the assailant's windpipe.

An ill-formed kick met Tavin's shin, no more than a sting. With a swipe of his leg, Tavin confined the fellow's lower extremities. He glanced at Gemma and winced at the sight of tears streaking her pale cheeks. "If he hurt you, so help me—"

"No." She shook her head.

Tavin skewered the man's shoulder with his elbow, freeing his hand to grip the assailant's domino. He tugged, revealing the sweaty, ruby-flushed face of Gerald Scarcliff.

"You." His voice was a growl. Did the Sovereign employ such ne'er-do-wells for unpleasant tasks? If Scarcliff were desperate enough, yes.

"Didn't know you'd claimed her, Knox." Scarcliff's speech was like gravel, with Tavin's arm against his throat.

"What a ridiculous defense for handling me with such intent. Catching me in the hall and telling me we could best view the fireworks from this room. And that Frances was on her way to join us." Gemma popped to her toes beside Tavin. "How could you do this to Frances?"

Frances? Tavin's stomach sank. If Scarcliff had met

Gemma in the hall, then he was not the man in the ball-room. Then—

Tavin couldn't yet force himself to let Scarcliff loose. The cretin may not be the man stalking Gemma, but still he had violated her trust. His arm pressed harder into Scarcliff's neck. "She told you *no*."

An odd, whimpering escaped Gerald's throat.

"'Tis over now." Soft hands touched his arms. Gemma's. "Let's go, please."

Now that she'd touched him, he couldn't bear losing the contact. Tavin's arms dropped. He turned and found Gemma's face, cupping her smooth cheeks in his hands. His thumbs swiped the tears from her cheekbones. Her eyes were wide and questioning, and her lips parted in query.

Unable to help himself, he lowered his head and gently laid his lips on hers. Just for one sweet moment. She was safe. She was well. She was his—no, she could never be that. He pulled away, and the vacancy left by her lips resonated through his chest.

He shouldn't have done it. Quick though it was, he should not have taken such liberties. He was as terrible as Scarcliff, doing that to her.

But her hands rested on his arms, and they didn't push him away.

In a flurry of black cloth, Scarcliff scuttled behind him. Tavin left Gemma to grip the man's domino. "Not yet, you don't. I have words for you. Ill using Miss Fennelwick and laying hands on Gemma—"

"I say." A masculine voice, shaky with age but firm in conviction, sounded from the door. Mr. Fennelwick. "Mr. Knox, what is this?"

Tavin dropped his hand. Murmurs and gasps filled the doorway.

"Miss Lyfeld?" Mr. Fennelwick moved to Gemma. "My dear, are you well?"

"A misunderstanding." Her smile was weak.

A strange gentleman in the doorway laughed. "I should say so. Who's in for a pound this 'misunderstanding' was over the girl's favors?"

"Watch yourself," another admonished. "Poor form."

"What's happened?" A woman's voice sounded from the hall. "We wish to watch the firework display and—oh, you do not say?"

Fabulous. Soon the entire party would hear something had occurred in here betwixt him, Scarcliff and Gemma.

Tavin felt a slight thwack on his sleeve as Scarcliff shoved past, muttering about satisfaction. Tavin forced down a retort. Much as he'd like a legitimate excuse to draw the man's cork and bloody his nose, he'd no desire to kill him in a duel.

Still, with a quick glance at Gemma, he followed Scarcliff from the room. Someone caught his sleeve. "Settle this at boxing, like a gentleman."

But it was not Scarcliff he wanted. He wanted—needed—to capture the other man.

He slid through costumed revelers, searching for anyone rushing in the opposite direction. It seemed like the entirety of the masquerade was gathered here, looking for places to watch the display of fireworks and finding a far different kind. There was Amy, her hand to her throat. The comtesse, her brow raised in regal disdain as she stood beside Frances Fennelwick, whose quivering chin was just visible.

And then, a flash of a slim-shouldered man in a black domino, slipping out the front door. No doubt Tavin would find a sovereign coin in the man's pocket.

He dashed outside after him. Skittering onto the street,

he peered up one end of Park Lane and then the other. And groaned.

Silhouettes of black cloaks fluttered down the street in both directions, dim as bats in the night sky. Dark-cloaked individuals climbed into carriages, ambled along the streets.

If it were me, I'd have tossed the domino. Disappeared into a crowd. Tavin sprinted down the steps—

"Knox." Wyling pulled off his hood and caught Tavin's upper arm. "What's happened? Scarcliff's ranting like a Bedlam-bound lunatic that you assaulted him."

Tavin shrugged free. "He was here. The Sovereign—his man. Following Gemma."

"Are you certain?" Wyling's face leached of color.

"Protect Gemma." Tavin enunciated the words, praying Wyling understood their import. "I'll call in the morning."

Piccadilly loomed, full of people and dark alleys. He dipped into one alley after another, searching for the lean fellow. His boot smacked into a pile of shadowy rubbish and—it wasn't rubbish. Tavin breathed a prayer.

A man slumped in the alley, his face obscured by dark liquid. Blood. "Can you hear me? Sir?" Tavin slid his fingers under the man's neck cloth, found a pulse fluttering in the fellow's throat. The back of his fingers brushed a smooth, hard circle, warmed by the man's body.

Tavin's jaw clenched as he lifted the object up to the moonlight.

A sovereign coin.

Chapter Thirteen

The next morning, Gemma's stomach still churned over the turn of events at the masque. Gerald Scarcliff's attempts, Tavin's reaction, and all of it causing such a mess. 'Twas bad enough. Now this.

The message crumpled in Gemma's fingers, the sharp edges of the foolscap pinching her skin. The sensation was incomparable, however, to the darts of pain inflicted by the words scrawled over the paper.

"Put that away." Eddie batted the letter with his pudgy fist. "You promised to play with us."

From her position on the nursery floor, Gemma caught Eddie's hand in a firm squeeze. "That does not excuse your tone or your slap, young sir. A gentleman does not order anyone about in that manner."

"Papa does." Petey nodded in a knowing way. "He struck Tom with a whip once, and he grows angry with Nellie all the time. He says it's her fault we vex Mama."

Gemma bit her lip. It was true. Peter and Cristobel both snapped at the servants and could be abusive. Tom, the groom, had received the lash for some trifling matter just before Gemma and the boys left for London, but when it came to Peter's horses, everyone learned the hardest way. One didn't cross the master.

Peter's and Cristobel's conduct perhaps explained why the pair exhausted valets and lady's maids, and hadn't kept a consistent nursemaid for the boys. Nellie was the most timid—and perhaps desperate—girl they'd hired. The poor creature couldn't say boo to a roasted Christmas goose.

Nor could she train a child in appropriate behavior. That left Gemma to instruct the boys.

"Striking and shouting are unacceptable behaviors, boys. Am I understood?" Gemma shoved her note into her pocket.

"Yes, yes." Arms full of wooden rods, Petey walked on his knees over the rug, no doubt speeding the process of wearing holes in his nankeen trousers. "Can we play *now*?"

"Not until I am certain you understand. I wish you to grow up to be kind men." She squeezed Eddie's fingers.

"Sowwy," he whispered, his eyes wide.

"I know. All is forgiven." Gemma kissed his head. Eddie snuggled close, smelling of soap and the unique scent of little-boy hair. She smoothed his short coat over his back.

The rods spilled from Petey's arms, clattering about the floor. "We shall try."

"Of course you shall. You are the best of lads. Now, shall we begin spillikins?"

The boys' enthusiastic agreement brought a smile to her lips if not to her heart. She loved playing with them, but today their antics could not distract her from the sick feeling in her stomach.

She had been having so much fun last night at the masque. And then everything had soured. She'd been caught crying in a room with two angry men. Who cared what the truth was? The idea that she was at the peak of a love triangle was enough to feed the gossips.

The truth was far more amazing. Tavin had *kissed* her. And he had disposed of Gerald without using fisticuffs or a weapon. She'd never seen anything like it, and although she found violence abhorrent, Tavin's speed and strength were impressive. In a matter of seconds, he'd rendered his opponent helpless without inflicting injury. Were all men as strong and efficient?

Judging from Mr. Scarcliff's weak attempt to kick Tavin, the answer was no.

"Your turn again." Petey grinned at her.

She, Eddie and Petey played several turns at spillikins, passing a thin, metal hook between them as they sat on the plush rug around the wooden rods, attempting to capture one with the hook without disturbing the other rods.

She maneuvered the hook under a rod but knocked others in the process. "Well, that was not well done, was it, lads?"

She muddled through her turn at the child's game, just as she muddled her way through life. It seemed she was destined to stare an objective in the face but not be able to achieve it, no matter her determination. But how hard should it have been to come to London, to see new things and make friends? Why couldn't she enjoy a normal Season like every other young woman?

Because nothing went right for her, not since she'd set the fire and all her hopes and possessions—and her parents' lives—had disintegrated to ash.

She handed the hook to Eddie and something thumped below stairs. The door knocker?

Had Tavin come? Her fingers pressed against her mouth. How would he look at her, after that kiss? Would his gaze hold tenderness or disdain? He had not wanted her to attend the masque last night. But *he'd* been the one who'd over-reacted. *He'd* caused the disturbance, laid his surprisingly

gentle lips on hers, set her reeling, and then had the gall to
storm from the comtesse's house without a fare-thee-well.

The whole carriage ride home last night, Wyling had
defended him, saying Tavin thought he saw trouble. What
nonsense. No smuggler could gain access to the comtesse's
masque. Hadn't Mr. Scarcliff said it would be harder to
gain entrée into the comtesse's than to Almack's?

Ah, Mr. Scarcliff. Gemma took the hook from Petey.
She'd thought Gerald Scarcliff a safe gentleman, enamored
of Frances. Recalling the puckering of his lips when he
tried to kiss her, Gemma grimaced. How wrong she'd been.

The sticks knocked together.

Petey laughed. "Aunt Gem, you are losing."

"So I am."

The nursery door opened with a soft creak and Barton,
one of the footmen, nodded at her. "His lordship requests
you in the library, miss."

"Aw." Eddie popped a finger into his mouth.

"I am trounced by you two, at any rate. Perhaps Nellie will take my place." Gemma stood and smoothed the
gauze fichu tucked around her neck. Through the thin
fabric, her pulse raced like a hunted doe's. "I shall see the
pair of you later."

If they all were not sent home because of her disgrace-
ful role in bringing two gentlemen to blows, that is.

Despite the cheery fire blazing in the grate, a cold gloom
settled over the library, causing Gemma to shiver. The
chamber's inhabitants—Wyling, Amy and Tavin—all rose
at her entrance. Wyling smiled, no doubt trying to set her
at ease. "Pray be seated."

Tavin moved toward the window, his arms folded.
Waves of frustration emanated from his tense shoulders.

She need not have worried about *how* he would look

at her. It seemed he had chosen to avoid all eye contact whatsoever.

She took a seat far from the fire. "How bad is it?"

"It made the *Morning Post*." Amy tried to smile and failed.

The little tea and gruel Gemma had managed to swallow this morning threatened to come up. "Oh."

Wyling tapped the sheet. "Listen to this. 'Besotted at last, Mr. "Black" forgets himself over Miss "Red," whose company he has oft kept in recent weeks, and fends off another suitor.'" He set down the paper with a gentle rustle. "It will not be difficult to add sums and come up with the two of you."

Amy's eyes moistened. "I expect it will blow over, dear, but our social standing is not so high that you are immune to exclusion by society."

Although the news was not unexpected, Gemma still sucked in a cold breath. She and the boys could be back under Cristobel's squat thumb in a sennight, if they returned on the morrow. "I am sorry. To all of you. I will see about packing at once."

"You misunderstand." Amy blotted her eyes with a lace-trimmed handkerchief. "We must wait and see if invitations are withdrawn."

"They already have been." Gemma pulled the creased note from her pocket. "Frances sent word this morning. She canceled our outing to Kew Gardens this afternoon."

"Perhaps she is ill."

"Her suitor lured me into an empty chamber with amorous intent. I embarrassed her and betrayed her aunt's hospitality by causing a scene. Frances's meaning is clear. She no longer wishes my friendship." She stared at the disarrayed curls on the back of Tavin's head. Why would he not turn around and face her?

"It was not your intention to wound her. Perhaps she will see reason?" Amy sniffed the last of her tears. A fresh round of guilt settled over Gemma. How could she so upset her sister?

"I intend to pursue reconciliation." Gemma tried to smile. "Whether she, or anyone else in society, accepts me is another matter, but I'd like to make things right with Frances."

Wyling shrugged. "I doubt a one of us will be invited to the comtesse's masques again, but as for the rest of the Season? Last night's occurrence will prove no more than a trifle. Remember the tidbit of gossip in the *Post*? Knox's actions are credited to lovesickness. The bon ton believes him jealous, no more."

The idea of Tavin as envious was ridiculous. He may have kissed her, but he regretted it now, considering he would not look at her. "And such a perception is not bad?"

"Every Season sees its share of duels, dilemmas and couples caught in the dark," Wyling said. "But Tavin's actions may come to be viewed as protective, considering what I heard from a few acquaintances I met in the park on my ride this morning. Apparently Scarcliff spent the night at a gaming den, losing more than he's worth. One fellow said he's already indebted to some unsavory sorts. I didn't know Scarcliff gambled, of course, but it sounds as if he's in trouble."

"It is bad enough he used Frances for her connections. Might he have pursued her for her funds, too?" Gemma's heart sank. "Poor Frances. I must make things right with her."

Wyling nodded. "In the meantime, as Amy noted, we must exercise patience. You're to attend the Hartwoods' ball in a sennight, I believe? Lord and Lady Hartwood are the highest sticklers of decorum. If they retract their invitation, then we will make a decision. Does that sound fair?"

"It does." Amy's shoulders relaxed. "And the *Post's* tittle-tattle about you and Tavin? It could be of help, Gem. If your names are linked, mayhap it will be easier for him to protect you."

Tavin didn't move. Didn't speak. How he much must loathe having his name joined with hers, to have others believe him infatuated with her.

"I see you do not care for the alliance of our names, Tavin." Her tone sizzled her tongue.

He spun around, his dark brows forming a low V over his eyes. They were not the tender, dark eyes that had gazed down upon her last night while his hands cradled her face.

"Not for me." His tone was cold as stone.

"You would prefer ostracism to a mention in the gossip pages?"

"I have survived both. I prefer neither."

Did he resent her so much? Obviously he regretted the kiss.

She had spent the night at turns mortified and thrilled. His kiss, brief as it was, had stirred memories of being held in his arms, her cheek against his heart, as he carried her from the pond so many weeks ago in the New Forest. She had wondered, after the brief kiss, if they would be closer now.

Instead, a large vein bulged in his neck, just above his neck cloth. So angry.

Gemma's spine straightened. It was worthless succumbing to the doldrums over a man in whom she inspired nothing but anger and remorse.

"Then go, please, Tavin. To Hampshire. To wherever you are sent. Godspeed." Although her words were scorched at the edges, she meant them. With God's help, perhaps he would be happy and complete.

Tavin turned his glare to Wyling. "I take it you did not tell her?"

Wyling's jaw tightened. "I told the ladies you interpreted a threat. That is all."

"All?" Tavin flung out his arm.

What were they talking about? Gemma leaned forward.

Wyling folded his arms. "I saw no use alarming the ladies, telling them you may—or may not—have seen a man stalking Gemma if it turned out he wasn't the Sovereign."

Amy's face pinked. "Stalking?"

"But I was not stalked by the Sovereign." Gemma skewered Tavin with a glower. "You attacked an innocent man last night—innocent of smuggling, at any rate. Mr. Scarcliff is a bounder and, I suppose, a gambler, but he is no felon. He is a man whom, I might add, I am capable of felling with my feet." If the words were stated with enough clarity, perhaps he would finally listen. *"The Sovereign is not in London."*

Tavin reached into his pocket and withdrew a gold coin. "I found this last night."

"A sovereign." Coincidence. "They are everywhere—"

"Not often near the mouth of a man found near-dead off Piccadilly."

A cap of cold settled over Gemma's head and worked its way down her spine. "What?"

"I came upon him last night, searching for the man who had shadowed you."

"Will he survive? Who was he? Poor man." Her fingers clutched on her lap. "But how do you know he was not set upon by thieves?"

"A cutpurse would not leave a coin behind." Tavin

passed the gold coin to Wyling. "Money was not the object of the attack. *You* were."

Her pulse beat hard in her chest. "I do not understand."

"The Honorable Mr. Theophilus Grenville, the victim, was a guest of the comtesse's. He decided to walk to the masque, but he never arrived because he had been struck on the side of the head, stripped of his domino and entrée into the masque and left in an alley with that sovereign on his neck. I expect the coin would have ended up in Grenville's throat, just as one has in all of the Sovereign's previous victims, but—"

"That is enough," Wyling interrupted. "No need to terrify the ladies with such talk."

Gemma gaped. 'Twas not the talk that terrified her. *He had been there?*

Tavin's head tipped. "Gemma should know what she is facing. She has taken this too lightly."

"We all have." Amy's hands were at her chest. "None of us thought for a minute she was in real trouble. Not even you, Tavin."

"Touché, madam. But I think it now. Her life is in danger."

Gemma sank back into her seat. The children. Peter and Cristobel. Wyling and Amy. Were they in peril because of her? Even strangers such as the unfortunate Mr. Grenville had been hurt because she'd had the misfortune to wear a red cloak and take a walk up a hill.

Father God… She licked her lips. Words to pray wouldn't form in her fogged brain. All she could think was, *Help me. Help us all.*

"Why now?" she squeaked at last. "After all this time?"

Tavin leaned against the mantelpiece. "The Sovereign either found you or determined you know something incriminating. He, or someone acting on his behalf, donned a domino and stalked you at the comtesse's."

God protected me. Gemma's hand pressed her roiling stomach.

"You left the ballroom for the hall, as did he. Then you both were gone." He tunneled a hand through his already untidy curls. "It took me far too long to find you, but when I did, you were in a closed chamber with a man in a black domino. The *wrong* man, it turned out, but I do not regret assisting you."

"Thank you." A swallow lodged, aching, in her throat. "For watching me. For tearing Gerald Scarcliff from me. Even if he was not the man you wanted."

Tavin's shoulders relaxed. Where had his anger gone? "Rake though he is, Scarcliff may have saved your life. If he had not pulled you into the room, the other man could have—" He broke off, glancing at Wyling.

But Gemma couldn't be protected from the gruesome facts. "Taken me. Killed me."

Amy rushed to her side, cupping Gemma's cheek with cool fingers. "Gemma, no."

"It is true. After all, back on Verity Hill, I saw his face." She stared at Tavin, trusting him to tell her the truth. "But I never saw the man in the domino. Where did he go, after the masque?"

"I would pay my last sixpence to gain that knowledge. He used the confusion of the, er, *incident* with Scarcliff to slip out. You can imagine what it was like outside the comtesse's house, men in black dominoes and cloaks going in both directions. I could not very well challenge them all."

Gemma squeezed Amy's hand, hoping to draw strength from her sister. As she did, she took in Amy's wide eyes, heard her sister's shaky breaths. Amy needed strength, too, especially after having been ill. Even now, Amy looked as if she might cast up her breakfast or burst into tears.

Recrimination settled, heavy and barbed, over Gemma's bones. She had taken from everyone for so long. Wyling's hospitality, Amy's patience and care, Tavin's protection.

And what had she given back? Nothing but defiance and selfishness.

That was not the woman she wanted to be. That was not the Gemma who had kicked the Sovereign in the leg and escaped him in the forest.

The anger she'd lost a few minutes ago surged in her veins and straightened her spine—but it was directed inward. She would make things right with her family, and Tavin and Frances, too. But she would not cow before a villain. How dare this Sovereign think to frighten her family? To harm innocent people?

His victims passed through her brain. Men back home, strangers to her but neighbors all the same. Tavin's friend, Thomason, who had striven to bring their killer to justice. Poor Mr. Grenville, who had just wanted to attend a party, the same as she.

The Sovereign had harmed them all—and probably more—to achieve his illicit goals. She could well guess how free the Sovereign was with the grim souvenirs he named himself after.

Poor Tavin. Smudged crescents under his eyes bespoke of his lack of sleep, and the faint lines around his eyes and brow deepened, making him appear older, wearier. All he wanted was to stop the Sovereign's reign, yet he was shackled to her as surely as if a chain bound their ankles.

His superior at the Custom House might not see fit to free him, but she would.

"I see no need to wait until our invitations are withdrawn." Resolve modulated her tone. "I shall return to Hampshire at once."

"Back to Cristobel?" Amy shook her head. "No."

But it was Tavin's response she wanted to hear. For a long moment, he stared at her, his gaze intense. "I can protect you here."

"I know you can. But if I return to Verity House, you will be ordered to accompany me, and from there, you will be able to catch the Sovereign and be done with this."

His massive chest heaved once as he took a long, slow breath. "You told me once you wanted this Season above all else. Now you would willingly abandon it?"

"Yes." She licked her dry lips, but her tongue had no moisture to spare.

Wyling and Amy's protests sounded, but she couldn't listen, couldn't respond. Her entire focus was fixed on Tavin. He quirked that brow of his.

"The roses are in bloom in the garden. Care to join me outside?"

It wasn't what she expected, but she nodded. "Certainly."

"Gemma," Amy pleaded. "You two will not make a decision without us."

"Do not make me behave the disgruntled brother-in-law." Wyling frowned.

"We shall not be but a moment, and you can watch us from the windows."

At Amy's reluctant nod, Gemma gathered her Kashmir shawl and preceded Tavin to the garden.

Tavin scanned the garden for flutters of white apron, or the straw of a hat—anything to indicate a servant at work among the plants. Nothing stirred but the bobbing heads of pink and purple flowers. He nodded in satisfaction.

The walled plot was not large, but it was private. And pleasant, too, with interwoven, pleached limes greening the garden walls. Box, rose, peony and lavender added color and fragrance, but its small size offered a stark contrast to his childhood home's garden, where the wide paths, fountains and mature trees had seemed to stretch into the wild beyond the estate borders.

Why think of Scotland just now? Far more pressing matters demanded his attention, and he had best get started before they were interrupted.

"Let us speak freely." He paced over the narrow gravel path. "It appears you have something to say to me, as well."

"It is as I said." The breeze stirred Gemma's hair, sending a lock of hair under her nose. She pushed it behind her ear and sat on the wood bench facing the garden's center, where a whitewashed pole served as a honeysuckle stake. "It will be better for us all if I return to Hampshire. If you convince Amy and Wyling of the merit of such an idea, they will allow it."

"You credit me with far too much influence."

Her laugh sounded more like a scoff. "I am in danger. Shouldn't my acceptance of the fact please you?"

"I should far prefer to have been wrong."

"Whilst we have privacy, I must speak." She squared her shoulders and stared up at him. "I am sorry."

He had not expected *that*. Did she refer to last night's kiss? He should be the one apologizing for taking such liberties. "'Twas not your fault."

"Enraging the Sovereign isn't, true. I could not help that. But I have made things difficult. I resented your advice. I thwarted your rules. And I insisted we attend the masque despite your protestations." She rubbed her cuticles with her thumbs. "I embarrassed us all—you, Frances, everyone. You must judge me a callous creature."

She hadn't mentioned the kiss, but the apology affected him almost as deeply. He could only return her honesty.

"Callous? No, but you are many other things. Patient with your nephews. Generous with your family. Defiant with me. But not callous."

Her head bobbed in time with the pink roses. "'Tis no excuse, but when Hugh chose to make other plans, I saw few options for my future. Cristobel's companion, a task I do not relish. I could live with Amy and Wyling, true. Or I could become a governess or wed. But I choose to stay at Verity House, with Cristobel, because of the boys. They need me and I…need them."

Would Tavin make the same choice? He'd left home, but then again, there was no one there for him to love. Or who loved him. "I see."

"So I made two decisions." Her lashes fluttered against her pale cheeks. "I have withheld them from you."

His heart stopped. "Does one involve those letters you have sent to your chamber?"

"I should have guessed you knew. When I realized where my future lay, I hired a solicitor. He makes investments on my behalf. Small ones, but I send him all I have. Perhaps by the time Eddie leaves for school, I will have enough to set up my own household. I will offer to care for the boys on their holidays, and I am certain Cristobel and Peter will allow it." She shifted on the bench. "I couldn't receive the solicitor's call without your or Amy's knowledge, so we correspond. But you knew, anyway."

"Only that you hid something from me." Not known from whom they came. He'd even told Garner about the letters. "I wish you'd told me."

"You would have told Wyling and Amy, and they would have offered me money. They've given me too much already."

Tavin's gaze fixed on the lavender. "There were two decisions, you said?"

She sighed. "The other, you know well. I chose to squeeze every moment of pleasure out of the Season as I could. No matter what, because this was my sole chance to experience adventure. Fun. I suppose that I pushed away any nagging of conscience, as if later, had I inconvenienced anyone, I could ask for forgiveness."

Something like resentment prickled under his skin. "Willingly sin, and plan to ask forgiveness later?"

"I was not sensible of it, did not plan it. But I justified my greediness. Such a light view of forgiveness smacks of entitlement, does it not? Not grace." She looked down. "Perhaps, because I was forgiven much, I forgive easily."

He resumed pacing over the gravel. Oh, if forgiveness were that simple. But whatever Gemma had done that needed clemency could not compare to *his* blotted past.

But they were speaking of Gemma, not him. Although he could not help but be curious about what she'd done that was *forgiven much*. Instead, he allowed himself another question.

"Is that why you are kind to Hugh, when you had every right to knock out his teeth?"

"Little good it would do me to knock out his teeth. Or gnash mine over him forever."

Gnashing teeth. Now that sounded familiar.

She sighed. "I was hurt, but it was my expectations, not my heart, that ached. I am confident now God has something else in mind."

Like scrounging pence so she could be independently poor for the rest of her days, with occasional visits from her nephews? His scowl pained his cheeks. "And you forgive your brother and his wife for the way they mistreat you?"

"Yes, but that is not why I stay with them. As I said, I wish to be with the boys."

"And it has nothing to do with *owing* Peter and Cristobel?"

"I do owe them." Her eyes went wide. "They took me in."

"As they should. It is called familial duty. Theirs, not yours."

"Familial duty extends both directions."

Not in this instance. Gemma had given up a large portion of her life for her brother. She'd also forsaken her future for her nephews. Chances were slim she would marry and have a family of her own if she waited much longer. It was cruel, yes, but the way of things in society.

And with that thought, Tavin's frustration dissipated like mist over a loch. "I do not wish to return to Hampshire. I wish to stay here, with you, through the remainder of the Season."

A huff escaped her shell-pink lips. "Catching the Sovereign cannot be accomplished here."

"It can if he has come out of hiding to find you."

"He will strike again?" Was it fear or determination that flashed in her eyes?

"Fear not, I will be with you." The words sounded too Biblical, and he shook his head. "Mayhap Wyling was correct. Let the world think I am 'besotted at last.' If I live in your pocket, I will better be able to protect you."

A flush pinked her cheeks to a becoming shade. "Agreed. On one condition."

He stifled the urge to roll his eyes. "Just one? I'm amazed."

She stood, tilting her chin to look him in the eye. "I will not cower before the Sovereign. I will help you catch him."

Chapter Fourteen

Tavin tugged at his ear as if the act could clear his hearing. "You did not just say, 'catch the Sovereign.'"

"I did." Gemma folded her hands before her.

Was the woman mad? "You are not a piece of cheese to trap a rat."

"Hunting a rat leads to bites. But setting a trap in the middle of the room lures him out."

His speech faltered again. "You are bound for Bedlam if you think I shall let you—as if you are capable—"

"Your face is purpling. Would you care to be seated?"

"I am not apoplectic. I am furious." He forced his fisted fingers to open. "You will not invite the Sovereign's attentions as bait, do you understand?"

"I do not need to *invite his attentions*. He follows me with a coin in one hand and a blade in the other, and I wish to stop him."

His boots crunched the gravel of the oval garden path, but the rhythmic pacing failed to soothe him. The space was too small to take him more than a few feet from her in this wee garden. Or cage, more like it, with its high walls and limited view. How could people choose this life, this confinement? He reached down to a lavender bush and snapped off a tender sea green stem.

"Pray do not attack the plants, Tavin."

"Better a bloom than someone's neck."

"I assume you refer to the Sovereign's, not to mine."

He glared. "Is this part of your thirst for so-called adventure? Playing at spy?"

"Of course not." She flushed crimson. "I want to help."

"Trained in combat, are you?" He tossed the lavender into the scraggly rosebushes. "Practiced boxing at Gentleman Jackson's? Or perhaps you think my work is simple. Guess how many knives I carry on my person at this moment."

"What a forward suggestion."

"Two. One at my back and one in my boot. But sometimes I carry three."

The pink receded from her cheeks and she laughed, the sound like her nephews' cackles. In any other circumstance, he might think her becoming, with her eyes alight. A charming image. But not today, with his vision swimming red.

"Think you this is amusing? Ach, lass, ye're more trouble than ye know."

Shame, hot and quick, flooded to his toes. Had he said *lass? Ye?* He chomped down on his tongue. How long had it been since he'd spoken like that? Like a Scot?

That is what you are.

No. It is what I was. That was how he had spoken when he was a bairn. And how he'd tried *not* to speak when he was a youth, his fingers swollen from lashings under Her Grace's instructions to replace his brogue with a refined English accent. He had been so careful, until that time at Eton school, when he got his nose broken by an older student for slipping and speaking like a Scot.

He was nothing now, not Scot, not English. Because he could not be both.

Had Gemma caught the words? He dared not peek to find out.

The crisp fabric of her gown swished, and the scent of lavender swirled in the air. Then her hands rested on his forearms. He braced himself.

"So *there* you are, Tavin. The real you."

No one knew the *real* him. No one would like him. Or forgive him. Not even God had done that.

Tavin cleared his throat as if the act could rattle all traces of brogue and pain from his throat. "We are not discussing me. We are speaking of your folly."

"Discussing my follies would take all afternoon." Her hands fell. "I know you mean to frighten me by your talk of knives, and I assure you, I am horrified. That is why I wish to end this. I may not have experience with weaponry," she said, her lips twitching, "but if I cannot serve as bait, I can do something else to help you."

At her quirking brow, he resumed pacing. "Such as?"

"Allow me to accompany you when you call on those sources of yours—"

"*Call?* We do not leave calling cards, I assure you."

"—and mayhap I will recognize my attacker among them."

"Never."

"I want to help you."

"If you wish to help me, you will do what I ask. Please, for your sake. Your family's sake. And mine."

Her gaze cooled, but she nodded. "Very well. I will not fight you. But do not forget, I am willing to return to Hampshire at any time."

It could not be that simple, but her eyes held no trace

of mischief. She meant her words. She was willing to sacrifice her Season.

"You will return to Hampshire. But you shall have your Season first."

"I have had it. And the cost of my thirst for *new experiences* was too dear." She spit the words as if they were curses. "No, from now on I shall do what the Lord wills, not what I will."

God's will. He had forgotten to seek it. He shut his eyes. *Lord, may Your will be for the Sovereign to be caught, for my sin to be atoned. For Gemma to be happy. But whate'er Your desire, not my will but Yours be done.*

A calm gentleness settled in Tavin's bones. With it came the assurance the Lord could redeem the situation. Tavin didn't wish to play as her suitor, but the idea did not panic him as it had an hour ago. He would be better able to watch her.

"I will not kiss you again." The words were too blunt, but when had he ever known how to speak well? "I should not have done that. It was improper."

"It was a hasty gesture of relief on our parts." Her gaze skirted her hem.

"I *was* relieved." Yet more than relief inspired him.

"So." Gemma's gaze rose. "Are you now my besotted beau, as the *Post* suggests?"

"Yes. Besotted and moon-eyed."

"One of us will be jilted quite publicly. I say it should be you."

Teasing lilted in her tone. Did she find the notion of his escort in public…fun? A twitch tugged at his lips. "No one would question your judgment."

"Perhaps this is forward, but if the invitation to the Hartwoods' ball is not retracted, will you escort me?" Did she bat her eyes?

"I should be delighted."

"And to view the Elgin Marbles? The boys would like to see them."

"Anything." Everything.

A flutter at the window caught his eye, indicating they were being watched, and he gestured they should return inside.

Her smile slipped. "I am to blame for all of this. All I wanted was a taste of freedom, and I caused naught but pain. I feel the ache of it deep in my soul, but there is not a thing I can do to remedy it."

He knew precisely how she felt.

A sense of peace curled Gemma's shoulders along with her Kashmir shawl the remainder of the afternoon. Once the boys settled for their afternoon rests, she sought out Amy, finding her in one of the morning room's comfortable armchairs. A length of bleached linen, taut in a tambour frame, rested on her lap. "May I join you?"

"There is no need for you to ask. Pray be seated." Amy smiled and plunked the silver needle into the linen. "Are the boys asleep?"

"They lie upon their beds, but that is all I can say." Gemma took the padded chair across from her sister even though it was too close to the fire burning in the hearth for her comfort—but not from the temperature.

Amy's brows furrowed. "There is no need for you to be close to the fire. Move to another chair."

"I wish to look on you." And this was the best way.

"Let us move to the table, then." Amy slipped a pair of scissors into the beaded huswife alongside her collection of needles and gathered up the linen.

"No." Gemma caught her sister's hand. "You must stay

warm. It is evident you are still unwell. And I have contributed to your illness."

"How so?" Faint dimpling appeared in Amy's pale cheeks.

"You are fatigued. You've lacked color in your cheeks for weeks now, and 'tis because I brought this trouble on you." Hot tears stung her eyes. "You and Wyling are good to me, yet I was greedy for more. I insisted we attend the masque. I made you cry. I am so sorry." She abandoned the chair and knelt at Amy's feet.

"Dear Gem." Amy's hands were gentle on Gemma's crown. "You know I named you, did you not?"

Gemma swiped her eyes, so as not to drip on Amy's needlework. "No."

"I had been reading something Italian and I thought *Gemma* the most wonderful name, so I convinced Mama. A gem is what you will always be to me. My precious sister."

The urge to make a harsh noise of disagreement rumbled in Gemma's throat, but she swallowed it down. Amy had taught her she was prized in the eyes of God, no matter her emotions. "I nevertheless regret causing such trouble by my selfishness."

"All is well between us, sweet sister."

Gemma rose to embrace her sister. "I do not deserve you."

"If it relieves you, you did not make me ill." Amy's cheeks reddened. "That is all Wyling's doing."

Wyling had hurt her? Her jaw slackened. "Amy."

"I am…increasing."

Gemma dropped to her knees again. "A baby?" After over six years of marriage?

"At long last." Amy was crying and laughing at the same time. "I know the subject is not fit for maiden ears, but how could I not tell you we are to be blessed by year's end?"

"How could God's blessings be unfit for my ears? Oh, darling." She crushed her sister to her. "What joy." *Thank You, Lord.*

"I agree." Amy's voice was muffled against Gemma's shoulder.

Gemma pulled back from her sister. "Have I hurt you?"

Amy's grin stretched over her cheeks. "I feel wonderful."

A baby, at long last. Gemma laughed. "So do I."

"He feels unwell." The woman reminded Tavin of a falcon—beak nosed, her hand clutching the staircase banister like talons. Brown in hair and dress, she peered at him with small, dark eyes. "You must not weary him."

Tavin nodded. He would do well to obey this daughter-in-law of Mr. Theophilus Grenville, for with one false word, he would be sent from the sickroom. And he needed to complete this interview.

Ascending the stairs, his fingers found the scrap of green ribbon in his pocket, his constant reminder of what had happened atop Verity Hill. Would he now learn another clue as to the identity of the Sovereign?

Gemma's features flashed before his eyes. As ever when it did, his heart pattered hard and fast, like rain against a windowpane. Tavin shook his head, focusing on the task at hand.

Mrs. Grenville preceded him into a stale, closed-up room decorated in shades of blue. A man of some sixty years was propped in bed against numerous pillows, a bandage wrapped about his balding head.

"Mr. Grenville?" Tavin bowed. "Thank you for seeing me."

"My daughter-in-law tells me you are the one who found me. Knox, is it?"

"It is. I am gratified to see you sitting up. You took quite a knock on the head."

"Might have killed me." Outrage emanated from Grenville's quivering limbs.

The daughter-in-law shoved past Tavin. "Do not excite yourself. The physician said to rest." She pulled the coverlet over Mr. Grenville's bony chest.

"I am not an invalid, Elspeth." He scowled at her, then at Tavin. "So I owe you thanks?"

He sounded more aggrieved than appreciative, but Tavin dipped his head. "I'm relieved you are well, but I would see your attacker brought to justice. Did you observe him?"

"As he struck me on the *back* of the head? How is a man supposed to see that?"

No help there. "Your domino and entrée were stolen, but not your purse. Perchance the attacker targeted you because he wished to attend the Comtesse du Vertaile's masque. Did you discuss your plans for the evening with a stranger?"

"Who are you, a Bow Street Runner?" Grenville harrumphed. "I *always* attend the comtesse's masques. Everyone of consequence knows that."

"Begging your pardon, then."

"Do we know one another? *Knox*, you said." Grenville's eyes sparked like flint in the dim room. "I knew your mother. Lady Cassandra Stanhope, before she wed. You favor her, with your dark hair and eyes."

Tavin's muscles stiffened. "Yes."

"A diamond of the first water, she was. Everyone's tongues wagged about her, even before she ran off with that Scot."

Hamish Knox. My father. A muscle worked in Tavin's jaw.

"Whatever happened to her?"

Tavin swallowed hard. It was always the same when peers remembered his mother. First, they recalled her beauty and popularity. Second, her scandal. The mention of the latter was impolite, yet everyone did it, perhaps because they considered Tavin—the younger son of an eloped couple who had hidden the rest of their too-short lives in Scotland—inferior.

Invoke Kelworth. His grandmother had taught him to remind everyone of his ancestry. But Grenville was not worth the effort.

"Until their death in a carriage accident some years ago, my parents were happy, which is what concerned you, I am sure." Tavin bowed. "Thank you for your time. Mr. Grenville, Mrs. Grenville."

He turned on his heel, quit the musty-smelling room and left the house. Heat pounded in his temples, his fists, in his feet as he stomped down the street.

He'd received no answers from Grenville, but he *had* gotten a reminder. He did not belong among the so-called bon ton, and he never would. He would have to pretend a confidence he did not feel openly escorting Gemma to the Hartwoods' ball and to view the Elgin Marbles and whatever else she wished to do while she crammed a lifetime's entertainment into one short Season. He did not belong in London but, for her sake, he would bear it.

And looking at it that way, the prospect of bearing the weight of his dislike of society didn't weigh as heavily on him.

In fact, it made him smile.

Chapter Fifteen

The morning after the Hartwoods' ball, Gemma stood near the great staircase at Montague House, where the Elgin Marbles were displayed, and smiled at Tavin. "I do not know what you mean."

"I am certain you do." His knowing grin was utterly charming despite his teasing. "I warned you last night that you'd regret dancing half the night away, yet you wouldn't listen. And here you are, weary already and we haven't yet begun."

Pity he was correct. Her feet did ache, but she'd not share such a private tidbit with him. Instead, she turned to the boys. "Are you ready to view the statues?"

"I have wanted to view them forever." Petey nodded.

"Me, too." Eddie said, his gloved finger at his rosy lips. "Ever and ever."

Forever and ever, yet the pieces from the Athens Parthenon had been acquired by the British Museum only a year ago. Gemma chuckled and tucked Eddie's hand in hers. "There are rooms upon rooms to explore." Even though the arches of her feet protested the plan.

"Rooms upon rooms," Tavin echoed, chuckling. The

sound drew curious gazes from other museum patrons filling the halls to view Lord Elgin's marbles.

A few female glances lingered on Tavin, and the impulse to glare at them narrowed Gemma's eyes. As if she was jealous. A choke tickled the back of her throat. Ridiculous. She had no *feelings* like that for Tavin Knox.

Oh, he was handsome. She had always thought so, from the moment of their introduction. His black coat fit his muscular frame to perfection; his dark eyes twinkled, and an errant lock curled over his brow.

But he was a government operative forced to protect her, and she was a spinster aunt with a murderer pursuing her. Their relationship was an arrangement based on security. Not l—

Love? The museum grew hot. And, oh, how tight had she fastened the Pomona-green ribbon of her bonnet under her chin, anyway? Her fingers fought the urge to loosen it.

Instead, she required both hands to grasp her nephews' fingers. Waiting at a discreet distance, the spindle-legged, young under-librarian assigned to escort them through the museum eyed the boys with suspicion, as if he did not approve of their presence. True, Wyling had needed to acquire permission to include the children this morning. But they were no trouble. Gemma smiled at them, pleased by their patience. "Another minute for Uncle Wyling to finish his conversation, and we will view the marbles and all the other treasures."

Wyling lingered a few paces behind, conversing the price of corn with Viscount Hadley. Amy suffered under the persistent tittering of Hadley's tiny viscountess, the phrase "young Mr. Scarcliff" repeated over and over. As if Gemma cared of him. Frances's lost friendship, however, was another matter. She frowned.

Tavin's gaze met hers, his brows scrunched in sympathy. "Do not listen to Lady Hadley. Remember, the Hart-woods welcomed you to their ball last night. Most of the whispers about you mention Tavin Knox, the Duke of Kelworth's odd nephew, losing his temper and escorting you to last night's ball."

"Did you dance with Aunt Gem at the Hartwoods'?" Petey rocked on his heels.

"Petey." Warmth lapped up Gemma's cheeks.

"Alas, I do not dance." Tavin smirked.

Of course he did not dance. He was too busy strolling about the room's perimeter and monitoring the grounds.

Gemma had not worried about the Sovereign at the Hartwoods'. No one wore disguises. If the Sovereign had joined the party, one nod and Tavin would have trounced the villain.

Although it must be difficult for him to guard her in a heavy crowd, like now, when it seemed all of London had turned out to view the Elgin Marbles. Did she make things yet more problematic for him by being here?

The ache in Gemma's feet sprouted to her stomach. *Father, You are with me. You've sent Tavin to watch over us. Please protect us all.*

Tavin's brow furrowed, his gaze raking her features. "Something wrong?"

"Perhaps we should have stayed at home, away from people."

"Stayed home for you to rest, mayhap, but if you refer to me protecting you?" He feigned a look of offense.

"Come, Aunt Gem." Petey stood on his toes and craned his neck. "I see the preserved giraffes on the landing."

"We must wait for Aunt Amy and Uncle Wyling." But both boys tugged at her hands. The under-librarian's eyes narrowed.

"We've waited forever." Petey sighed.

"Ever and ever." Eddie nodded.

Gemma willed herself not to grow impatient, too. Pity the under-librarian didn't whet the boys' appetites by informing them what they'd see, but the fellow no doubt dismissed the children as insignificant and preferred to await Wyling. She exchanged looks with Tavin.

He smiled. "While we wait, let's look at the curiosities in that cabinet over there."

Eddie sucked his free finger and Petey scowled, but they obediently accompanied her to peer into the display case. A few manuscripts did not hold their interest, but then Tavin gasped. "I say."

"What?" Petey hopped to his toes. Eddie bounced. Even Gemma leaned down, but all she saw was a cluster of minerals, side by side.

Tavin made a show of squinting. "I recall a tale from my youth of the seven gemstones. By order of King Richard the Lionheart, a long-forgotten brotherhood of knights was tasked with protecting the gems from a mysterious foe while the king went on crusade, and when he returned, he would sell the gems to create an even larger army of knights."

Smart, that Tavin. Anything to do with knights was bound to hold their attention. Gemma smiled at his foray into the world of imagination. "Is that so?"

"'Twas only a tale."

A tale he'd just made up, jiffy-on-the-spot, no doubt. Tavin shrugged, but winked at her.

Petey blinked. "I count seven. And see, that one is purple. Is it an ameth-oh, that purple stone?"

"It is," Gemma answered in truth.

"I say they are King Richard's gems." Eddie hopped.

"The knights served the king to the death." Petey rocked from one foot to another.

"I am King Richard," Eddie declared.

"You are not." Petey spun. "He was the eldest, like me. And he had a beard."

"So do I." Eddie curled his index finger over his top lip, like a mustache. "I shave it."

"How many days a week?" Tavin asked, looking serious.

Gemma giggled, then caught Amy's eye. At last, Viscount and Viscountess Hadley nodded their farewells, and Amy and Wyling came alongside them, their mouths turned down in apology.

"Forgive me. We had hoped for a meeting with the Prince Regent, but he has gone to Brighton." Wyling's brow creased. "With the price of corn continuing to rise and men gathering in protest, this is not the time to—" He shook his head. "This is neither the time nor place for politics. Or anything else. Shall we?"

Amy's eyes communicated she knew well what else was, and she'd tell Gemma the moment she had the opportunity. Then they ascended the stairs at last, and Petey cast a last, lingering look at the cabinet. Gemma bit back her smile.

After viewing rooms of manuscripts, vases and minerals—which did not belong to any knights, according to the under-librarian when Petey asked—they at last entered the rooms where Elgin's marbles were displayed. They passed a series of metopes depicting scenes of life in ancient Athens, replete with warriors. Since the under-librarian was more concerned with impressing Wyling, she took on the role of the boys' guide. "The Earl of Elgin brought these back to England from Greece, and now we may view them. Are they not remarkable?"

"What is that?" Eddie pointed at a broken frieze.

"Charioteer." Tavin's voice was gentle, as if there was

nothing he'd rather be doing than accompanying a female and two children through a museum. "See here, the front wheel of the chariot, and the man's arms, holding the horse's reins."

"These friezes were at the Acropolis, fixed to the Parthenon, when Jesus walked the earth."

"Did He see these?"

"No, but Paul visited Athens and told the people there about God." Tavin tipped his head and related the Bible story.

His words jolted Gemma. Not many individuals spoke of faith outside of church. St. George's, Hanover Square, was oft packed on Sunday mornings, yet many of the parishioners looked down their noses at one another. Her first Sunday in London, Gemma had smiled down the pew at a young woman with the looks of a fellow comeout. But Gemma's smile had not been returned. The lady had scrutinized her clothing during the prayers and sighed during the homily.

The Lord was not much discussed among the beau monde. Yet He was discussed among spies, it seemed. Tavin had made reference to his faith before, but did his beliefs run deeper than most of his peers?

What a strange man he was, up to his neck cloth in secrets and danger. Why was he a spy? His pockets were plump enough without a government salary, so it wasn't money.

Gemma's feet protested every step, but she urged her nephews toward a long frieze of warriors on horseback, their togas flowing behind them.

Tavin put a hand on Petey's shoulder and gestured toward a warrior carved into a frieze. "See the quiver on his back, and the bow in his hand? How I should like to have my hands on those weapons. I should feel like Robin Hood. Have you shot an arrow before?"

They shook their heads, but Petey's eyes glowed. "I wish we could do it now, right here."

Tavin smiled. "The notion is tempting, but we haven't a decent target in here."

Eddie frowned. "And Aunt Gemma would grow angry with you."

"True, and her wrath is considerable." Tavin winked at her.

Petey's arms twitched, as if eager to pull a shaft from an imaginary quiver. "I would shoot the arrow across the Thames."

"Here is another bow and arrow, Mr. Knox." Eddie tipped his chin toward the frieze. "And another."

"Indeed. What sharp eyes you have, lads." Tavin nodded.

Then he turned so his back was to the frieze, his gaze on the others in the chamber. A casual move, but there was nothing relaxed about the set of his shoulders. His gaze scanned the crowd. The thought that the Sovereign might visit her here in so public a place, with the boys at her side, lifted the hairs at Gemma's nape.

How quickly she had forgotten. She had not paid attention to her surroundings, but Tavin had never ceased. How did he manage to distract the children and watch the crowd, all while managing to show her kindness?

He was a far better man than she'd first judged. A fresh rush of guilt washed over her. "I am sorry you must keep watch like this."

"We are all sorry for something." His glance flicked at the direction of her hem. "I, for one, am sorry your feet are sore from last night."

So he wished to keep the conversation light, did he? "Pah. I could *still* be dancing."

"If I had danced as many sets, I would not be walking about London today."

"As many sets? You did not dance a single one."

"I was clear on that point. I do not dance."

"All gentlemen dance." She pretended to scrutinize a sculpture of an armless, headless woman. "But my discomfort is nothing. I promised the boys we would come today. And I am not tired." Her toes were another matter.

His gaze stayed fixed on the passersby. "At least your popularity at the Hartwoods' ball proved one thing. I did not ruin your social standing. The gentlemen lined up to dance with you."

A hum escaped her lips. "Wyling's friends were tricked into partnering me, I am certain."

His mouth curved open in the way she had come to associate with a tease, but before he spoke, Amy fell behind and drew them back.

"I have learned most distressing news, and I feel you should be aware in the event an acquaintance spies us and makes mention. I would not wish you caught unawares." Amy leaned toward Gemma and Tavin. "There was a duel last night. Mr. Scarcliff."

Tavin's head tipped forward. "Who was the other party?"

"Mr. Edward Dillard. Did you know him?"

His eyes darkened. "Ned? Yes, I did. Many years ago."

Amy frowned. "Mr. Dillard, I regret to say, is deceased. Mr. Scarcliff is nowhere to be found. Remember how Wyling heard he was deep in debt? He must have tried to get out of it by cheating at cards. Mr. Dillard caught and challenged him."

Gemma's hand pressed her heart and stared at Tavin,

whose features remained inscrutable. "I am sorry for the loss of your acquaintance."

"He lived by the sword, and died by it, too."

"Mayhap we should go home, after hearing such news," Gemma offered.

Tavin shook his head, but smiled at her. "I will not disappoint the children."

"Then let us attempt to enjoy ourselves. I am sorry for bearing ill tidings. I'd no idea you knew him." Amy sighed and moved toward the children. "What have been your favorites so far, gentlemen?"

"The seven gemstones of the brotherhood of knights," Petey said. Eddie nodded. Little imps.

Amy took Eddie's hand, and Wyling set a hand on Petey's shoulder. Walking ahead, they left Gemma to walk alongside Tavin.

"Receiving shocking news is difficult, but in public? There is no need to continue on."

He shrugged. "I no longer knew Dillard. And how can I leave the museum? Look at the boys. They are good lads."

"You are kind to them."

"I am not an ogre. I was once a child."

"Alas, patience with children does not spring from having once been a child one's self."

"If it did, everyone would make a proper parent."

So he had noticed the distance between the boys and Peter and Cristobel was not just in miles? "Our parents were loving and generous with us. I cannot explain why my brother does not show the same interest in his children."

"I did not refer to your brother or parents." His eyes darkened. "I referred to mine."

Oh. "You were not close?"

"They were seldom at home. They were in love and

could not be expected to devote their attentions anywhere but on one another. Then my grandmother made arrangements for my schooling in England. When they died, I had not seen them in two years."

"I am sorry." If only she might touch his hand.

"Thank you. But it was many years ago." Wrinkling his brow, he paused beside another sculpture of a headless female form, his gaze on a solitary man passing by. Gemma sensed the discussion would not continue.

Eddie turned around and grinned at Tavin.

Tavin smiled back, but Gemma bit the inside of her cheek. Of course the boys liked Tavin. They had also grown to care for Hugh. Mayhap they liked any gentleman who showed them attention. In a few weeks, there would be no man in their lives except their father. She had better pray more often for Peter to see what gifts he had under his roof.

Tavin leaned toward her. "What do you think of the marbles?"

A safer subject than wounds inflicted by parents' negligence. "I do not like thinking of how they arrived here, hacked off the Parthenon. But they are beautiful. Walking past these antiquities, it is easy to picture myself among the ruins in Athens. Bright sun, hot breeze, the dust of a past civilization swirling about me." She took a deep breath through her nose and imagined it carried the scents of exotic spices.

"Perhaps a journey to Greece is in your future."

She shook her head. "My imaginings are impractical, but I cannot help myself. I would like to see new things. A castle ruin in Wales would excite me to no end. I have always loved castles in books. Go on, laugh."

"I am not laughing." His gaze fixed on her, dark and

calm as the deep pond where she and Hugh had fished as children. "You should go."

He thought himself kind, but his suggestion cut to her marrow. She had made her choice. She would use every last shilling to care for the boys. There would be no adventure for her.

"You know I cannot."

The way he stared at her eyes, her lips, the hair curling about her ears, sent Gemma's stomach thrumming. His mouth was set in a serious line, but he did not appear the least bit angry. Why did he not look away?

Her reticule slipped from her hand and fell to her feet in a soft thump. Tavin bent and retrieved the fist-sized, beaded bag.

"How clumsy of me." She took it from his hand. "Thank you."

An odd look crossed his features. "What about this? Is this yours, as well?"

He pulled a green ribbon some six inches in length from his pocket. Similar to the medium-green shade of her bonnet trimmings, the adornment was duller and wider than her ribbon, and edged in a ragged cut. "A pretty hue, but no. Was it on the floor?" She glanced down.

"It has been in my possession for weeks. I found it pinned under a stone atop Verity Hill, that day you met the Sovereign. I have since wondered what it means, if it is the promised clue from my contact."

"I doubt the Sovereign kills over shipments of ribbon."

He stuffed the ribbon into his pocket. "But its edge was intentionally weighted by the stone. That is why I think it might be important."

"A woman in red is not the quarry after all, then? Mayhap it was a woman in green." She grinned at the silliness of the notion as they followed Wyling, Amy and the boys through the exhibition hall.

"Is this your way of helping me with my case?"

"You are allowing my help, after all? Delightful! Let us reason this out, then." She clapped while a tolerant grin twitched at his lips. "Could the ribbon's origin be a hint?" Her thoughts flew like sparrows. "What about the color? Perhaps it has literal significance. Could there be a Mr. Green? A location with the word *green*? The comtesse! *Vert* means green in French, does it not?"

"You suggest the comtesse is involved?" His eyes narrowed.

"'Twas merely a thought." She waved her hand. "Perhaps the ribbon symbolizes something. A political matter? What was it they used in France? For the revolution."

His brow furrowed. "The guillotine?"

"No, the rosette." Her fingers flapped over her collarbone.

"The tricolor cockade?"

"Before that. Did not green symbolize something to the citizens?"

His eyebrow arched, as if he thought her dotty.

A thud against her shoulder pitched her forward. Tavin's firm grip encircled her upper arm, and just as quickly as he caught her, he let her go. She had not been watching where she was going. "Pardon me, I was not attending—"

The woman she had encountered wore a cloak of pale blue and a velvet bonnet over sunrise-gold curls. "Frances."

Her friend's blue eyes widened. And then she was gone. The sweetness of her violet scent stuck in Gemma's nostrils even as her form retreated.

"I am sorry," Gemma said, but Frances could not have heard her.

Tavin's full lips turned down in sympathy. And even

though they stood in the middle of the museum, his hand extended to hers.

And, without considering why she wished to so badly, she took it.

Chapter Sixteen

When Tavin made his farewells, after visiting Montagu House, with an offer to take her riding the next morning, Gemma agreed, although she no longer required his instruction. Nor did she plan to ride again with Frances. There wasn't single excuse for them to ride together other than because they enjoyed it.

Which she could not admit to anyone, but she did.

The ride was pleasant, but cut short once the gentle mist gave way to a heavy rain shower. They returned to Berkeley Square, where Tavin dismounted and rushed to her side.

Gemma's breath hitched as Tavin's hands went 'round her waist. His touch lasted just long enough to assist her from plump Kay, but the brief contact turned her legs to sponge. She stared up at him, breathing in the odors of wet horse and leather and rain, for far too long.

Rain dripped from his beaver hat onto the collar of his ink-black greatcoat, but his teasing smile was warmer than an August afternoon. "At a loss for words, duckling?"

What must the grooms who handled Kay and Raghnall's reins be thinking, to hear Tavin call her such a name?

Still, she could not stop a smile from tugging at her cheeks. "Pray tell, how am I duckish?"

"What other creature would be out in this weather?" He tapped her soggy bonnet. "I should have returned you home once it started sprinkling."

"I am not afraid of rain. Perhaps I am part duck, after all."

He grinned. "Let us get you inside."

She shook as much rainwater from her vermilion habit as she could, so as not to drip all over the gleaming stone floor inside the house. "May I persuade you to stay for tea?"

"It sounds just the thing. I must speak to Wyling, at any rate."

She excused herself to change while he handed his damp coat to a footman. When she returned downstairs, Tavin stood in the drawing room, his hands extended to the fire in the grate. His head swiveled toward her and he smiled. "Look at you. From a duckling to a swan."

Her fingers fumbled at the high neck of her white muslin gown. Corbeau ribbon, so deep a green as to appear black in the dim of the rainy afternoon, trimmed the ensemble. "Perhaps in color, but in all other respects, I am nothing like one. One would require a modicum of grace for that."

"And swimming skill, which you seemed to lack in the New Forest." His teasing manner erased the faint lines around his eyes. "I had to carry you, as you recall."

Her blush brought much-needed heat to her chilled cheeks, but she would not thank him for it. "If you had been more forthcoming at Verity House, I would not have been out of doors to fall in the swollen pond."

"If I had not pulled the leech from you, you would have been bled dry before breakfast."

"If you had not slipped, the leech would not have sunk its teeth into me."

Their quantity of their bickering had not lessened over these past weeks, but the intent behind the words had altered. At least for Gemma. The tone behind their words had shifted from accusation to pleasant repartee. Tavin seemed to feel the same, for he wore a wide grin, and Gemma's cheeks cramped from smiling so much.

"We are at a draw, then." His eyebrows wiggled, which always made her laugh.

"Where is my family? The house is quiet."

"Stott says Wyling and Amy took the boys toy shopping. They should return at any time, arms weighted with metal soldiers." He glanced at the mantel clock. "I hope you do not mind I stayed despite their absence."

"Of course not. You have earned a cup of tea."

He stepped aside in invitation for her to join him at the hearth. "Come, warm yourself."

"The heat reaches me here."

"You have been both a duck and a swan today. Do not be a goose." He bent to poke the logs, coaxing a wing of feathery flames to unfurl. Orange and sizzling, the flames grew in proportion to the rapid pace of her pulse.

"I am warm enough."

"You shiver where you stand." With a clank, he set the poker beside the hearth and reached out his hand.

She stared at the smear of ash on the pad between his thumb and forefinger, small, insignificant, black as his coat. Just a dusting, but it brought to mind the memory of that day, when flakes of ash had fluttered about the ruins of her home, all that remained of her possessions. Her parents.

She could not take his hand.

"What is wrong?" His voice was soft as the ash.

Words clogged her throat like smoke. She should sit, but her legs refused to move.

Tavin was at her side before the first tear slid down her cheek. Wrapped around her, his arms were solid, warm, more comforting than any blaze.

"You always stand away from the fire." His breath warmed her ear. "I thought you sacrificial, leaving room for others to warm themselves. But I've missed something, haven't I?"

His heart beat under her cheek, keeping rhythm with the mantel clock. Steady.

He would hate her, but she couldn't bear keeping it in any longer. "I killed my parents."

To her surprise, his arms neither tightened nor slacked. Nor did he speak, but held silent, as if allowing her to tell him when she was ready. If he judged her, he concealed it well.

She breathed in his woodsy scent. "Petey had just been born, and my parents wanted Peter and his new family to have all the rooms he needed. That is why we switched residences. Papa, Mama and I took Peter and Cristobel's rooms in the dower house, and Peter moved into Verity House."

"That was kind." Tavin's thumb traced lazy circles on her shoulder.

"My parents were that way. But I disobeyed them." The tears flowed thick and fast. "Mama told me to go to bed, to not to stay up reading in the library. She said I would fall asleep. But I was so comfortable on the chaise with a novel by Mrs. Radcliffe, and not the least drowsy. Except, of course, that eventually I did close my eyes."

He laid his head atop hers. "There was a fire."

"I woke up, not knowing where I was. I stumbled to

bed. I do not recall anything but darkness. I do not recall my candle. But it must have—I must have…"

His thumb continued to rub her shoulder.

Gemma extricated a hand to wipe her tears. Tavin's neck cloth was a soggy mess. "I woke to fire. I ran outside, but Mama and Papa were not there. I ran back in after them, but it the smoke was so thick I could not see. And it was my fault. The fire started in the library, underneath their bedchamber, and I was the last to use it."

"Yet you woke to darkness. It could not have been your candle."

"I have told myself that so many times one might expect me to believe it by now."

Tavin's thumb stilled and his arms fell. A handkerchief appeared in his hand, and she took it. She'd never used a man's handkerchief before. The large linen square smelled of starch.

"I know I am forgiven. Amy reminded me that if the Lord cast away my sins, who am I to hold on to them?" She dabbed her eyes. "But I still feel guilty. And I do not like fire."

Tavin stepped away, and the room felt cold. "I am sorry I stirred such memories."

"You could not have known."

"I am not sorry you told me, however."

"Nor am I." Their eyes met, held. The world seemed steadier, as if a bridge spanned the gulf between them.

Sharing with him had been easy. Perhaps because he was a trustworthy man, adept at keeping secrets. Yet this was something more. Like friendship, although she did not feel this sort of vulnerability when she was with Frances. On the contrary, she would like nothing better than to return to Tavin's arms for a while longer and listen to his steady heartbeat.

The clatter of silver announced the tea's arrival. Gemma set about cutting slices of plum cake and pouring cups of the steaming brew.

His warm fingers brushed hers when he took the tea-cup from her hands. "Have you errands for the day? Other than, er, tonight, that is."

"Ah yes. Tonight."

Since the arrival of the vellum invitation to dine with his grandmother, the Dowager Duchess of Kelworth, they had spoken little on the topic. No doubt the dowager believed the tittle-tattle in the paper about "Mr. Black" being enamored of her. Gemma sniffed. If the dowager expected a love match, she would suffer great disappointment in a few weeks.

He grimaced. "My uncle, the duke, will be in attendance, with the duchess and their eldest, Helena."

Eyeing Gemma, no doubt, judging whether she was suitable to marry into their illustrious family. Not that it mattered. It would never happen. Crumbs of plum cake stuck in her throat. She washed them down with a too-large sip of tea.

"I will be ready." For the dinner, and for their scrutiny. "If it is well with you, I should like to call upon Frances today. My written apologies have not been well received. I should like to try in person."

His fingers shredded the hem of his serviette. "Reunion is not always possible."

"Nevertheless, I should like to try. God has forgiven me, but I wish for Frances to, as well."

His brows knit low over his eyes and he stared into his teacup. "God's forgiveness—how do you know when it happens? Does something feel different when He bestows it?"

"I *felt* differently when I accepted His forgiveness for

setting the fire." At his lifted brow, she sighed. "For *perhaps* setting the fire. But forgiveness is not an emotion. His pardon was there the moment I asked for it. But I had to accept it."

He opened his mouth, but the outer door opened. A noisy rush of rain, chatter and the stomps of small boots sounded from the hall. Amy's gentle scold about wet cloaks and hats elicited a grin from Gemma, but not Tavin. She leaned forward. "Is something—"

He was on his feet. "Now that Wyling is home, I must attend to business. But when you call upon Miss Fennelwick, take footmen with you. And Wyling."

Eddie ran into her arms, waving a mechanical monkey in her face. He flopped onto the floor and wound a small key with short, grinding sounds. "Watch this, Aunt Gemma!"

But she couldn't, not with her gaze on Tavin. She forced her attention to the floor, and when she glanced up again, Tavin was gone.

The sharp odor of ink met Gemma as she crossed the threshold of the Fennelwick home, as if someone had dropped an inkwell in the entry hall. Wyling must have detected the odor, too, for his long nose twitched when he offered his calling card to the graying butler.

While they waited in their rain-damp cloaks, Gemma leaned toward Wyling. "You are good to come with me."

"'Tis my pleasure, but if I'd let you come alone, Knox would have my hide for a saddle."

The butler returned. "The master is at home and will see you in the library."

"Splendid." Wyling grinned at Gemma. "I imagine Fennelwick has an astonishing collection of volumes stored there."

Mr. Fennelwick did indeed boast a vast assortment of books. Bookshelves spanned from floor to ceiling, bowing under the weight of numerous leather-bound tomes. A massive oak desk supported a mound of clutter, and beside every chair, book-topped side tables stood testament to the utility of the space. The odor of ink intensified.

Dressed in a simple gown and cap, Frances stood from the window seat and set down a sheaf of papers. Her gaze rose no farther than Gemma's tan kid boots.

Mr. Fennelwick bowed. "How pleasant to see you, Lord Wyling, Miss Lyfeld. Tea?"

"A welcome suggestion on a gloomy day." Wyling's nod of encouragement to Gemma was discreet but pointed. This was her chance to speak to Frances. He'd do his best to give her ample time, but she shouldn't squander a moment. Wyling smiled at his tufty-haired host. "I had hoped we might continue our discussion of your work on the Roman occupation of Londinium while the ladies enjoy a comfortable coze."

Frances's smile was forced as she gestured for Gemma to join her on the window seat.

Gemma perched beside her. "Thank you for receiving us."

"Papa does not mind the interruption to our work."

Mr. Fennelwick might not mind, but Frances seemed to. Gemma swallowed past the lump in her throat. "What are you studying?"

"A mosaic unearthed in Kent." Frances chose a paper from the stack at her side. "Or rather, a sketch of one. This is a rough drawing of the discovery."

The sketch, while simple, revealed a winged horse surrounded by a geometric border. "How intriguing."

"But imprecise." Frances pointed to objects surrounding the horse. "Papa's friend said these lumps are ocean creatures, but here they resemble bags of wool."

"Mayhap pillows." Gemma tilted her head. "Or haystacks."

Frances's eyes creased in amusement, and hope sprouted in Gemma's chest. In the past minute, something had shifted, like ice thawing on the surface of a pond. Gemma prayed and reached her hand to Frances. "I am sorry. So sorry. As I said in my letters, I regret causing you such distress. The scene at the comtesse's. And Gerald Scarcliff. He was *your* suitor."

"I would not have tolerated his suit much longer. The man did not know *tessarae* from *terra-cotta*." Frances exhaled an unladylike snort. "Besides, he preferred you."

"I think not—"

"He was vile, drink or no drink, to use us both to gain entrée to the comtesse's masque. I regret if my plain-spoken words wound you, but they are the truth."

One thing Gemma had long admired about Frances was her forthright speech. "It is your wounds which concern me. I have damaged our friendship."

"Is it friendship? Or did you use me to gain entrance to the masque, too?"

Gemma's lips parted with a soft pop. "I wished to go… but not at the cost of your friendship. I do not care if I ever go again."

"Good, because you shan't be invited. The comtesse is not pleased with you."

"I imagine not. But all I wish is your forgiveness, Frances."

Frances's chest deflated in a ragged sigh. "You have it. But I was never angry about Mr. Scarcliff. I was angry you lied to me."

"I did not plot to renew our acquaintance so I could attend the masque."

Frances scowled. "Not that. Mr. Knox. You said he was no suitor, but he is everywhere with you. I heard you are dining with his family tonight, too."

Frances had her there. Tavin would have her change the subject, but Gemma's spine straightened. The Sovereign may have altered her life, but he'd not change her. She might be forced to allow others to believe a charade, but she was no liar.

Gemma plucked at her Kashmir shawl, praying for courage. "I wish to tell you something. But it is a secret and must remain so."

Frances peeked at her father and Wyling across the cluttered library. They were deep in conversation over an open book. "I am trustworthy, Gemma."

Gemma nodded. "My friendship with Mr. Knox will not extend beyond the Season."

Frances's pale brows rose. "How can you be so certain he will not remain steadfast?"

"Because—" the word soured her tongue "—he is paid to befriend me."

Tavin shook rain from his sleeves as he shut the door to Garner's antechamber behind him. "Sommers, tell Garner I am here."

Sommers glanced up. "Alas, he is not here to receive you."

"Again?" Tension clawed up Tavin's shoulders, settling around the base of his skull. "His schedule cannot be so full."

Sommers withdrew a scrap of foolscap from a file. "He left this for you."

Tavin scanned the note, which offered little but an utter

lack of concern for Gemma. Garner—who had wanted Gemma watched in the first place—would not grant more agents to protect her despite the Sovereign's attack on Mr. Grenville.

"Did you give him the other *sealed* missive I left?" Sharing Gemma's secret desires to enjoy her Season and seek a solicitor for the sake of her nephews had been a necessary though unpleasant obligation. But the note was *not* for Sommers's eyes.

Deep lines formed around Sommers's puckered mouth. "I left it for him and it is no longer here. Any other insults of my character?"

"My apologies." Tavin made for the door. "But tell him I need to speak to him. 'Tis urgent. And I need more men."

"He trusts you to handle things according to your unique set of skills." From his tone, Sommers did not offer a compliment.

Tavin pushed out the door he'd just entered. He had a woman to protect 'round the clock, a case to solve and no one to authorize additional protection for Gemma.

Lord, will You not hear me until I put the Sovereign in chains? When will You answer me? I cannot do this alone.

A cool blast of wind hit his face as he exited the Custom House, setting his resolve. He'd catch the Sovereign. He'd make things right.

But until then, he was on his own. He'd see Gemma well protected, even at his own expense. And he had little time to hire anyone before dinner at his grandmother's tonight.

Chapter Seventeen

The Dowager Duchess of Kelworth's dinner was exquisite—at least, the ample dishes appeared that way to Gemma. She'd eaten her food, even if she'd been too nervous to taste it under the tension palpable at their end of the table. Tavin and his uncle, the duke, interacted over the steaming platters of food with a cool politeness. Even Wyling's diplomatic attempts to divert the conversation did not help, his witticisms falling lifeless as the buttered trout on Gemma's plate.

Now some dozen ladies gathered in the dowager's drawing room while the gentlemen remained at the table. Amy joined a gathering of matrons by the windows. A second group was comprised of come-outs, younger than Gemma. The third group, containing the dowager, the duchess and her haughty daughter, Helena, was by far the more intimidating group to join. But Gemma squared her shoulders and approached the dowager duchess's cluster.

I kicked a murderous smuggler in the shin. I am no coward when it comes to this woman.

Regal in her tall chair by the drawing room fire, a tiny smile played on the dowager's thin lips. A toque sat atop her graying curls like a diadem, and the train of her violet gown swirled at her feet. An immense amethyst ring shimmered in the firelight as she extended her hand. "Pray be seated here, Miss Lyfeld. I would know you better."

The indicated chair was far from the fire. Gemma smiled, for she wouldn't wish the dowager to misinterpret her fear of the flames for fright of the woman. "Thank you, Your Grace."

"Your paternal great-uncle is Lord Lindsay, is that correct?" The Dowager didn't wait a moment to begin the inquisition.

"Yes, Your Grace." Cristobel might not have married Peter had he not been in line to inherit the title of baron.

"I do not know him." The dowager waved her ringed hand. "Do you, Caroline?"

"No." The current duchess, a delicate-featured woman, frowned at the delicate string of tiny pearls around Gemma's neck—a simple necklace for a simple, unimportant baron's grand-niece. But the treasured strand had been Mama's.

"Uncle Lindsay is not oft in London." Gemma glanced at the door. *Tavin, where are you?*

No doubt he paced the dining room, aggravated by his roles as grandson and government protector intersecting tonight. Perhaps he had even excused himself and sneaked outside, watching for trouble, relieved to be away from this dinner party.

"Something amusing, Miss Lyfeld?" The dowager's snap yanked Gemma from her reverie.

"No, Your Grace."

"No doubt Miss Lyfeld thinks of a certain gentleman." The duchess licked her lips.

"A man in black?" Lady Helena, Tavin's cousin, though not yet of age to come out, was old enough to lift her nose at Gemma. Despite herself, Gemma's cheeks warmed.

"She blushes. I daresay she does think of him." The dowager's eyes narrowed. "Is he taken with you?"

The folds of Gemma's crepe gown hid her clenching hands. "Pray forgive me, Your Grace, but I do not know what you mean."

"Do not play coy. My grandson avoids society, so it is no surprise that now, when he is at Almack's, routs, parties of all sorts—and even mentioned in the *Morning Post*—everyone wonders why he has changed." The dowager grinned like a cat with a rodent between its paws.

"I cannot say, Your Grace." And it was true. Tavin had understood when she'd told him she'd shared the nature of their relationship with Frances, but he'd asked she not divulge the Sovereign—or his work—to anyone else. So Gemma would not.

The rumble of masculine voices carried through the doorway, and Gemma's neck craned. She should not be so obvious, but the yearning to see Tavin pricked her skin like a needle. Twelve gentlemen filed through the door, but Tavin's was the face who held her gaze. A fierce line creased his brow until he spotted her among the feminine company, then it soothed, as if kissed away.

He worried about her, and, despite what she'd told Frances, it was not just because he was paid to. From the way he glanced between Gemma and his grandmother, it seemed he feared Her Grace's attacks more than the Sovereign's.

Oh, how she cared for him. How she wished to soothe the crease in his brow every day and tell him all was well.

Impossible, of course. Nevertheless, she smiled when he strode toward her.

With a rustle of satin, the dowager duchess rose, halting his progress. All conversation ceased, and with every eye upon her, Her Grace smiled at the company. "Now that the gentlemen have joined us, let us enjoy some entertainment. With so many young people present, dancing seems in order. The carpets are rolled in the gallery, and Lady Albright has agreed to play the pianoforte."

It was known far and wide Tavin did not dance, Not even for his grandmother, so he doubted anyone missed him when he slipped outside while everyone else adjourned to the gallery.

His check of the grounds complete, he brushed beads of mist from his black coat sleeve and reentered the house through the library's French door. He crossed the darkened chamber to the hall door and knocked, the sound no louder than an acorn's fall. No one in the hall would hear it unless they awaited the noise. Which Wyling did, and the trustworthy fellow would not open the door unless the hall was void of servants or the dowager's guests.

The portal cracked open to reveal the illuminated hall and Wyling's eager face. "All is clear within. And without?"

"Quiet." Tavin stepped into the hall. "Booth reported no disturbances, and there has been no message from Tott, so all is well with the boys at Berkeley Square, as well."

"Are you certain these men are trustworthy?"

"Aye. I've worked with them before. So long as they are paid well, they will do what is asked of them."

"And you pay them well, indeed." Wyling led Tavin to the long gallery upstairs. Strains of conversation and the keys of a pianoforte grew louder by the step.

"If Garner will not give me more men to protect Gemma, I must do it myself. And, no, for the tenth time, I will not accept your coin."

Wyling paused at the threshold. "I still say you should inform Gemma you've hired two men to assist you."

"And have her grow yet more concerned? No." Tavin

strode into the gallery, where a handful of couples twirled to a spirited tune. "She is safer with three of us watching. Four, if I count you, which I do part of the time."

"Thanks so much," Wyling said drily.

Tavin smirked. "I trust no one more than I trust you. But even the lofty Earl of Wyling requires sleep. Besides, you will need to be rested with a child coming."

Wyling's lopsided grin gave him a boyish look. "I wish you could know this happiness."

A child? Tavin had never believed he could be a father, although when he spent time with Petey and Eddie, he wished he could. "Mayhap when I have earned it."

"You cannot earn it, *fool*." Despite Wyling's harsh word, his tone was bathed in pity.

They parted and, true to his custom, Tavin strolled the gallery's perimeter. He counted the number of guests, found no one missing and felt his shoulders relax.

Gemma had not yet noted him. She spun on the arm of his mother's brother, the duke, while the mathematically precise strains of a cotillion sounded from the pianoforte.

A flash of purple caught the corner of his eye. He turned. "Your Grace. Your entertainment for the evening has proved to be a success."

"Dancing allows a young lady to demonstrate the degree of her education. Does she possess musicality and refinement? How does she compose herself?"

"And you wished to test Miss Lyfeld's accomplishments." A muscle worked in his jaw.

"She dances the cotillion with ease, managing to converse with the duke despite the complexity of the figures. That indicates skill and breeding."

"Skill and breeding do not compare to her kindness. Few females are as tender of heart, regardless of how she dances."

"If you want a softhearted creature, why not meet other females who hold the same quality?" Her Grace fluttered her lacy fan. "Lady Jane Appleby is caring. See her there, in the ostrich headdress? Perhaps you might ask her to dance."

"I do not dance."

"What you do not do is consider possibilities. You are set on Miss Lyfeld, then?"

"We are friends, Your Grace. No more."

"A blatant lie. See how she steals peeks at you?"

"She does no such thing."

The last strains of the cotillion fell away, and Gemma curtsied to his uncle Kelworth. Someone announced La Boulanger, and Wyling stepped forward to claim Gemma for the circle dance. Uncle Kelworth partnered with Amy. And then Gemma caught his eye, flushed and spun to join the circle.

The dowager sighed. "She is sweet, if a trifle old." At the furrowing of Tavin's brow, she trilled a laugh. "Ease that look of thunder from your countenance. I must ensure this is not some fabricated, cream-pot love on her part, generated to gain entrée into this family. I would not see you in a *mésalliance*."

"Think you she is after my fortune? My mother's name?" Though his fingers clenched to snap something, he willed his voice to sound light. "Miss Lyfeld craves neither."

"Then she is old *and* imprudent. Your purse and connections are estimable." Her Grace frowned. "You could do better, but so long as she cares for *you*, I approve the match. It is long past time you were wed and occupied with something other than your business interests in— whatever it is."

"Foreign import." Tension slid away, as if wiped by a thick cotton towel. *She cares for me?* Ridiculous. But when their eyes met again, a giddy sensation expanded in his chest.

Her Grace sniffed. "Foreign import, Parliament, no matter. Ladies do not care to know the subject of gentlemen's business so long as it provides security."

Tavin laughed. Gemma would disagree.

"Grandson, you are of a humor tonight."

"Perhaps I am happy."

"Do try to contain such embarrassing emotions before you become a subject of gossip."

"Too late for that." He bowed and took his leave.

Accepting a glass of orgeat punch, he watched the dancers circle. When the tune ended he stepped toward Gemma, extending the almond-smelling drink. "Orgeat?"

"Thank you." Their gloved fingers brushed. "Do you not care for any?"

"Too sweet for my taste." Then again, his tastes were changing. He had never thought he'd feel this way, whatever this feeling was. Hopeful. Drawn to her.

The groups formed sets for a contra dance. Gemma set her glass on a passing servant's tray and grinned up at Tavin.

"Dance with me."

"I do not dance."

"Every gentleman dances."

The old argument that he was no longer a gentleman tasted stale on his tongue. "Is that an absolute truth? I have another one for you. Ladies do not ask gentlemen to dance."

"Then perhaps," she said, leaning toward him an inch, "you should ask if I would be so gracious as to honor you."

He couldn't. Could he? But, oh, how he wanted to ask her—

The thought caught him 'round the legs like a snare and threatened to send him tumbling to the ground.

He wanted to dance with Gemma. To hold her for more than the instant required to lower her from a horse. To look down into her eyes and breathe in the lavender of her perfume and the almond-sweet scent of the orgeat on her lips. To pretend there was no need to stand back so he could protect her, to let go and do something without fretting about how fast he could unsheathe the knife in his boot.

To just dance. To pretend he was a normal fellow, with a normal life, free to love her.

His breath caught. Love? He had naught to offer her, just the heart he had not noticed beating in his chest until the day he noticed *her*.

"It has been a long time since I danced. Years. I might make a mistake." He'd made so many mistakes. Perhaps he should not willingly make this one.

"As might I. I could injure your foot."

"You did the Sovereign's."

That made her laugh, and several heads turned their way. "For shame." Her tone teased. "Now everyone is looking at us."

"They were, anyway."

"There are unspoken rules for dancing, Tavin. You are supposed to smile, as if you enjoy yourself, but not too much."

"I care not a whit for such rules. If I wish to laugh, I shall." He bowed over her hand. "Do me the honor of dancing with me, Gemma?"

The sparking light in her eyes dimmed into a smolder, which somehow seemed far more hazardous than her flirtations. She placed her gloved hand in his, sending a shock up his forearm. "How long I have waited for you to ask."

And though he did not wish to, he believed her.

They stood somewhere in the middle of the twin lines of dancers. He bowed, she curtsied. They stepped together and apart, all without breaking their gazes. Then he took her hands, turned in a misshapen circle and lifted their right hands for another circle. Her body was within his loose, public embrace, warm and close.

Their hands stayed linked across their midsections while they took steps forward in the line, then back, but their gazes held.

Lord, what is happening to me?

Parting to glide around the outside of the lines, she disappeared behind the line of women, but he watched her still. The hem of her white gown swirled like script on a page, spelling out a story he could not help but read.

Tavin's missteps were small but present in every figure. She seemed not to notice or care. Three times, they followed the figures. Too soon, the tune ended. At the end, he did not let go of her hand.

She wanted her Season, to live in the moment. And for the rest of the night, Tavin would do the same.

"Will you dance with me, Gemma?" His voice sounded tremulous. "Again?"

The squeeze of her fingers assured him of her assent. "Until my slippers are worn through."

In the end, however, Gemma did not dance that long with Tavin. He excused himself far earlier than her slippers wore out.

A foolish fashion, these slippers. Pretty, true, but there was nothing appealing about how the white kid made Gemma's feet feel as she hopped and spun to the strains of the reel. Would it not be sensible to pad a dancing shoe rather than provide naught but a thin barrier of leather between the foot and the floor?

Gemma's toes ached, as did her heels and ankles and lower back, the muscles clenching tight beneath her perspiration-damp chemise. Her airy gown of white gauze did little to keep her cool tonight. The long gallery could serve as a hothouse if the dowager duchess were so inclined. Had this room no windows, no way to allow an evening breeze to cool the guests?

With the tune's final strains, she curtsied low and smiled at the duke. Cristobel would be apoplectic to learn Gemma had danced with so lofty a personage, not once but twice. Cristobel would not even care that the duke only danced with her to glean more information about the woman they believed had brought Tavin back to society.

If any woman had that power, Gemma might covet it. But just one man, the Sovereign, held such sway over Tavin.

A wave of thinning, fair hair flopped over the duke's brow as he bowed. Tall and narrow faced, the duke was nothing in looks like Tavin; nor did their manners mirror one another's. The duke's questions about her upbringing were more subtle, but no less persistent, than those of his mother. "Thank you for the dances, Miss Lyfeld."

"I am honored, Your Grace." Her curtsy pained her ankles and knees. *And thank You, Father, for the respite.* A few moments on the terrace would do well to cool her.

Should she tell Amy before she went? Gemma hesitated by the gallery door. Both Amy and Wyling were engaged in spirited conversations, and if Gemma lingered to interrupt them, she might be claimed by another of Tavin's nosy relations.

Besides, Tavin was outside. The thought of spending a moment alone with him on the darkened terrace hurried her steps. And her pulse.

Misty air enveloped her on the small terrace at the rear of the house. Flanked by two plants in alabaster-white urns, Gemma peered into the garden for a glimpse of Tavin.

Shrub- and tree-shaped lumps in various shades of gray became clearer, but no Tavin.

She would wait. Tavin would find her. In the meantime, she would enjoy the brief escape.

Beneath the screen of her gown, she flexed one ankle, then the other. Blessed relief. She ached so. But if Tavin asked her dance again, she would.

A snap of wood. The flutter of leaves. The bulky form of a man along the garden wall.

"Tavin?" The moment she breathed his name, the hairs on her arms lifted.

The man was not Tavin. Nor a liveried servant, not in that dark attire. He slunk along the side of the house, toward the street. Away from her, which was the opposite direction a knave sent to stalk her would go. Unless—

A cur sent by the Sovereign was here to hurt Tavin before taking Gemma. She fisted her hand to her mouth to cover her gasp. What had he done with Tavin?

The plant potted in a ceramic urn weighed against her palms, stretched the extension of her fingers. But it was no heavier than Petey. Her arms were strong.

She crept to the edge of the terrace, lifted the heavy pottery and heaved it over the garden wall.

Chapter Eighteen

The splintering crash of the urn against flagstone was followed by a masculine grunt. The dark-clad form bent over. Gemma lifted the second urn to her chest. Mayhap it would be wiser to scream, but that would provide the man enough time to run away. She would rather render the intruder unconscious before crying for help.

The bulky man staggered to his feet, his hand pressed to his hip. So that was where she had struck him. Good. He could not chase her or flee so easily now. His head swiveled to face her. Even in the dim, his glare was menacing. She memorized the thickness of his neck, the smallness of the eyes, while the muscles in her arms flexed to hurl the urn.

"You li'l baggage." He lurched forward. "Small wonder someone wants you dead."

Before she could throw the urn, a second dark form barreled between her and the intruder, a flash of bleached neck cloth gleaming like a beacon in the moonlight. Tavin. Their bodies tangled over the flagstones.

Shall I scream now? Tavin wouldn't want her to cry out. He'd want to protect his family by keeping them ignorant. Gemma clutched the urn.

Tavin spun the man from him. "Enough, Booth. It is I."

Gemma dropped the urn to its pedestal with a thud. "You know this man?"

The stranger rubbed his stubbly jaw. "You owe me double, Knox. She hit me, she did."

"I do not recommend you boast of it." Tavin hurdled over the terrace rail to come alongside Gemma. "This is Booth, Gemma. He is here to protect you."

Her stomach sank to her aching soles.

With a click, the French door to the house opened, spilling light onto the terrace. *Please be Wyling.* But the form in the doorway cast too short a shadow. The dowager duchess hastened toward them, her lips pressed together so tightly they might have been stitched closed.

"Your Grace." Gemma curtsied, her sore feet protesting the act.

"Grandson. Miss Lyfeld." No mention of Mr. Booth. Where had he gone? Disappeared into the night, leaving her alone with Tavin on the terrace. Gemma bit her lower lip. Hadn't she wished to be alone with Tavin, not ten minutes ago?

She almost laughed. When would she learn her dreams came to her already broken?

"How do you fare, Your Grace?" Tavin's smooth tone insisted nothing was amiss.

"Better than you." The dowager stared at his lip. "You attempted to take liberties? Little wonder Miss Lyfeld struck you."

A needle prick of guilt stabbed Gemma's conscience as Tavin swiped blood from his lip with the pad of his thumb. Mr. Booth had hurt him. And it was her fault.

"Your relations seek you, dear girl." The duchess's tone was laced with kindness, but Gemma was not fooled. "My grandson and I shall be along in a moment."

Thus excused, Gemma returned inside. But not before she caught an emotionless mask slipping over Tavin's features.

Tavin didn't dance with Gemma again. Instead, he loitered with Wyling at the chamber's edge until the evening's end, when he escorted them home to Berkeley Square. At Wyling's invitation, Tavin joined them in the drawing room and leaned against the side of the mantelpiece as young, crackling flames flickered in the hearth.

"Your grandmother expects a proposal is forthcoming? You must tell her one isn't." Dismay tightened every muscle in Gemma's body, including her voice, which better resembled a screech.

"I tried, but it is not as if I could tell her the full truth." Tavin rubbed the back of his neck as the mantel clock struck two.

Long, flickering shadows danced to eerie effect on the green walls. Perhaps that was why it looked as if Wyling and Amy exchanged smirks as they sat in chairs near the fire. Certainly they didn't find this amusing. Gemma's arms folded.

Wyling stretched his legs. "You are both overreacting. As far as the dowager duchess is concerned, Knox must have attempted to kiss Gemma and was chastened for his efforts. I was guilty of no less when I courted Amy." A sly smile spread over his lips.

"That doesn't explain the urn." Tavin slumped onto the settee beside Gemma. He didn't come close to touching her, but her right side—the side closest to him—prickled, as if he did.

"As we were leaving, I informed Her Grace it was an accident." Gemma fussed with a flounce on her skirt. "She accepted my excuse of clumsiness."

"She appeared to, but do you think her so gullible as to believe you picked up a soil-filled urn for no reason, walked with it and tripped several feet from where you started?"

"Your Mr. Booth prowled about the garden like a thief—or a *certain smuggler's* henchman. If I had been told your superior had sent a man to protect me, I would not have thrown an urn at him."

"I didn't wish to worry you."

Gemma opened her mouth to protest and stopped when Amy rubbed her temples. "Must the pair of you bicker? You are worse than Petey and Eddie."

Wyling patted her arm. "Remind me not to allow our offspring to be as quarrelsome as these two."

"We are not quarreling." Gemma rubbed her prickling arm.

"No." Tavin pinched the bridge of his nose. "We are discussing Gemma's admirable but misplaced sense of self-preservation. Hurling that urn was unnecessary."

"I was not preserving *myself.* I feared for *you.*" The dolt. "I thought that skulking creature had injured you—or worse—and I had best render him immobile for the magistrate. What else was I to think when I saw him but not you?"

"That I know what I am doing. You do not need to protect yourself when I am with you."

Amy sighed, her features etched with fatigue. Poor Amy. She—and the babe—required rest. "Go on to bed, both of you," Gemma urged.

"Not yet." Amy's smile did not reach her eyes. "Besides, we cannot very well leave you two alone anymore, can we? The dowager is not the first to expect an announcement. More than one acquaintance of mine has anticipated a betrothal betwixt you two."

Gemma ground her teeth. Tavin rubbed his hand over his jaw and lip, grimaced and stared at his fingers. Fresh blood. He'd reopened the wound.

Gemma tugged a lace-edged handkerchief from the beaded reticule still dangling around her wrist and twisted toward him. "You are making quite the mess."

He scowled and stared at the floor, but allowed her ministrations. With gentle dabs, she mopped the last traces of blood from his cheek and chin, just as she had done countless times for her nephews. It was a simple, nurturing task. But the comparison of experiences ended there. Tavin did not howl, for one thing. Nor did he lean into her for comfort as the boys did. Instead, he watched her, his breaths warm on her hand.

When the blood was gone, she lowered her hand. The lace of her handkerchief caught along his whiskers.

Amy cleared her throat, signaling Gemma to move back. Wadding the handkerchief into a ball, Gemma cleared her throat. "If you're worried about talk or your grandmother, you don't need to come with me and the boys tomorrow." They'd planned to view the curiosities displayed at Bullock's Egyptian Hall.

Tavin snorted. "I will not break my promise to those children."

"It will be good for you to be apart in the evening, however, as planned," Amy insisted. Tavin hadn't wished to interfere in Gemma and Frances's show of support to Hugh and Miss Scarcliff by joining them at Drury Lane theater tomorrow night. "You will prove to the ton you and Tavin do not live in one another's pockets."

"But you'll be outside, will you not?" Gemma peeked at Tavin. "Does your superior have any others watching me besides you and this Mr. Booth?" Her voice, unlike her emotions, was crisp and businesslike.

Tavin stared at the floor. "There are two men in total."

"But they're not Garner's men." Wyling folded his arms. "No more half-truths, Knox. Tell her the rest, so we can go to bed."

Gemma's grip on the handkerchief tightened. "What half-truth?"

"Garner did not hire Booth to watch over you." Tavin fixed his gaze on his knee. "I did, and a fellow named Tott, too. Garner is not convinced the Sovereign was behind Grenville's attack. Therefore, he does not believe you in serious danger. But I do, and I *cannae verra* well watch you 'round the clock."

Cannae verra? Smooth and lilting, the pronunciations shouted of his Scottish upbringing, something he'd always hidden to perfection. But the words slipped from his weary body, unfiltered and, judging by his unchanged expression, unbeknownst to him.

Poor, weary man.

"Tavin—"

"Do not fight me." His tone was soft as worn cotton. "Please. I will not keep any information from you again. And I will keep you safe."

Perhaps it was the late hour. Perhaps it was the lines of exhaustion creasing Amy's face or the tinge of Scotland on Tavin's generally guarded tongue.

But she could not keep fighting him.

Despite how it looked to the others, she inched closer to him again and laid her hand on his. Tavin needed to see her eyes when she spoke to him. "I only wished to thank you. I told you I would help you, Tavin. And I shall."

Firelight danced in his dark eyes. "Good" was all he said, but she knew he understood.

She would do whatever was necessary to end this, even

though it would mean ultimately telling him goodbye when the case finished.

It was not as if she had pinned her hopes to Tavin as she had to Hugh. Quite the contrary. Then why did the prospect of never seeing him again prick at her like needles?

Despite having slept little the previous evening, Tavin's steps were light as he walked alongside Petey, Eddie and Gemma from the museum hall housing Bullock's intriguing collections. At this early hour, Piccadilly was not crowded, but Tavin would be a fool to take his attention from the street as they progressed from the Egyptian Hall toward Wyling's house.

Not that he was alone accompanying Gemma and the children. Wyling and Amy followed, trailed by the boys' nursemaid and Wyling's most strapping footman. But Tavin had learned long ago he could not rely on others to do what was required.

He glanced back at Wyling and Amy, who chatted but kept their eyes on the street, helping him protect Gemma. Could he ever repay Wyling and Amy for all they'd done for Gemma?

Paying note to the passersby, the shadows, the foot traffic behind them, he tipped his chin down toward Petey. "What did you like best? Napoleon's carriage? Captain Cook's treasures from the Sandwich Islands? Or the animals?"

"Yes, sir. The pwe…pwe—"

"Preserved," Gemma prompted. Despite faint lines around her eyes testifying to a lack of sleep, her face shone with pleasure, framed by the pretty bonnet she'd worn at Montagu House. The trim was green ribbon—much the same grassy hue as the ribbon from Verity House he kept in his pocket, but thicker. One trailing band, borne on the breeze, spiraled over her cheek, and the instinct to sweep it aside twitched in his fingers. Instead, she brushed it away with an efficient gesture. "The animals were *preserved*."

"Preserved." Petey nodded. "And bang-up to the mark, too, sir."

"Bang-up," Eddie echoed.

Although his gaze fixed on a man lingering over a flower-seller's fragrant cart, Tavin smiled at the children's mild use of cant. *Bang-up to the mark,* indeed. Where had they heard such talk? From their father?

A father who, like Tavin's own, for the most part ignored his progeny.

Tavin swallowed back a painful lump in his throat. How could Peter Lyfeld be such a fool as to disregard the two freckled treasures hopping down the street?

The boys bounced, fidgeted with their collars, chirped like parakeets. And their actions, their words, their smiles twisted something in his belly.

Why, he'd come to care for the imps. Just as he had for their aunt.

Tavin's clenched fingers relaxed and with the lightest touch, he rested his hand on Petey's shoulder. "The preserved animals were bang-up to the mark, indeed."

Gemma's gaze flitted from the boys to him to the passersby. It wasn't just fatigue creasing her eyes, but worry, too, although the boys would never guess she felt concern from her light tone. "I have never seen anything like that giraffe. Its neck and legs were longer than the height of a man."

"Why are they so long?" Eddie's hand crept under his miniature neck cloth, as if afraid his throat might stretch.

Tavin grinned. "A long neck is better when one eats from trees, and I suppose long legs are better than short ones when running from lions."

Eddie's eyes narrowed with a mischievous gleam. "I can run fast."

"Indeed you can, but you shall not demonstrate for us now." Gemma held out a hand, seemingly to catch him should he try. "It would not do to lose you in this crowd."

"I am a giraffe!" Walking with locked knees, Eddie stretched his neck and tilted his chin in the air.

Petey put a fist over the bridge his own nose and spun back toward Amy and Wyling. "I am a rhino-sisser-us. Look, Mr. Knox."

"So you are."

"Me, too." Eddie's fist landed over his nostrils and he skipped to join them.

Amy took Eddie's hand and the four of them walked, side by side, discussing the animals. A sweet smile curved Gemma's lips, and Tavin couldn't help but watch her longer than he should have.

They walked on, weaving through pedestrians and carts laden with savory-smelling meat pasties, jewel-hued fruit and fresh blooms, their fragrance taking him away from London to grass-filled meadows and lush heaths of heather. For a moment, a sense of freedom loosened his limbs and allowed him to feel the warmth of the sun seeping into his black coat. It was a hopeful sensation, a small gift from the Lord. Tavin was not forgotten. He had reason to hope in God's plan, mercy and provision.

When this was over—when the Sovereign was caught— maybe he could have a life. A wife like Gemma. Children like Petey and Eddie, whom he'd take with him everywhere so he'd never miss an amazing word that fell from their honey-scented mouths.

A wife like Gemma? When what he wanted was Gemma herself?

The boys dashed back to show their rhinoceros noses

to Amy and Wyling. Gemma peeked up at him. "Thank you for accompanying us. Even after last night. The dowager duchess will have expectations if she hears we were out today."

Tavin shrugged. "I disappoint her regularly."

Her tongue clucked like a hen's. "Come, now. She holds you in great affection."

"She sees my mother when she looks at me. If I still spoke like *me auld fither*, or had inherited his ginger locks, she would leave me in peace, as she has my brother."

"Forgive her, for your own sake." She glanced back at the strawberry-headed boys. "And there is nothing wrong with ginger hair. I am quite partial to it."

"Not me. I prefer the lightest shades of golden brown, like the flank of a fawn."

Her hair, and she knew it. Her eyes went wide. Ach, how he loved her. He'd deny it no longer. Her, and those rascals she loved. He'd take them all if he could.

But he couldn't, not today. He first had to repay his debt to God and Crown, and that could take years. His lifetime, perhaps. Still, he wanted it. Wanted a life with Gemma.

She flushed, brushed the errant green ribbon from her cheek and looked away, anywhere but at him. Then her gaze fixed in the direction of his ear. And she gasped.

After all her dancing last night, she must be sore. "Is it your ankle? Shall I summon that carriage, after all?"

Her head shook a fraction.

"Would you care to take my arm, then?"

"No." It was a strangled cry. And her eyes were not fixed on his ear, but across Piccadilly. "He—"

The hair on his neck lifted. And he understood.

He swung Gemma behind him with his right arm. With his left, he reached to push the boys into Wyling's arms. All the while his gaze darted, hunted. "Where?"

"I can't see him now." Gemma's voice was high-pitched, despondent. "But it was he. Those eyes, the height, oh, Tavin, it was he. *The Sovereign.* In a brown coat. Right there. But now he is gone!"

Chapter Nineteen

Where? The air was too thick, her throat too tight to breathe, but Gemma willed herself to calm. She'd be no help to Tavin if she quivered or cowered. This could end now. Here. She forced as deep a breath as she could muster and searched the crowd for the man who'd attacked her on Verity Hill.

"He's wearing brown? Light or dark?" Ordinary words, but they were clipped, anxious, from Tavin's lips. His clutch on her arm was firm, tethering her behind him.

"He's here?" Amy's voice was so high she clearly knew whom they meant.

Keep your wits, Gem. "Brown like mud. Sludge. Not a pretty shade." *Pretty, indeed.* She searched her memory for more details. Helpful ones. "Graying hair and a brown beaver hat. About your height, I think. He left that store, with the bay window, and ambled west—"

"Did he get into a carriage?"

"He was on foot. I didn't see—"

"Who's on foot?" Petey wiggled in Wyling's arms.

Tavin craned to peer west. "Did he see you?"

"Your form blocked his view of me." Besides, she wore a poke bonnet that shielded her face unless he'd eyed her straight on, but he'd given no indication of that. Oh, this felt so helpless. Where had the Sovereign gone?

"I'll see the ladies and boys home." Wyling's tone brooked no argument as he shifted the boys to Amy's arms and reached for Gemma's hand. "Come—"

"No." Gemma's head shook so hard her bonnet scratched her ears. Tavin needed her. "You don't know what he looks like. I can search with you."

"Absolutely not." Tavin's grip slackened as he spun to Wyling. "I'll call when I can."

Her jaw gaped. How dare he! She alone could identify the Sovereign. He needed her. "Tavin—"

But he didn't look back as he dashed westward down the street.

Tavin's search of Piccadilly and its surrounding streets and alleyways proved fruitless, as had his inquiry into the shop with the bay window—a boot maker's, which would have yielded helpful information had the Sovereign actually made a purchase or kept an account. According to the proprietor, however, the gentleman in the brown coat remembered an appointment before he could settle on a style.

Within the hour, Tavin's boots stomped in time with the pounding in his temples as he paced Garner's planked floor. How could his superior be so dense?

"He was on Piccadilly. *The Sovereign.* And you shrug?" Tavin's fists tightened.

"Miss Lyfeld glimpsed a gentleman who resembled her attacker. He strode the far side of the street, wearing a brown coat and hat. Everyone wears brown. Even me." He gestured at the limp coat hanging beside his desk, with a coffee-colored beaver hat resting on top. "You know as well as I do the man might have been anyone."

"She insists it was he. And I believe her."

"I think it most unlikely, now that I've learned of new activity in Hampshire." Garner stood from behind his desk. "I've a pressing appointment now, Knox, but you shall be glad to hear that I've decided you should return there, too."

"The Sovereign is in London, not Hampshire. I'll not go back now." Tavin was long past the point of using respect in his tone.

Garner shrugged into his brown coat and set the hat on his graying head. "How long did you beg to return to the New Forest? Yet now you balk?"

"I begged to go before I knew Gemma to be in danger."

"*Gemma*, now, is it?"

The most polite answer Tavin could muster was a glare.

Garner sidled past him to the door connecting his office with Sommers's. "Your job was to glean information while protecting her, not to fall in love with the chit."

"There is naught between us." There couldn't afford to be. "But I'm staying here."

Garner paused, hand on the door latch. "Miss Lyfeld is in no danger whatsoever, but your source in Hampshire was executed. Where do your priorities lie?"

"Where God places them. And He has put Gemma in my hands. I'll not leave her when she is threatened, which she is, whether you believe it or not."

Garner's glare turned icy. "Depart for Hampshire on the morrow. And you will no longer hire my men to do your bidding on their off hours or I shall see to it you are exposed for the accomplice to murder that you are. Do we understand one another?"

Tavin's arm dropped. "Entirely."

Gemma or his job, his reputation and his family's name.

When Garner pushed through the door, Tavin did not stop him. After the span of several deep, coarse breaths, he acknowledged defeat, slamming Garner's door behind him with a gratifying smack.

Clank! None too gently, Gemma set her untasted tea on the drawing room side table. But how could she exhibit ladylike serenity after such a harrowing afternoon? She'd spied the Sovereign. Rushed home, wide-eyed and watchful. Then she'd waited two anxious hours for Tavin to complete his search. And now that he'd finally called, he was unbearably unreasonable.

"It is not necessary to change my plans for tonight." She huffed across the drawing room floor toward Tavin, brushing past Wyling and his rolling eyes. "I will go to the theater with Hugh and Frances as arranged."

"Are ye mad, woman?" Tavin glared at her from his stance at the window. "I'll *nae* see you killed because you insist on squeezing every last drop of pleasure from your Season."

Not even the tinge of Scots in his speech softened her resolve. "I'm not going to the theater for me. I'm going for you, so the Sovereign might follow me again and we can catch him. Will you not even consider my suggestion?"

"Oh, I considered. In the time it took me to blink. Then I disregarded it as the most bird-witted proposal ever to scorch my ears." He returned to the window, brushing aside the sheer white curtain and peering down at the maples below.

"Wyling, please." Gemma turned to her brother-in-law. Like her, he still wore his outer garments from their visit to the Egyptian Hall, as if he expected to flee the house at a moment's notice. His toes tapped against the drawing room floor and his gaze darted at the door. Waiting for Amy to come down, or wishing to go to her?

This tension was not good for Amy in her condition.

Or the boys, whose questions at being hurried home without a farewell from Tavin had been unsatisfied. This had gone on too long. *Soon, Lord. Please make this end soon, for everyone's sakes.*

Perhaps things would move faster if Tavin allowed her a say. "Wyling, please convince him of the merit of me as bait."

"Oh, no." Wyling stretched his long legs. "Knox and I are of one mind. To call your idea imprudent is an understatement."

"But we discussed this, Tavin. In the garden." His brief glance told her he remembered, too. "The Sovereign knows who I am. That means he knows about the boys, and he is wicked enough to harm them just to spite me. So let us finish this. Let me stand in the open so he will come for me."

Wyling's fingers steepled before his closed eyes. "Tell me you did not agree to such an outlandish scheme, Knox."

"He didn't, precisely." Gemma's arms folded over her chest. "But we are partners."

"Even if I was inclined to agree, everything has changed." The curtain fell from Tavin's hand like a deflated sail. "My superior does not believe you."

Tavin's flat tone sent shivers up her arms. "He doubts my sincerity? Or my sanity?"

"His reasons are not important. Garner's decision is final. He orders me back to Hampshire. Even though the Sovereign is here. Even though my leaving will leave you vulnerable. I must go or lose my position."

But I need you.

She bit back the words along with the tip of her tongue. Mild saltiness filled her mouth, accompanied by an underlying bitterness. Remorse. *Dear Father, forgive me.* How could she continue to be so selfish?

Her fingers fiddled with the ribbons of her pelisse. "Do

not concern yourself with me. I shall be fine here, with your Mr. Booth to watch over me."

Tavin's head hung low. "Mr. Booth's services are expired. I've been prohibited from hiring custom men. I can hire others, but we cannot afford to make a mistake, hiring the wrong man. The process takes time I do not have."

Wyling stood. "Gemma is my responsibility. I will make inquiries, and in the meantime, my footmen will serve."

More expense. More people endangering themselves for her. Gemma rubbed her temples.

"No."

"I agree. Your men are trained at carrying parcels, not weapons." Tavin's fingers raked through his hair.

There was but one option. Gemma touched his sleeve, just enough to capture his gaze before she drew back her hand. "Then I shall bow out of the theater tonight and return to Hampshire on the morrow, as well."

Tavin's eyes dulled to jet. "I cannot be close enough to protect you there, either. Not with the work I now have to do."

So that was final. He would be free to do his job without the added weight of her everywhere he went. But he would no longer be with her. The sudden ache made her clutch her hands to her chest.

"We still have the advantage." She forced her tone to brightness. "The Sovereign will not know I am there, not yet. And I will stay inside. No walks up the hill. No red cloak. I promise. I will not…need you."

As he nodded, a ragged sigh escaped his chest. "I am sorry. For accusing you of wanting the pleasures of town when what you wanted was to help me. Not that I should blame you for wanting a bit of fun. This was your one Season."

Gemma's lower lip caught between her teeth. Adventure. Fun. How shallow it all seemed. "You knew who I was right from the start. Selfish and bold."

"No." Tavin's thumb lifted her chin, forcing her to meet his eyes. "I've said it before, and I'll say it again. You are giving and kind."

At the emphatic clearing of Wyling's throat, Tavin's hand fell away.

"It is settled, then." Wyling nodded. "We leave for Hampshire on the morrow. Perhaps Peter can be persuaded to release you into our care, Gemma, and you may accompany us to Portugal. The Sovereign will not follow there."

Gemma returned his brave smile, but she knew as well as he did that she would never leave the boys.

"I shall inform Amy and have Nellie prepare the boys." Wyling's long legs carried him to the door, where he paused to cast a pointed glare at Tavin. "I shall need you in the library in ten minutes, Knox. *Ten.*"

He shut the drawing room door behind him, leaving them alone. For what purpose other than to say farewell?

Despite the added layer of her pelisse, Gemma shivered with cold.

"Do not be afraid." Tavin's voice was soft. "I would do anything to keep you from fear."

Was that why she shivered? Fear? Gemma rubbed her arms. "God is with me."

"I am relieved you will not go to the theater tonight."

"Guarding me would have been difficult," she agreed.

"When will you accept that is of no consequence? I can protect you." He folded his arms. "But I didn't care for you being with Beauchamp."

"Why ever not? After what Gerald Scarcliff did, Hugh and Pet must be suffering. Frances and I wished to extend the hand of friendship to them."

He shook his head and muttered something like "fool

Beauchamp" before sinking into a chair, resting his head in his hands.

"You must be exhausted." Her hand rested on his shoulder, another brief, light touch that was nonetheless far too bold.

"There's no one like me, serving the way I do. When I have ended the Sovereign's reign, mayhap I can tender my resignation. Things are changing now that the navy assists in routing smuggling vessels. But for now, I am trapped." His broad shoulder bowed under her hand. "I am so tired of it."

She sat beside him before her fingers betrayed her and curled into his hair. "Could this restlessness be from the Lord, calling you to something new? Think on it, Tavin. He may have other work for you to do."

He shook his head. "I cannot stop this work."

"I know no one who shows the commitment to one's duty that you do. But there is no dishonor in changing course when God directs us toward a path."

"Honor has little to do with it. I am indebted to the Crown. And to the Almighty. Working for Garner is the one thing that can earn me any peace."

"Peace? Shouldn't you seek God for that?"

"He withholds it. I have not yet earned it."

She eyed the mantel clock. "Do not speak in riddles. What is this talk of *earning* peace?"

He leaned his head in his fists. "A man's blood is on my hands."

A swallow worked in her throat. She should not be surprised he had been forced to hurt someone. When he had subdued Mr. Scarcliff without harming him, however, she had appreciated his strength, as well as his choice to avoid a violent end. "A smuggler?"

Tavin barked a mirthless laugh. "A revenue agent."

A sick sensation swept her stomach. Then, with the hesitation of a mouse creeping whiskers first from beneath a cupboard, her hand snuck out for his.

He jerked away. "Don't. I don't deserve kindness."

"After all I shared with you, you must realize I do not condemn you."

He stared at her so long, she half expected Wyling to burst through the door with his eye on the clock. "How can it be so easy for you?"

"To go on when you're responsible for someone's death? You know how I struggled to forgive myself."

"You did *not* kill your parents, for one thing. But what I did was worse." Tavin's eyes shut. "I fell in with Ned Dillard at Cambridge."

"Dillard." She searched her memory. "The one killed by Mr. Scarcliff in the duel."

"I was raw in knuckle and in soul then. I fought with my schoolmates. Fought against my grandmother's desire to snuff the Scot from me. Then my parents died. And then there was Flora."

A thrill of unease shot through Gemma's limbs. "Fl-Flora?"

"Flora McInnis. My neighbor. There was nothing between us, spoken or unspoken. Still, I imagined there was, and I went home to see her."

Gemma busied her fingers with the lace rosettes on her gown. "So someday, will you make her Mrs. Knox?"

"She is Mrs. Knox already." Her gasp scratched like thistles in her throat, and Tavin tapped her cheek. "She married my brother, Hamish."

Heat flooded Gemma's face. "Oh. I am sorry."

"I am not, anymore. But I broke from my brother, left Scotland and have yet to return. I engaged in an ugly period of brawling, gaming and drink. None of it numbed the pain, so whenever Ned Dillard thought of a grand scheme, I was eager to take part."

Gemma squeezed his thick fingers.

Tavin squeezed back. "He seemed as eager to forget his life as I. One holiday we stayed at his home along the Dorset coast, and late on an evening we spied casks of brandy bobbing in the channel tide. It would be a bang-up lark to take some, would it not? Dip our toes into the dark world of smugglers? We had a few casks on the beach when the rum runners greeted us."

Gemma's free hand covered her mouth.

"I responded with my fists. I did not know Ned carried a pistol until he shot a man on horseback, galloping down the beach toward us. Neither of us knew the man was a revenue agent."

She shut her eyes, holding back tears. "How very sad."

"Nothing happened to Ned, of course. Too highborn to hang, and he claimed confusion in the darkness and self-defense against the smugglers. I may not have pulled the trigger, but I was there, encouraging it, and I share the blame. Had I pulled Ned away—"

"Ned Dillard made his own choice. He fired the pistol. Not you." She shook her head. "I know you, Tavin. I suspect you tried to help the revenue agent."

His eyes darkened. "There was no point, after long. The fellow bled into the sand."

"What happened then?"

"Nothing. The affair never became public. Ned went on his own way. I returned to Cambridge." A faint smile toyed at his lips. "There, Wyling drew alongside me, befriended me. I was drawn to his wit and his easy manner. When he told me about the one way to redemption, I clung to the news. Much of my anger ebbed over time, but never my guilt. The conviction to repay what I'd done consumed me, so I made inquiries. And I met Garner."

Ah. "He put you to work?"

"I was skilled for it. I knew well-connected people, yet I had a reputation for keeping low company. Whenever a complicated issue arose that required more delicacy than a revenue agent possessed, I handled it."

"But this conviction you mentioned, to repay the Crown?" Gemma's thumb traced circles over the back of Tavin's hand. "What was demanded of you?"

"Nothing. It is a matter of conscience. To the Crown and to God. To earn forgiveness for my sins."

"Penance has its place, but you will never earn forgiveness. Only accept it. You think you must stop a murderer for God to love you."

"I know He loves me. But He must be so disappointed."

"It pains me that you believe that."

She peeked at the mantel clock. Twelve minutes had passed. The boys' footsteps pattered in the outer hall, echoing the raindrops pinging against the window. "You should rest tonight, before your long journey on the morrow."

He shook his head. "There's no one protecting you."

"The Sovereign did not see me, but even if he did, the house is locked."

"Aren't you afraid of anything, woman?" His brows knit.

Oh, yes. And if he kissed her again, he would know what it was.

The door opened, admitting a tight-jawed Wyling bearing an opened missive. He offered Tavin a quick scowl and handed the sheet to Gemma. "No need to cry off your commitment to Hugh. He's been called on urgent business to his estate. He is already left for Hampshire."

Tavin gently pulled his hand free.

"I hope nothing is amiss." Gemma scanned the letter, penned in Hugh's loopy scrawl. "I shall jot a quick note of cancellation to Frances, then. And our London adventure will be over."

"I am sorry it was not all you wished it to be." Tavin stared at her. "Thank you for what you said."

So many things she wished she could say. *Thank you. I hope you find peace.* Instead, she dipped her head. "I will pray for you."

Wyling's throat clearing recalled them to the present, and with a last look and a bow, Tavin departed. Gemma plopped before the escritoire to write to Frances. The smell of ink filled her nostrils as she smoothed the foolscap paper. "Cancel…return home…my apologies… Remember what we spoke of, when I told you what happened when I wore the red cloak?"

She looked up at the wall, unseeing. Then she dipped the pen in the inkwell again. "Oh, Frances. You were correct. My feelings are as you suspected, but a favorable outcome could never have been accomplished."

She'd resolved to accept God's will and not fight against Him. Yet as she sealed her letter with wax and tears, her heart railed against that decision. This was too hard. Yet this was how it must be. How would she endure it?

Chapter Twenty

Staring out at the darkness, Gemma sighed, her breath fogging her bedchamber's windowpane.

She was safe. One of the footmen stood guard at the front door, and no one could slip past without awakening him. Another watched Berkeley Square from the drawing room. She could not be better protected within the house, and yet there was Tavin, standing in the garden below her window, under the acacia.

Not that she could see his face. The branches obscured most of him, but not his legs. One leg bent at the knee, boot bracing against the tree trunk at his back, while the other was planted on the gravel, bearing his weight. His black clothes melded into the shadows, but his fingers, leached to gray in the dark, fiddled with something. A twig, perhaps. Not in a frantic way, but relaxed. Perhaps he was bored.

And cold and damp, no doubt. Small sprinkles fell against her window in little taps.

Go home, Tavin, before you come down with a cough.

The house creaked as rain fell steadier now, pattering like fingernails against the pane, and the clock below stairs pealed twice. All was still, except in the garden. And in her heart.

* * *

Through the feathery leaves of the acacia, Tavin peered up at the soft ocher glow of the single candle wavering from the second-story window. The curtain fluttered and the flame danced, illuminating a female form at the window.

"Go to bed, Gemma," Tavin whispered. The vapor of his words swirled into the rain dripping off the leaves onto his boots and coat sleeves.

He should be sleeping, too, with the long journey tomorrow. If Garner knew Tavin had disobeyed him by guarding Gemma, he would no doubt send Tavin to reprimand tea smugglers in the Outer Hebrides, where the only excitement was catching eels for supper.

Nevertheless, he shifted his backside against the slender trunk, folded his arms and crossed his ankles. He was not going anywhere.

Neither was Gemma, it seemed. Her silhouette leaned against the sill, postured to gaze out into the garden. Could she see him in the dark? The acacia was not an ideal hiding spot, but it offered better shelter than the pleached limes, and he wouldn't squat beneath the hedges all night. Still, he stood motionless, his chest the lone part of him moving.

The acacia blooms smelled sweeter in the rain, but then, everything did—the flagstones, the leaves, the air, washed clean. Unlike him.

I do not feel forgiven, Lord. Is Gemma right? Does it have naught to do with the truth? Tavin shifted to lean his shoulder against the trunk. Forgiveness seemed far too embarrassing—too intimate—for his parents to discuss with him and Hamish. Not that they knew what he'd done. They'd died before he'd traversed down his current path.

And the dowager duchess, with her grudges and schemes?

Her scolds were shaming, not edifying. The only parent Tavin had witnessed extending grace to a child was Gemma.

She was no mother, but he knew of no other who poured herself out for another the way she did. When Eddie or Petey fell short, what did Gemma do?

He scrunched his eyes, and in his mind he saw her cling to the boys' small hands. She did not withhold affection or love. Like God?

He might not have a Bible at his disposal, but he'd committed some Scriptures to heart. God's promises of unending love were certain. Tavin had repented, grieved over his sins, begged for forgiveness. Mayhap it was time Tavin believed God granted it and lived accordingly. As a changed man.

Changed. Yes, that was it. So much in him had changed. Gemma had more than something to do with it, but the peace filling his chest came from the Lord.

With rain speckling his boots and cuffs, he began with the Lord's Prayer. And then, gazing on the candlelit window on the second story, he asked the Almighty to help him believe. And then he chose to believe it.

He puffed out a breath. He may be free from the shackles of his sin, but he was not released from the burden of his duty. Not yet. He'd committed to arresting the Sovereign, and he would do so. Not because he must to earn God's grace, but because he'd given his word. But after he finished with the Sovereign?

Tavin's chin tilted up. What should he do when he had fulfilled his obligation? *Do You want me to continue on for Garner, Lord? Or do You have something new for me? Grant me patience as I await Your word and Your provision.*

Gemma's silhouette shifted at the window. He resisted

the urge to toss a pebble at her window. But he was no callow youth. Nor was he free. Not in *that* way.

Nevertheless, a smile tipped his lips. *If I did not have this occupation preventing me, I would call on you, Gemma Lyfeld. I would woo you and marry you. I would take you and the boys and show you a grand adventure far away from here.*

As if Gemma whispered in his ear, he knew what she'd want him to do. Go home to Perthshire. He uncrossed his ankles and stared up at her window while the thought took root and grew like gorse along his bones. Home.

Summer in the Trossachs was a fine place, among the lochs and oak-covered hummocks where his *fither* hunted roe buck. The tors would be covered in wildflowers soon: saxifrage and clumps of purple heather. When he was small, his clothes had been scented with their spicy blooms—a better smell than mud-damp boy, or so his nursemaid had insisted.

He should go home and see Hamish. Tell him he loved him despite the harsh row they'd had, where Hamish had blamed Tavin for turning English and Tavin had accused Hamish of stealing everything he loved.

Gemma's silhouette receded and the ocher glow disappeared. *Sleep well, my sweet. The Lord and I will watch over you.*

With a groan, the kitchen door opened. The small figure of a woman exited the house and hobbled along the puddled garden path curving toward the necessary. One hand clutched a shawl as she disappeared behind the vine-covered brick privy.

Tavin tucked his chin into his chest, better obscuring his white shirt collar. The rain spatters thickened, as did the breeze, and he pulled his coat collar more snug around his nape. After a minute, the maidservant dashed past in a streak of white nightclothes. She struggled to open the door, but it appeared stuck. Swollen from the damp, no doubt.

Tavin envied the maid when she dashed inside, at last. A warm kitchen or a dry attic had its comforts, to be sure.

But he'd chosen his lot tonight, and he'd stay until dawn. He was not tired. The rain would pass. Already, shafts of moonlight poked through the leaden sky like silver threads through a dark coat.

Tavin shoved his hands into his pockets and found the green ribbon. Ah yes. He fingered the length. The key to this riddle—

A lime bough rustled, bowed, as if a cat pounced on its branches. The hair at Tavin's nape rose.

The knife from his back was in his hand before the two silhouettes dropped from the boughs of the neighbor's draping sycamore, far closer to the servant's door than Tavin. Muttering a prayer, Tavin burst from the shelter of the acacia. He'd have his arms around their necks while they struggled with the locked door—

Which gave way with a single yank. They slipped inside. The maid had left it unlocked?

His heart thudding in his ears, he pulled on the door. Stuck. Stuck. He shouldered into the door. His bones rattled, but the door held. He rammed his shoulder into it again. Again. How had the house not been roused by the noise?

Gemma's face on his mind, he breathed a prayer and kicked.

The coverlet rustled over Gemma's head as she rolled over, the sound like a seashell pressed against her ear. *Swish, swosh.* How long since she'd seen the sea? When her parents had lived, she'd often visited Christchurch, touching the gray waves with her fingertips while cutters sailed past. Where did they go? Exotic ports, distant lands, where palaces and castles crested the hills.

Creak. No seashell sound. No clicking of the settling house. She sat up in bed. *Creak.*

Icy stings pricked her mouth, her arms, her spine. *Tavin.* She slipped from the sheets, her feet recoiling against the cold floor. Waving the drape aside, she peered into the darkness, searching for a shift of his leg, the fiddling of his hand, a glimpse of his white collar under the acacia. Nothing. Where had he gone?

A footfall outside the door. She dropped the drape. Tavin? Or someone else?

What if they found the boys? What if—

No. I do not play that game anymore. I do not ask "what if?" I ask God. Though her stomach swirled with nausea, she forced herself to pray. *Help me.*

The knob jiggled. Metal scraped. Covering her mouth, Gemma staggered from the window to the dressing table. Her fingers curled over the silver-plated candlestick. The door opened. Dark figures poured into the room like spilled ink. "Greetings from the Sovereign," one whispered as they slunk to the empty bed.

She sucked in a breath to scream.

A growl erupted from the door. *Tavin.* As if he could see in the dark, he moved straight to her. His large hands gripped her arms, pushing her against the wall so fast her head spun. Sheltering her with his broad back, he kept one of his arms extended around her like a wing. "No," she breathed.

Then he disappeared to plow headfirst into one of the intruders—there were two, she could see that now. One engaging Tavin, one leaping over the bed. The second invader grabbed her. His fingers were cold around her wrist as he tugged her toward the door.

She struck his face, his neck, anywhere she could reach with the candlestick. Tavin gripped the man's collar, yanked him away from her while his boot met the other intruder's gut.

"Who is he?" Tavin's shout sent shivers up her arms. "Who pays you?"

Shuffling. Her nightstand crashed. An *oomph* escaped Tavin's lips. Then more gasps, but not his. *Scream, you ninny!* Gemma uttered a weak cry.

"You do not have to die." Tavin's voice was calm but menacing. "Tell me who he is."

Gemma gasped, then at last cried out. She stomped her bare feet, smacked her hand against the wall. Someone would have to hear her.

Tavin thrust her behind him again. One man lay on the ground, unmoving, and the other lunged for the door. Tavin's foot hooked the man's ankle and brought him to the ground. He planted his boot on the intruder's back as he bent to grip the hair at the back of his head.

"Who?" His demand was almost buried under the thunder of padding feet.

The intruder laughed, wheezy and wet. "Ye think ye'll ever know?"

The bobbing light of candles bounced against the walls and her chamber filled with forms and shadows, their horror-etched faces grotesque in the lights held under their chins. Wyling and footmen and even the aged butler, Stott, his hair in tufts, stormed into the room. Wyling called for rope and the magistrate.

"Let him go, Knox," he ordered.

After a heartbeat, Tavin's arms went around Gemma, warm and solid, smelling of rain and wool and acacia. Her ankles wobbled beneath her, but he steadied her, laid his head over her cap, murmuring nonsense words like she did when the boys scraped their knees.

"Are you hurt?" she managed.

"No." But blood spattered his shirtfront. "You?"

She shook her head, rubbing her forehead against the knot of his neck cloth. Then she peeked up. Oh, my, how many people gathered in her chamber? Housekeeper, footmen with rope and Wyling, ordering the footmen to bind both intruders. Then Wyling touched her shoulder. "Come, Gem."

Pain sluiced down her arm, and she winced.

"You are hurt." Tavin's fingers reached for the collar of her night rail, but Wyling brushed them aside.

"Amy will tend her, Knox."

At once, Gemma understood why everyone stared at her. It had less to do with the intruders than her, donned in a night rail, wrapped in a gentleman's arms.

She stepped back and recovered her wrapper from the foot of the bed. "There will be a bruise on the morrow, but I am well."

"Gemma." Amy, her light brown curls framed by a nightcap, peered into the crowded chamber. "Come away now, dear."

Wyling turned to the doorway. "All is well upstairs?"

Gemma gasped. "The boys!"

"Safe and sound," Amy assured her. "They slept through the whole nightmare."

Gemma's breath left her chest in a painful whoosh. "I would like to see them, nevertheless."

Wyling stood aside. "An excellent idea. This is not the place for you, Gem."

No, her own chamber was *not* the place for her, with every man in the household crammed into the space. It seemed Tavin took up the most room, with his broad shoulders and wide stance. A muscle worked in his jaw. "Before the magistrate arrives, I've some questions of my own to ask these two. Starting with who they are."

"We don't recognize yer authority." The wheezy man spit blood onto the polished floor.

Tavin's hands gripped the intruder's coat. Wyling held up a hand, but Tavin shook the bound intruder. "You tread on thin ice. Now speak."

Gemma's bare feet froze into the floor. She had never witnessed Tavin like this, veins bulging in his forehead and neck, his hands like talons, his mouth curled in rage.

"Who am I?" The man's cracked lips spread into a grin. "A citizen of Britain, yer equal, and there's naught ye can do to stop us."

Tavin glanced up, blanched when he saw her still there. He nodded to Wyling. "Get her out of here."

The footmen blocking the doorway stood aside, and at the same time a moan echoed from the far side of her bed. The footmen lifted the semiconscious attacker, who had crashed into her nightstand and whom they had bound at wrist and ankle.

"Maybe this one'll speak," the younger footman said.

"No need." Gemma crept forward until she stared the bleary man full in the face. "I know you."

Chapter Twenty-One

Tavin's arm extended around Gemma like a shield. The blackguard might be bound and muddleheaded, but he could come to his senses at any moment. Tavin's limbs twitched. The brigand on the floor would not receive another chance to touch her. Not even with his teeth.

"You know him?" He worked to keep his voice gentle. For her.

"Saul. One of Hugh's grooms back home." She squinted at the bruise-mottled face. "Or he *was* his groom. I have not seen him in some time."

In response, Saul opened one eye. His companion, the taller, wheezy man, struggled against his bonds. "Not a word, fool!"

"I know it is you, Saul." Gemma's voice was honeyed, as if she bade to her nephews to awaken. "You accompanied us when Hugh and I tooled the carriage to the lake."

Sympathy? For one of the men who had accosted her in her chamber? Tavin pointed at the door. "Enough, Gemma. Go lie down."

"Ha." She spun and reached for Amy's hand. "Let us go to the nursery."

When the patter of their footsteps faded down the hall, Tavin eyed Wyling. "Leave me alone with them."

"Are you mad?" Wyling shook his head.

"Five minutes. 'Tis all I require."

"Five hours won't help ye." The taller intruder laughed, a snarling sound. A trickle of blood slipped down his chin and landed on his lapel, pooling on a slim green ribbon pinned there. A ribbon like the one in his pocket, found atop Verity Hill.

"What is this?" He tugged the trimming from the black-guard's coat with a satisfying rip.

The man rolled his eyes.

"Answer me." Tavin leaned close enough to smell the man's rotting teeth. "What does this ribbon mean?"

Wyling took his shoulder again. "Do not do something you will regret—"

"Who hired you?" Tavin moved to stand over Hugh's groom—former groom. "Does Beauchamp know where you are?"

"Wait for the magistrate, Knox." Wyling's arms folded. "Remember where you are."

"I remember all too well where I am. A chamber of in-nocence. I will know who they are if I have to pummel it out of them."

"You will not." Wyling had never spoken like that to Tavin before. "You will let the magistrate do his job. You will not repay violence for violence."

Tavin gaped as if trying to breathe under water. His fingers flexed, curled, released. The anger did not diminish, but he nodded. Deep breaths of Gemma's lavender-scented things cleared his head, and he stared at his hands. *Dear God, I thought I was a new creation not ten minutes ago. Help me tame this anger within me.*

He glanced at Wyling. "You are a wise friend."

"Not so wise. But we will do this the correct way. I'll not have the ruffians who invaded my home set free, I assure you." He inclined his head at the footmen holding the down pair. "Take them to the library. If they so much as twitch their noses, stop them. Am I clear?"

"Yes, Your Lordship." The footmen hauled the attackers out the door, half dragging Saul.

Wyling studied Tavin, his eyebrows high on his forehead. "I daresay you cracked the little one's brain-box."

"And your furniture."

"Better that than Gemma. I cannot imagine what they intended with her."

Tavin shook out his frosty hands, still chilled from being outside. He held the green ribbon he'd taken from the intruder against the empty hearth. What did it mean?

From the threshold, the white-haired butler bowed. "The magistrate is here, m'lord."

"Put him in the drawing room. I will be down in a moment."

"A moment? We go *now*." Tavin started for the door, catching the eye of two maidservants huddled in the hall. They dashed away, giggling. Ire renewed in his muscles, like ember to flame. Gemma had been almost killed and the maidservants *giggled*.

"I will speak to the magistrate. Not you." Wyling held up his hands. "You have a problem at the moment, and it is not that green ribbon."

Gemma didn't catch much sleep on the cot set up for her in the nursery. After a few hours, she'd arisen to dress and pack. Now she helped ready the boys, despite her weariness. "No arguing, gentlemen. When we leave for Hampshire, you will ride in the carriage with me."

"But Raghnall is tethered outside." Petey pointed out the rain-spattered nursery window.

"We want to ride Raghnall!" Eddie stomped.

"Mr. Knox is in a hurry, and he can travel much faster if he does not have to keep pace with our carriage."

"That is not fair."

Nothing is fair. Gemma laid out Eddie's traveling cloak. "Finish your bread. Nellie will bring you down when it is time."

Gemma had her own preparations to make. All her possessions were packed except those of immediate necessity, and they awaited her in Amy's dressing room. She'd not ever go into her bedchamber again.

David, Wyling's youngest footman, smiled when he spotted her in the hall. "His Lordship requests your presence in the drawing room, miss."

"Thank you." She hastened there, curious.

Wyling did not await her, however. Tavin stood at the window overlooking the square, his stance wide, hands behind his back. He looked hale, whole, unharmed by last night's events. Her breath left her in a rush, and at the sound, he turned to face her, a tiny smile playing at his lips. "Good morning."

"Good morning. I thought Wyling would be here, but I am glad to see you." She licked her lips, tasting the lingering apple sweetness from her snack of the children's black butter. "Thank you for saving me. Once again. You always save me." Hot tears pricked at her eyes.

"Not always." He drew closer and wiped her eyes with the callused pad of his thumb.

She leaned into his hand. "I cannot think of a time."

"I can think of several." His hand lowered.

How brazen she was to feel disappointed that he did

not pull her close. She dropped her gaze. "Do you soon depart?"

"In a few minutes. My things and fresh horses have gone ahead. I plan to be at the village well before you arrive."

She nodded. "Did you glean information from the intruders? Something to lead you to the Sovereign?"

"Those brigands' mouths are shut tighter than oysters, but they may yet speak." His eyes clouded. "Unfortunately, Garner is away from the office, so I cannot speak to him before I leave."

"Once home, I should like to call on Hugh. He must be warned of Saul's part in the Sovereign's scheme."

Tavin's eyes narrowed. "Has it not occurred to you that Saul could *still* serve Beauchamp—even in the capacity he supplied last night? That Beauchamp could be the Sovereign and the man who accosted you on Verity Hill could be his lackey?"

"Hugh?" Gemma almost laughed. "He would not dare."

"Soil his hands with murder? No. He has a plethora of alibis, but he could be the coin and brain behind all of this."

That was enough. "You have always disliked Hugh—"

"The way he treated you was abominable."

"—but I cannot believe you would stoop to such accusations."

Tavin rubbed his forehead. "I do not wish to spend our time arguing."

"Nor do I." It might be all the time they had.

"Will you sit with me, Gemma?"

How she wished to, but now? The house was occupied with preparations to leave. "I do not think I can. Wyling called for me."

"For my sake." With a formal motion, he gestured to the settee.

The fire popped, the lone sound aside from the ticking clock in the chamber. The only sound in the house, it seemed. Someone had shut the door behind her. Shut her up, alone with Tavin? She perched on the end of the settee, her mouth suddenly dry.

He sat beside her, swallowing against his neck cloth. "Gemma. You are a…fine woman."

"Thank you." It came out more like a question. Was this his awkward way of bidding her farewell? "You are a fine man. Do not ever forget how much the Lord values you. How much I esteem you."

If she could give him just that one gift, she could be satisfied. She prayed so, at least.

His hands were hot, taking hers. "Knowing of our mutual estimation and respect, perhaps our friendship could be something more."

His knee edged the settee, as if prepared to hit the floor. The memory of Hugh in a similar posture robbed her of breath.

Was he proposing marriage?

A liquid thrill pooled in her stomach and gushed through her bones. Marriage between them seemed impossible, with his profession and her commitment to the boys, and yet…

I love him. I love him. I—

Tavin's eyes darted to the door, to the ticking mantel clock, to their joined, damp hands. And the thrill in her stomach twisted into something nauseating and cold.

Just like another rainy day, in another drawing room with another gentleman. She had perched on a settee, expecting a proposal, ignoring the discomfiture on a man's face—and she'd looked a fool. She'd not disregard the signs now. She pulled her hands away.

His gaze lifted, his eyes wide.

"If you would consent to be my wife, I should be most happy." He did not sound it.

She had not dared admit to herself how much she wanted this. Wanted a life with this man, even though such a prospect suffered so many obstacles it could never work.

Nor, did it seem, that he actually wanted to marry her, anyway.

She licked her lips. "Why do you wish to marry me?"

His hand flapped on his lap. "I could better protect you."

The rain hit the window in sheets. Its dull sheen was safer to look at than Tavin while she muddled together a response. "You wish to marry to keep me safe?"

"It's a good idea, you must admit. You would no longer need Peter's permission for anything. I would send you to Portugal with Wyling and Amy. Warm clime, and you would be with her when the babe came."

"I would honeymoon with my sister?" Just what every bride longed to hear.

"When the Sovereign is caught, you can come home. If I am still hunting him when Wyling's tenure is finished abroad, I will arrange for you to travel anywhere you wish. With all the protection you require."

She stared at her hands. "And after he's caught, and I come home?"

His swallow was audible. "I would furnish a home for you, wherever you like. The boys would be able to see you whenever your brother allows it." The pace of his words increased, like a nervous child's. "I know how you love Petey and Eddie. And I have come to love them, too."

So he loved *someone*. At last, she dragged her gaze to meet his. "Thank you for your generous offer, but I will not marry for purposes of protection."

His lips mashed together and he hopped to his feet.

"There is something else you may wish to consider. I had hoped to keep the burden from you."

"I thought we no longer kept secrets from one another." Except for how humiliated she felt that he did not care for her like *that*.

"Well, it is not as if I am comfortable telling you I have compromised you."

Her jaw went slack. "I beg your pardon?"

"It seems when I was in your bedchamber at half past two in the morning, my presence drew some curiosity from the staff."

"You were protecting me from murderers." Her screech had carried, no doubt, through the keyhole, and she covered her mouth.

"After watching from the garden. But no one believes that. You know how these things work. When the gossip spreads from the cook to the butcher and the scullery maid to the peddler, which it will, half of London will think I was already in the house. The footmen know I was not below stairs. The maids know I was not in a guest chamber, either. So where else would I have been?" He spread his hands. "I cannot allow others to think you compromised. Wyling believes this is for the best."

Spots filled her vision. *Ah, Lord, everything I ask for is given to me twisted and broken.*

"Wyling asked you to offer for me."

The clock ticked. How long had Wyling granted them privacy? Enough to get the job done.

She exhaled a ragged breath. "I shall never be leaving Verity House again, and no one within its walls cares if all of London titters about me. Besides, they will forget me."

So, it seemed, would Tavin.

"Long memories have a way of fertilizing the seeds of scandal. My mother—"

"I am no duke's daughter. I am the great-niece of a reclusive baron, and although Wyling believes I might be compromised, anyone who pays attention will know two criminals were set on murdering me in my bed, no matter where you happened to be before it occurred. No, my reputation will remain intact." She couldn't look at him anymore. Fussing with her lacy cuff kept her eyes and fingers occupied. "But I thank you for your kindness."

"Your answer is no, then." His face, when she peeked up, was a blank mask.

Her nod was curt. "You are free from any misguided sense of obligation Wyling placed on you."

"I have done naught but obliterate every opportunity for happiness you possessed."

"Not you. The Sovereign—and my choice to wear a red cloak."

If she'd donned her black one, she would probably not have been in danger. She would not have known Tavin. Or come to love him.

But he did not love her. That much was clear. He puffed out a long breath and strode out the door without wishing her farewell.

Chapter Twenty-Two

Three days passed, and Tavin still stung from Gemma's rejection.

Oh, she'd been correct to reject him, of course. He had proposed out of pressure from Wyling, not of his own volition. But he had not realized until she'd refused him how much he wanted her to accept.

Not because of duty. Not just to protect her. But because he loved her and wanted the sort of life she deserved, the kind he couldn't give her while he held this job. But he wanted that life. Wanted to marry her. The past three days, traveling to Hampshire and scouring the New Forest, he'd thought of her every moment. Missed her. Even though she wouldn't marry him to save her life.

Mud splattered his coat sleeves as he galloped from the village to Verity House. Wounded pride, broken heart and all, he had to see Gemma. It could not wait.

Wyling's note informing him of their arrival yesterday had reached him at the posting inn not twenty minutes ago, just after he'd returned from a night of prowling the New Forest. Any weariness he felt dissipated at the thought of seeing Gemma and the boys today.

Oh, yes, he hoped the boys would be allowed to see him.

He turned Raghnall onto the familiar drive of Verity House. At the sight of Verity Hill looming green in the distance, he shuddered, half expecting to see Gemma donned in a red cloak and climbing to the crest.

She was not on the hill, of course. She stood on the front drive alongside a saddled bay gelding, her vermilion riding habit waving in the wind like a flag.

He dismounted with a leap. "What are you doing?"

"Good day to you, too."

"You promised to stay indoors."

"The ride is not for pleasure. I must warn Hugh."

She would be the death of him. "Calling upon him is not necessary."

"This sort of news cannot be written in a missive, should a servant peek at the page." She patted the gelding's neck, avoiding Tavin's gaze. "I informed you of my intentions back in London, and it is not as if the Sovereign is here."

Tavin's jaw clenched. The distant stare of the young groom holding the gelding's reins did not fool him. The lad had heard every word betwixt them. Gemma sighed and turned to the groom. "A moment alone, please, Jed."

The groom nodded and stepped away, his hands behind his back.

Tavin yanked off his beaver hat and smacked it against his thigh. "Why isn't Wyling accompanying you?"

"He is otherwise occupied, arguing with Peter since breakfast about my future." Gemma's voice was low, her gaze down on the grass tickling her hem. "He is trying to take me and the boys with him and Amy to Portugal, but Peter is insistent."

Surprise expanded in his chest. "Peter wants the boys close?"

"No." She tried to smile, but her chin quivered. "I should have said the boys have his permission to go. But I do not. Cristobel has need of me to nurse her through her supposed attack of nerves. So Petey and Eddie may leave, but I must stay."

His chest deflated. "I am sorry." For everything. If he had executed his proposal better, perhaps she might have agreed. Perhaps she would not have been parted from the boys, after all.

And he would have been within his rights to haul her into his arms and kiss her, and then, when he had regained a sense of time and place, to keep her safe.

With a snort, the gelding nudged Gemma, and she patted his neck. "Patience, Jasper." Her clear gaze met Tavin's, revealing the strength and determination he admired but, in this instance, feared. Her headstrong ways could get her killed.

Perhaps another tactic would help. "Have you ever ridden Jasper? He seems far more spirited than Kay."

"I can handle him. After all, I had a credible, if surly, riding instructor." Her lips twitched. "If you will excuse me, I am going to Hugh's. Amy did not like my decision to visit him any more than you do, but she does not believe Hugh capable of such malice, so she agreed, as long as I take a groom with me. Which is sage advice, even when one is not pursued by a murderer."

"It is not amusing, Gemma. Someone wants to harm you."

"But not Hugh."

Tavin stifled the urge to tear his hair from the roots. "Do you have such affection for him? Are you so blind to the connection between him and the Sovereign?"

"*Circumstance*, not connection. And I never loved—" She shook her head, jiggling the pheasant feathers decorating her hat brim. "This is none of your affair."

She'd never loved Beauchamp?

"Fine." He crouched and cupped his hands for her boot. "Put your foot in my hand and climb up. I cannot stop you from going alone. So I will go with you. *And* Jed. Get on the horse."

Her boot landed with a smack against his palms. A tiny half grin pulled at his cheek.

The errand might be foolishness itself, but he'd be spending time with Gemma again.

He had grown familiar with the hedgerow-lined road between Verity House and its neighbors when he'd stayed here so many weeks ago investigating the Sovereign. Before Gemma became involved. Before she was *Gemma* to him. Back then, she was Miss Lyfeld, the pretty miss who came to represent all the things he thought he could never have: a home, a heart.

Although, riding beside her with Jed the groom trotting behind them, he wondered how he could have thought he'd ever forget her. He loved her with every sinew in his body.

Overhead, the clouds thickened to an ominous gloom. "Is there not a shorter route connecting your homes?"

Gemma pointed to the rolling hills on their right. "There is a small stone wall I used to climb. Then I ran over the grass, down the slope."

Her blue eyes softened, and for a moment Tavin pictured her climbing the wall as a child. What had she looked like then? Gap-toothed, bedraggled, her hair flying loose? How he'd love to see her childhood face reflected in one of her children.

He shifted in the saddle in an attempt to also shift his dangerous thinking. "You must have been a hoyden then."

"Then?" With a laugh, she flicked Jasper's reins and took off at a run, leaving the road for the knolls.

He dug his heels into Raghnall's flanks and gave chase. She did not go far. At the rise of the tallest hill, she paused, a vision cloaked in flaming orange-red for the entire world to see.

"Have you forgotten already?" He pulled up alongside her.

"I am not overlooking Smuggler's Road." Exertion, not embarrassment, flushed her cheeks. "The Sovereign is in London. And Hugh is ignorant of Saul's actions."

"Ho, sir, madam." Jed's voice called from behind them. Tavin turned as Jed leaped from his mount and knelt on the grass.

"What is it, Jed?"

"Not certain, sir, but 'e started dragging 'is toe after that run."

"Oh, 'tis my fault." Gemma's fingers splayed over her chest. "Poor creature."

"Looks like a sprain, miss, nothing serious." Jed's gentle smile did little to ease the expression of guilt on Gemma's face. "I'd best take 'im back, if you don't mind."

Tavin shook his head. "We shall all go back." *Thank You, Lord, for providing the means to bring us home.*

Gemma's lips twisted. "No, you go on without us, Jed. We'll return shortly."

Creaking the leather, Tavin turned in his saddle so he faced her. He reached out and rested his hand over hers. Not to take her reins but to touch her, even if just once more. "Be sensible. We should not call on Beauchamp without a chaperone. Or a party of men."

"I know Hugh. You do not. I owe him this much."

"You owe him nothing."

"He is my friend."

"And what of me?" He released her hand and cupped her chin. "What about me?"

Her lips parted. She could not very well tell him she loved him—

Heat rushed to her cheeks. She must be the color of her riding habit. "You are my friend, too, but Hugh must be told about Saul keeping dangerous company. Please." She licked her slightly raw lips. "His house is not far. Five minutes is all I ask."

He did not look at all pleased when he nodded, but his thumb brushed her chin before his hand fell and he urged Raghnall onward.

The ride to Beauchamp's estate was brief, indeed, and within a few minutes, Tavin stood on the drive, helping Gemma dismount. He held her about the waist longer than he should have. "Five minutes, you said."

She laughed, not moving from the circle of his arms. "So I did."

Letting her go, he handed the horses to a slim groom who appeared as if from the air.

A crusty-faced butler led them upstairs, past marble sculptures and exquisite tapestries, to the drawing room overlooking the back of the house. Gentle flames danced in the hearth, and a large gilt-bronze candelabrum was alight with six candles.

Tavin's lip curled as he surveyed the gold-hued chamber. Heavy drapes the color of mustard and honey wallpaper covered the stone walls under a high plaster ceiling dripping in gilt. The furniture and lacquered tables were accented with gold, too, and arrangements of creamy yellow blooms festooned a pair of gilt-bronzed jardinieres.

"Too much gold is not a good thing." Tavin paced the perimeter, his boots sinking into the plush, pollen-hued rug. "Has he not heard the story of Midas?"

"Or perhaps not heeded its moral." Gemma peered about the chamber, her brows lifted. Did she consider how she might have changed it had she married Beauchamp?

"I can see why you had hoped to live here."

"Do not tease, Tavin." Her mouth set in a line.

"Not for the decor, but the proximity. It *is* close to the boys."

She moved to the window and fingered the drapes. "Things have a way of working themselves out. I have every confidence the Lord will surprise me yet."

That was his Gemma. "I think—"

She spun from the window, her eyes wide, her finger extended in a point. "Tavin."

The hairs at his nape rose as he dashed to her, sidling against the gold drape. Sliding the panel aside an inch, he peered down. Beauchamp faced the house, engaged in a heated conversation with a brown-garbed man.

"Who is the other man?"

"Him."

"The man from Verity Hill and Piccadilly? The man who struck you?" He spared her a glance. She nodded, her lips mashed together, her face leached of color.

Every muscle in Tavin's body flexed as his brain discarded strategies. If he were alone, he would not hesitate to do what was necessary. But with Gemma here, his options were few.

"You were right." Grief laced her whisper. "Hugh is the Sovereign. He ordered those deaths. Even mine."

He lowered the drape and cradled her cheek, forcing her gaze to meet his. "They did not see us arrive, and they will not see you leave."

"Me?" She gripped his lapel. "No, both of us must go. Now."

"I submitted my card. If he doesn't yet know I was here, he will shortly, but I will wait here and tell Beauchamp we had an argument and you returned home without me.

That would not be so unexpected, would it? Nor would it be a lie. We bickered just this morning."

Her grip on his coat strained the seams of his coat. "How can you jest?"

"Because I do not want you to be frightened. Now go. Get Wyling, your brother, anyone you see along the way. If you *cannae* get to the horses, run the way you showed me, over the wall. I will keep Beauchamp occupied long enough for you to reach home." He dropped his hands.

"Tavin." There was something other than fear in her eyes.

He cradled her bonneted head and pulled her to him, brushing a swift kiss on her brow. His eyes squeezed shut as he memorized the moment, praying it would not be their last. "May the Lord go with you."

Her fingers traced his cheek. Then she fled out the door. *Guard her, Lord, for I cannot.*

He faced the door, rehearsing his words. *Play jealous about Gemma; that should not be hard. Engage his pride—*

The door opened, revealing Beauchamp, the shoulders of his pale blue coat lifted in a sheepish-looking pose. "Mr. Knox. Forgive the delay. I fear I was occupied."

"I can return later." With shackles and a dozen armed men.

"Not after you have come so far." He stepped all the way into the room. Behind him trailed Gemma. And Beauchamp's companion.

Gray-headed and icy-eyed, the brown-garbed man held Gemma's arm. "Hello, Knox."

Garner.

The fireplace poker was in Tavin's hand before Garner could take another step. He'd have Beauchamp's legs out from under him in a trice, then Garner's—

The click stopped him cold. He had no choice. He dropped the poker.

Garner pointed a pistol at Gemma's throat.

Gemma winced at the raw sting of rope against her wrists as she wiggled against the chair where Hugh had bound her. But her pain couldn't compare to Tavin's, his jaw and temple red from Garner's repeated blows. Why did Garner continue? Tavin was already shackled in hideous manacles and chained to a metal ring in the fireplace grate.

"Stop, you monster!" Her screams and stomps should have alerted someone.

"The staff is too well paid to stop polishing silver and come to your aid." Hugh patted the crown of her head, bonnetless, thanks to Garner's insistence it obscured her features, and he wanted to fully see the girl who'd thought to end his reign.

She shrank from Hugh's touch on her head. To think she'd planned a future with him. At least Hugh sported a bloody nose. And Garner had not gained the upper hand without cost. One arm curled against his chest, and a bruise blossomed under one eye.

At last Garner stepped back. He pointed at Tavin. "He keeps a knife at his back, Beauchamp. Take it."

Grimacing, Hugh flipped Tavin's coattails and unsheathed the knife from his waist. "I do not know whether to be horrified or impressed."

The loss of the knife was a blow, true, but not a crippling one. Did Tavin's superior know of the blade in his boot?

"Remove his Hessians, as well." Garner waved the pistol at Tavin. "And do not think to lash out with your feet, Knox. Miss Lyfeld will pay the price if you do."

Tethered to a crouch by the short chain linking his

wrists to the hearth, Tavin glared as Hugh yanked off his boots. "Do not touch her."

"Is this affection I hear? I always thought you two smelled of April and May." Hugh discovered Tavin's small knife. "Excellent deduction, Garner."

The rope binding Gemma to the chair strained her chest, forcing her to breathe in shallow pants. Then Tavin's chain rattled. She met his steady gaze, forcing herself to use her head. To pray. To help Tavin.

Tied up, all she could think to do was distract Hugh. With great reluctance, she tore her gaze from Tavin's.

"I came in *friendship* to warn you about Saul, never guessing you were the one who had sent your groom to kill me in my bed."

"I'd never hurt you, Gem." The irony was laughable, but Hugh, oblivious, glared at Garner. "If I'd known—"

"You'd have changed nothing, because she could have ruined your enterprise." Garner sneered. "The description of me you offered Knox was, to my relief, vague enough that he'd not suspect me, but then I learned of your clandestine letter-writing, dear girl. How was I to be sure you were not some sort of agent for a rival smuggler? Or worse, for the government, which could only mean that others were aware of my intent to start a new order. So I had no choice but to find you at the masque. I was so close to you then. I had hoped 'twould be enough to frighten you into leaving town while I went about my business there. But once Knox told me you'd recognized me on Piccadilly, you had to be dispatched."

"Pity for you both it didn't work." Gemma spoke loud enough to cover the faint rattling of chains sounding from near the hearth. Not enough to draw Garner's notice. *Keep on it, Tavin. Whatever you are doing—*

Hugh spun to Tavin and tsked. "It will not work."

Tavin snorted. "I was about to say the same of your objectives."

Hugh's eyes goggled in mock confusion. "Oh, you mean the smuggling. Gemma, the most amazing thing happened when Father died. I learned there's a tunnel that extends from my wine cellar to the village posting house, with a fork that leads into the New Forest. I wish we'd known about the tunnels when we were younger. How we would have enjoyed exploring them."

Bile rose in Gemma's throat. "With far different intent than you use them now."

He turned back to Tavin. "When one has as resourceful a partner as a Custom House official, well, it is difficult to see the negatives of such an arrangement. Everyone wins."

"Not everyone." Tavin shifted his weight from one stockinged-foot to the other. How uncomfortable he must be, forced to his haunches, chained at the wrists to the fireplace. "Garner's motives do not match yours. He wants men. And money, too, for his cause."

Gemma bit her lip. Tavin had better know what he was doing. Whatever it was, it kept all eyes from her, so she resumed twisting her wrists. The soft *scrich* of rope against the chair chafed her skin, but mayhap it would weaken the bonds.

"What cause?" Hugh frowned.

"You don't know what Garner is about, do you?" Tavin's voice was pitying.

"You try to turn us against one another," Hugh said.

"No, he's correct." Garner turned from the window. "How did you come to this conclusion, Knox?"

Scrich, scrich.

"That you are the Sovereign?" Tavin did not take his eyes from Garner. "All signs pointed to Beauchamp, except for the green ribbon. I admit it took me weeks to fathom, but it is obvious now."

"Not to me." Hugh dropped Tavin's knife on a lacquered table with a petulant thunk.

Garner stepped toward Tavin. "How did you learn of the ribbons?"

"I found one atop Verity Hill, the day you attacked Gemma. I wasn't certain if it was a scrap or a clue until Bill Simple's murder. Then, too, Gemma mentioned France, but it was not until your men, wearing similar ribbons, attacked her that I grasped your goal."

Garner smiled. "You withheld that ribbon from me. To think I found you trustworthy because of your professed faith. Now I see you are just as deceitful as everyone else from your class."

"Will someone not tell me what is going on?" Hugh raked a hand through his hair.

Scrich. Gemma eyed the knife.

"More than brandy and tea came through your cellars, Beauchamp." Tavin's voice was soothing, as if he spoke to Petey and Eddie. "Garner smuggled people, too."

"Utter rot."

"There were never Frenchmen in your cellar?"

"To collect payment, of course. But the war against Napoleon is over."

"They were not here to gather intelligence." Tavin grimaced. "They came to help start a revolution."

Hugh's brow creased, but Gemma fully understood now. "Before the tricolor in France, green cockades served as a symbol for the populace. These green ribbons must be a signal for Englishmen planning to challenge the government."

"Not just challenge," Garner snorted. "We will dispose of it. Parliament, all the so-called 'betters' who trample the citizens under their heels. And it will begin with the assassination of the Prince Regent."

As Hugh's jaw went slack, Tavin's leg shot out.

Chapter Twenty-Three

Now.

Jerking like a snared bird, Gemma fought against the ropes.

Tavin's foot hooked Hugh's ankle and yanked. As Hugh landed on his backside, Tavin pinned Hugh's arms with one leg and planted his other foot atop Hugh's throat.

Gemma tugged. If she could break loose and reach the knife—

The reverberation of a pistol shot stole her breath. *Tavin.*

Hugh crawled out from the cage of Tavin's legs, rubbing his neck. Something Tavin would not have allowed, were he strong enough.

"Tavin." Was that her voice? Or did she merely gasp the word?

Then a crimson flower blossomed through the length of white neck cloth high on his chest.

She screamed, stomped, wrestled against the rope. Popping to her toes, she hobbled like a half-dead crab toward Tavin, her chair dragging on the thick gold rug.

"'Tis well," Tavin lied, his eyes dull.

A plush cushion lay on the floor from the tussle. She

stretched out her leg and kicked it toward him. "Use this to stanch the flow."

He pressed the pillow to his body.

"Now see here." Hugh's chest puffed out. "I did not agree to this."

Gemma glared through hot tears. "If you've any decency left, Hugh, unbind me so I may tend to him."

"I was not the one to shoot him, Gem." Hugh's voice rose. "I don't wish to kill anyone. Certainly not the prince. His Highness is a personal friend. Are you mad, Garner?"

Garner brushed aside the curtain and peered out. "No time for histrionics. They are here."

"Who?" Gemma's wrists twisted. She would forfeit the skin on her forearms if it meant getting out of these ropes and helping Tavin.

"A shipment of goods." Hugh stormed back to the window. "But are men with seditious intent under those tarps, too, Garner?"

"And weapons." Tavin's voice was weak, but his glare was piercing.

"Must I shoot you again, Knox? This time in the gut?"

"Enough." Hugh pulled at his hair. "Give me my money and then we're finished."

Garner hastened to the door, pistol in hand. "Wait while I will send the free traders in the correct direction. If you grow weak-livered now, Beauchamp, you'll get nothing. Hear me?"

Hugh grimaced, but then offered a reluctant nod. As Garner's boots stomped down the hall, Hugh sank onto the settee, his head in his hands.

Tavin shuffled against the chains, pressing the blood-soaked cushion to his chest.

Gemma wriggled against her bonds. "Hugh, look at me. He shot Tavin. He will kill the prince, and me, may-hap within the hour."

"That was talk." Hugh tugged at the hair at his temples. "He wouldn't hurt you."

Tavin was pale as snow. "He had me protect Gemma. Not for her sake but his, to ensure she posed no threat to him. He may kill you, too."

Hugh rose to his feet. "He won't. He needs me. I can persuade him to spare you, Gem, but you must not speak of this, not of me or my part. Ever. Promise?"

Of course she couldn't.

"She will keep silent." Tavin nudged her leg with his. Her gaze met his. "I will not let you die. You will agree. For me."

"I won't go without you." She turned back. "Please, Hugh."

"I'm sorry." Hugh turned away. "Knox is shot, anyway."

Tavin gritted his teeth. "Beauchamp, put that knife to good use and set her free."

Garner's return clamped all their mouths shut. "More visitors for you, Beauchamp. Get rid of them, before this day ends in utter disaster."

"Who is it?"

"The Earl and Countess of Wyling."

Gemma sucked in a breath to scream, but Garner's slimy hand smothered her mouth. "If they do not leave this house in two minutes, unaware of your presence, they will die. And so will those two lads of yours."

She'd bite him if not for his threat to kill her family. Be-cause if she knew anything about this so-called superior of Tavin's, it was that he had no hesitation to commit murder.

* * *

The wound in Tavin's chest burned, but it was also curious. He had been stabbed, punched, kicked, bitten and thrown from a horse, but he had never been shot.

At least the wound was high, closer to his clavicle than his heart. Either Garner was a poor shot or he preferred watching Tavin bleed to death on Beauchamp's yellow rug.

"Do you think they will be safe?" Gemma's voice was low. "Wyling and Amy. And Jed, oh!" She bit her bloodless lips.

Poor lass. He'd get her home with his dying breath.

"They'll be home with the boys soon. And so will you."

"Since you are in the mood to talk, Knox, explain something." Garner collapsed into a lyre-backed chair. "Your family failed you. They ignored you, then used you, tried to break you, but you overcame. When you came to me, repentant over that middling agent's death, I was astonished. A gentleman, remorseful? But you made your own way rather than *inherited* it. You didn't lean on your family's name or power to accomplish good. Can you not see how much better Britain will be once every man earns his lot?"

Breathing ached. Speaking ached. But every minute was another gift from Providence, another opportunity to save Gemma.

"There are other ways."

"Ah yes, your Wyling *tries his best*. I will grant you that. But he must die when the time ripens."

A cry escaped Gemma's lips. Tavin did not dare look at her. Seeing her grief would do him in, and he would not be able to continue. "So you will slaughter the nobility, steal their possessions. Usher in a new era."

"The Prince Regent gorges his gullet and ignores responsibility. Wouldn't your God rather clothe the poor in the prince's finery and feed the starving from his larders? Sounds like heaven, does it not?"

"Not quite."

Hugh slunk into the room, his shoulders hunched. "Amy and Wyling are gone. I said Gemma and Knox were not here."

"Good." Garner smiled.

"But there is a problem in the cellars. The men are sparring over the weapons."

Garner cursed and stood. "Watch them, Beauchamp, or I will have to shoot you, too."

As Garner left the room, Hugh moved to the window. After a minute, he turned around, his gaze on the rug. "I cannot stop him. But you and I will be safe, Gem, if we keep quiet."

Tavin's knife lay on the lacquered table. Hugh ran his hand over the hilt, slow and pointed, and then he left the room.

Gemma snorted. "Why did he not cut me loose?"

"So he could state in all truth he did not do it when Garner points a pistol at his chest." But excitement thrummed in Tavin's chest. "You can reach the blade."

"I am tied to the chair." As her brows rose, her fingers wriggled.

"Carry the chair with you, like when you brought me the cushion."

Pressing her toes into the rug, she scuttled in awkward thumps to the lacquered table. She stretched behind her, her fingers fumbling for the blade. Determination lined her face. She had never looked more beautiful.

"That's it."

The mantel clock ticked. Her fingertips skittered over the slick table surface and then brushed the handle. She almost had it—

The knife slipped to the floor and bounced under the settee.

Sending him a look of exasperation, she set the chair down on all four legs and tried to scoop it out with her boot-shod foot. "I cannot."

Perspiration glistened over her face. He felt damp, too. Was it sweat or blood? "You can."

"I am so sorry." She continued to stretch her foot for the knife.

"I'm the sorry one, lass. I'm supposed to protect you."

"You have. God sent you to keep me safe."

"Until now." His eyes shut. "Perhaps we should beseech His aid now, Gemma."

He thanked God for Gemma. He prayed for strength and wisdom. And then the light of the candelabrum flickered through his closed lids. He opened his eyes.

"The candelabrum."

Her eyes narrowed. "What?"

Lord, give her strength to do what I ask of her. "Use the flame to burn the ropes."

"But my hands are tied. I cannot carry it to you."

"You *maun* be brave, lass. Back up to the candelabrum and lean your bonds into the flame."

Her jaw slackened. "I will catch fire."

"No. The ropes will—"

"And then the chair." The pitch of her words rose. "And then me."

"The rope will burn and you will be free." His words were slow, even. "The fire will be so small we can extinguish it with the water from that vase. We can do this, Gemma."

We? Tavin chewed his cheek at the word. Shackled to the hearth, he'd not be the one to overturn the jardiniere for the water. But he would do everything he could to help her. "My gaze will never leave you. I promise." He wished he could brush the errant lock of hair from her cheek. "Will you try it?"

She licked her lips. The mantel clock ticked away the little time they had left. If she did not act soon, she would die here with him.

At last she nodded, her eyes squeezed shut. She inched backward.

He leaned forward, his head swirling with fogginess at the sudden movement. "There are still several inches to go."

She scraped back another measure. Still not far enough.

"You are so brave, lass. The bravest female I've ever known. Remember how you thwarted Garner that first day? And he is not an easy man to foil. Now try to rise on your feet and lean back."

She grimaced, holding the awkward posture. "I'll burn."

"The rope, not you. Now lean."

She muttered something and inclined back. Flame danced a hairbreadth from the rope.

"Almost, Gemma."

A ghost of a smile played at her lips. "See how I succumb to your flattery?"

"'Tis not flattery, but truth." His gaze fixed on the flame. "I have never admired anyone as much as I do you."

Screwing up her face, she leaned farther, and the rope began to smoke.

"There, it's catching." He kept his voice soft as lamb's wool. "Twist away, if you can. I must see when the rope falls away."

The odor of singed fibers assaulted his nose. Tiny, orange-gold tongues of flame lapped the rope, licked the chair's upholstery. What memories it must spark in Gemma, whose chest rose and fell in panicky breaths.

"Now twist so you can see the fire, on your left side?" She obeyed, but sounds like a wounded animal's escaped her throat. "That arm is looser, is it not? Because it's smoldering. Lift a wee bit."

Grimacing, she did. And the rope turned black just as the flames on the back of the chair grew high enough to scorch her hair.

"Now!"

She leaped from the chair, although her right arm was still attached with rope that had yet to burn. She wrested against it and pulled free. A deep, painful breath left Tavin's lungs.

Gemma hastened to the closest of the jardinieres. Yanking out the bouquet it held, she gripped the zinc water bowl and tossed it at the burning chair. The water landed short, soaking the rug.

Every muscle in Tavin's body seized. He forced a single breath before speaking again. "You must get closer. Use the other jardiniere to quench the flames."

"Tavin," she protested, but she did it. Water splashed over the chair. Small flames still lapped at remnants of the rope. She ripped cushions from the settee and beat the flames until all that was left was smoke and charred furniture.

Her eyes met his. "We did it."

"'Twas all you. How brave you are. Now run. Fast as you can."

"Not without you." Her eyes glowed like the fire she'd just extinguished. "I'll pick that lock on your wrists with the knife."

Like a true spy. "You haven't time. Leave me the knife and run."

"Never." She dropped to her knees, stretched for the knife and rose. Her backside hit the lacquered table, tilting it on its spindly legs. The candelabrum tipped, scattering candles like chaff. A few extinguished. But the others landed at the hems of the golden drapes.

She stared at Tavin, eyes wide, as flames lapped up a drape.

"Run, Gemma. Don't stop."

Instead, she held up the cushions and took a hesitant step forward.

"Don't attempt to beat it out." Not with her fear. Besides, she'd fan the flames rather than smother them. He rose on his haunches. "They will see smoke and come. Beauchamp will help me." But probably not. "Go."

"I lost my parents this way. I cannot lose you, too." She scrambled to his side and poked at his shackles with the knife. Every other second, however, her gaze darted to the drapes. Then she grasped the poker and struck the chain.

Futile. He reached for her, but she stuffed his hands back against the blood-soaked cushion at his chest. "Behave and keep this pressed against you."

As if it mattered. Bleeding to death was preferable to suffocating in smoke. He cupped her face. The act tore at his wound, weakened him, but strength wasn't something he'd require much longer. "Please go."

Her wet cheeks heated under his fingers. "I can't."

Ach, how he loved her. But he wouldn't add to her grief by declaring his heart. If he did, she'd never leave. "You must. For the boys. Go."

With a whoosh, the second set of drapes caught fire.

She screeched, an unholy sound. "I've killed you."

He held up his shackles. "You did not do this. I am not angry. Never forget that, lass."

Tears streaked her face.

"Gemma, I now trust that I am forgiven. I have peace

from God. That's what you wanted for me all along, is it not?"

She nodded, her lips pressed in a grim line.

"What a gift you are, lass."

She pressed her face to his, wetting his cheeks with her tears. His head spun from the agony and joy of this farewell.

"Now go." He urged her back before he caused her death.

She stared at him for a moment and then disappeared out the door.

Chapter Twenty-Four

Hot. So hot.

Gemma fled the room, yet there was no escaping the stench of smoke filling her nostrils. She gasped to scream, but she coughed instead. Not that anyone would come to Tavin's aid, anyway.

Tavin. She'd left him to die.

But he'd wanted her to. He wanted her to live. To care for Petey and Eddie. With slick hands, Gemma dashed down the stairs. Her boot slid, and she caught the banister, her upper body twisting over the rail.

Her muscles locked as if ice captured her instead of fire.

Images flashed before her eyes. Petey's face. Then Eddie's. Amy's, Wyling's, Frances's, even Peter's and Cristobel's. Tavin's, his brow arched in that saucy way.

They are Yours, Father. I release them to You. At last, I give them into Your capable hands.

In Gemma's mind, the Lord's hands appeared. Scarred, strong, cupped, as if waiting to hold something. She imagined Petey and Eddie. As if they were babes in her arms, she placed them in the Lord's hands. *They are Yours, Lord.*

Then she gripped the banister and pulled herself upright. And she kept on pulling until she had ascended every stair.

Thick smoke coiled from the drawing room door, but she plunged in.

Fire lapped the two far walls. She veiled her mouth and nose with her sleeve. "Tavin!"

"Get out." He had dropped the pillow from his chest.

She dropped to her knees, shoved the cushion against his wound, pressed his hand to it and then crawled away. Her eyes stinging, she peered through the smoke. The air was clearer down here, but not by much. At last she saw it, a reddish lump close to the fire, but she reached out, anyway.

"You returned for your bonnet?" A cough consumed him.

Her fingers worked at the brim, plucking around the pheasant feather. Then she pressed the hatpins into his fingers. "Are these sturdy enough? You must tell me what to do if I am to pick the lock."

His eyes rolled back. "No. You must—"

"I must hurry, is what I must do. So tell me."

The lines around his eyes softened. Then he held up his wrists.

"Insert the first pin into the keyhole. Push up. Now insert the second. Do you feel the change in resistance?"

She nodded, then manipulated the second pin according to his instructions. Jiggled. Nothing happened. "Tell me again."

"There's not time."

"Once more." First pin, push up. Second pin. Find the barrier, feel for the change. Wiggle.

She could not hear the click or the rattle of the chains as they fell away. But Tavin's hand was firm around hers as he hauled her to her feet and pulled her from the golden room.

* * *

Never had air tasted sweeter. Like scythed grass and dew. Bent over, palms against his knees, Tavin drank the spring-cool air in heaving gasps and choked them out again. Beside him, Gemma sank to the gravel drive, her red riding habit looking less like a flame than a sooty rag. He swallowed, his throat rough as splintered wood. Speaking would hurt, but he couldn't stop himself.

"You are beautiful."

Her eyes narrowed. "Blood loss has addled your brain."

She gave way to another fit of coughing, and Tavin rose with care. Everything hurt. Pain from the shot radiated down his arm and up his neck. The imprints from Garner's boot in his back would take a while to diminish, as well.

But the wounds would wait. He scanned the yard. What few servants Hugh had in residence scrambled with buckets in hand. Hugh shouted instructions and tore at his hair. Raghnall and Jasper weren't visible, but in the distance, an ink-black horse galloped toward the New Forest, Garner on its back.

Pity Tavin had lost his boots. Ah, well. He nudged Gemma with his good shoulder and led her, jogging, to the stable. "Pick a horse, lead him to the block and climb on. Get Wyling and as many men as he can muster."

"What are you doing?"

The stable was dark, empty of grooms, but it took mere seconds to find a saddled gray gelding—belonging to a smuggler, perhaps. He shoved his left foot into the stirrup. With his right arm, he hoisted himself atop the tallest of the mounts. "Ending this."

He dug his heels into the gray and sped after Garner.

At the rise, he spotted the black horse and rider. Tavin clucked his tongue. The gelding was no Raghnall, but he responded well enough to Tavin's commands. The pain of his wound jarred with the horse's gait. He cradled his left arm closer to his chest. *God help me.*

He slowed the horse's pace at the tree line, peering into the gaps between trees. He paused to listen for the snapping of twigs, the rustle of leaves.

And then he heard it. The jingling reins of a cantering horse. Probably riderless.

Tavin slid from the saddle and tethered the gray to a branch. The desire to cough was overwhelming. So was the desire to sink to the earth and rest. Instead, he studied the ground for signs, equestrian and human. His stockinged feet made little sound crossing the carpet of damp leaves. He waited, listened.

A mammoth fallen oak blocked the widest space between the other trees. A twitch of a smile curled at his lips. Garner had thought to jump it?

With his left arm still curled into his chest, he pressed his right palm against the oak and leaped over it, spinning back around, his boot connecting with some part of Garner's prostrate form hidden under the trunk.

"Oomph!"

Garner slithered away, one hand on the tree trunk, the other curled in a fist. No pistol. Tavin must have knocked it from his hand when he'd kicked him.

As one, they both lunged under the fallen tree.

Garner reached out, but Tavin had no interest in the weapon. One armed, Tavin grasped Garner's coat and hauled him away from the pistol.

"You intend to fight me with one hand?" Garner grasped a fallen branch and swung.

Tavin blocked the branch with a kick. "I will fight with no hands, if I must."

Garner eyed the pistol on the ground.

Tavin circled him away from it. "Are you afraid? Sir?"

"I am the Sovereign." Garner's nostrils flared. "All Hampshire fears *me*. And soon England will, too."

"No one in London even knows you. Recall Theophilus Grenville, that fellow whose entrée to the masque you stole?" Tavin shifted. Once Garner lunged, he'd have him where he wanted him. "He'd never heard of you."

A muscle worked in his cheek. "He will."

The pain in Tavin's chest and shoulder deepened. Tavin stood tall, but his vision started to blacken. "You chose him for a reason, though. Whom did he harm? Your lady love?"

"My sister. A maid in his house." Garner spit. "He cast her and her babe out with a few coins. She died begging for mercy, from him, from God. There's no injustice in Grenville's death."

"You'll be sorry to hear it, but Grenville isn't dead. And justice is not yours to dispense."

"Then he'll be the first to die in the new order." Garner lunged for the pistol.

Tavin's foot caught Garner's ankle, tripping him. His right arm gripped Garner's wrists, pinning them behind his shoulder blades.

Garner writhed against Tavin's hold. "You will die from blood loss before you can drag me out of here."

"Test me."

Tavin swept his leg under the fallen oak, drawing out the pistol. Garner grunted, twisted, snapped his jaws, but Tavin's grip did not loosen. His left arm tore with ragged pain as he gripped the pistol and examined the chamber.

Loaded. Ready to fire.

Garner laughed. "I suppose 'tis fair, you killing me after I tried to kill you. But if you murder me, your God will reckon with you."

"Who said anything about murder? I am apprehending a smuggler."

Tavin cocked the pistol. Garner's eyes grew wide.

Extending his wounded arm hurt more than anything Tavin had ever done. His skin seared. Black spots appeared before his vision, but he could still see the fear in Garner's eyes.

The fear of a man with no hope.

Tavin fired the pistol. Straight into the air, to signal Wyling.

Shouts penetrated through the trees. "Knox! Thataway!"

"You couldn't kill me." Garner's brows knit together.

Tavin pulled Garner up to stand, his right hand still clenching Garner's wrists like a cuff. "I never intended to."

"I will be more powerful imprisoned than I am now. My followers will grow in number and zeal. I will change the course of human history."

Tavin nudged his superior toward the sound of the shouts.

"There is one true Sovereign, Garner, and He is not you."

Chapter Twenty-Five

The evening passed in a flurry, with Tavin, Wyling and Peter behind closed doors with officials and the physician, preventing Gemma a minute alone with Tavin. Determined to wait up until he was able to see her, she'd bathed, changed into a clean muslin gown and curled onto the drawing room sofa where she'd sat with Hugh all those weeks ago. She opened her prayer book.

"Ah Lord GOD! behold, thou hast made the heaven and the earth by thy great power and stretched out arm, and there is nothing too hard for thee."

"'There is nothing too hard for thee.'" Gemma's words were soft as vapor in the air. She resolved to pray and trust through the night. But sleep overtook her, and when Amy cupped her shoulder, dawn's gray tendrils crept beneath the drapes.

"Tavin?" Gemma bolted upright.

"He's well. Determined to make an early start."

"He cannot travel with that wound." She hurried to stand.

"The bullet went through. He's been patched and caught a few hours' rest. I learned he wished to see you but thought you were asleep in bed. He's leaving soon for London." At

Gemma's grunt, Amy smiled. "Gentlemen grow irritable when they have work to finish."

"His work *is* finished." Gemma wadded the light blanket she'd snuggled beneath. "He was shot and beaten. Someone else can transport Garner to London."

"But he would see it as leaving the job unfinished, and then he would not be Tavin Knox, would he?"

No. Gunshot wound, bruises and all, Tavin completed his tasks. She loved his dedication, but it meant she'd have to let him go—today and every day, just as she had prayed while bent over Hugh's banister.

She let out a ragged sigh. "When does he depart?"

Amy helped her to stand. "Once he's returned here from the village. He's overseeing the, er, prisoners' placement in the wagon."

Gemma could only nod before marching upstairs to wash and repin her hair. She'd break her fast later. Why waste a moment when she had so few left with Tavin?

The boys, who as yet were blissfully ignorant of the full scope of the previous day's events, were awake, fed and dressed, so she and Amy took them out front to frolic on the dewy lawn. Within a few minutes, Tavin, atop Raghnall, trotted into the yard. Aside from the left arm curled into a white sling and the shadow of a bruise on his jaw, Tavin looked hearty and whole as he dismounted on the drive, watching her.

Until the boys barreled into his side and grabbed his knees. "Mr. Knox!"

He laughed and winced at the same time. "What a greeting!"

Gemma choked down the emotion thick in her throat.

"Can we ride Raghnall today?" Petey abandoned him for the horse.

"Not today, lads. I'm for London."

Eddie pouted. Petey returned and tapped Tavin's arm, making him wince. "What's this?"

"Just a trifle."

Eddie rubbed his own jaw. "Why is your face splotchy?"

"Er." Tavin looked at her, helpless.

"Shaving with a dull razor?" Petey nodded knowingly. "Papa's valet says dull razors hurt."

"My razor isn't dull." Eddie curled his finger over his lip to make a mustache, like he had when they'd viewed the Elgin Marbles.

"Indeed not." Tavin laughed, and despite herself, Gemma did, too.

Amy patted her arm and beckoned the boys. "Come, help me find the package of cake Cook prepared for Mr. Knox's travels. I think she left bites for us."

"Cake before noon?" Petey's jaw dropped. "Hurry, Eddie."

Gemma didn't watch them go. Her gaze was on Tavin, her steps toward him slow. He moved toward her at a faster pace. "I feared I'd miss you."

"Are you in pain?" She stared at the buttons of his black waistcoat.

"Only when I ride. Or breathe. Or when Petey and Eddie greeted me." He laughed. "I will miss them."

"When will they see you again?" When would she?

His touch was gentle on her cheek. "I don't know, lass."

Her body betrayed her by filling her eyes with tears. "What about Garner's men?"

What about me?

He owed her nothing. She knew better than to expect something more from him. Yet still she hoped.

He wiped her tears, but then his hand fell. "They're being rounded up by local authorities. Word went ahead of us, warning the prince. But Garner has created quite a mess. I must assist the Board of Customs to set things right."

"You will have much work to do." She tried to smile. "And I daresay Miss Scarcliff may not wish to marry Hugh now." Her little joke inspired the smallest of smiles. There was no use prolonging this. "Go with God, Tavin."

He took her hand and placed the briefest of kisses on her wrist. "And you, Gemma."

She wasn't going anywhere, but she smiled. It was easier this time.

He released her hand just as Amy and the children returned with a paper-wrapped parcel.

"Cake!" The crumbs on Eddie's lips revealed that he'd sampled his share.

"I think you will like it, sir." Petey handed it to Tavin.

"Thank you, lads." He tucked the parcel into a pouch on Raghnall's saddle, mounted up and, with a final wave, trotted away.

There is nothing too hard for Thee, Lord.

Not even forgetting Tavin Knox.

Gemma became adept at saying goodbye over the passing weeks. Amy and Wyling departed for Portugal—without the boys, after much discussion—and Gemma's world returned to what it had been before she met Tavin Knox. Loving the boys. Serving Cristobel.

Now, as summer waned into autumn, Gemma entered a new season, too. Acceptance of her lot and trusting God to care for her and her broken heart. Sending sums from her small investments and allowance each fortnight to her London solicitor to invest on her behalf. Praying for Tavin.

And she'd been blessed with peace. Most of the time, anyway.

Bent over the table in the morning room, Gemma held

the creased foolscap to her nose, as if she could smell Portugal on the pages. Instead, the faint aromas of ink and Amy's tuberose perfume lingered there—not exotic fragrances, to be sure, but soothing ones all the same.

I miss you, Amy. Missed conversing, asking questions she was too afraid to put into writing. Did carrying a child hurt as much as Cristobel said? Had Amy and Wyling received any news from Tavin?

At the fresh ache in her chest, Gemma dropped the letter. It had been a few months since he'd gone back to London, but his face was clear in her memory.

With a loud sigh, Cristobel entered the morning room and sank into the coral-pink armchair by the fire. "September is too premature for this chill. Why is there no fire laid?"

"I was comfortable without it, but I shall ring for one, if you like." Gemma rose and pulled the bell.

Cristobel scrutinized the remnants of Gemma's light repast and a pair of letters lying on the table. "News from Portugal?"

She nodded. "Shall I read Amy's letter to you?"

"For certain." Cristobel huddled under her shawl in the padded chair. While a footman coaxed a fire from the logs, Gemma read Amy's letter, smiling as she reread Wyling's diplomatic endeavors and Amy's preparations for the baby. "It sounds as if Amy and Wyling's adventure is off to a wondrous start."

"That is all?" Cristobel pulled her paisley shawl tighter over her shoulders. "Has she found a reliable physician to deliver the babe?"

"She does not say, but I am certain she will attend to the matter."

Cristobel grimaced. "What is that other letter?"

"It is from my friend, Frances Fennelwick."

"The one who drones on about tiles and pottery shards?" Cristobel sniffed, either from the chill or in disapproval of Frances's studious pursuits.

Assume it is the cold weather and not a spirit of judgment. "Would you like me to read Frances's letter to you, as well? She invites me to visit her in Kent, where she and her father are studying a Roman mosaic."

Not that she would accept. Gemma had made her choice. She would stay here to care for the boys and wait on the Lord.

"I have no interest in hearing about that lady digging in the dirt." Cristobel held her hands to the growing flames.

Grant me more patience, Lord. "The boys would love it."

"The boys have worn me to a sliver today with all their stomping." Cristobel rubbed her forehead. "I do not know how I manage."

Gemma had been part of the stomping, too. They'd played as horses this morning, racing about the nursery. "While they rest, you may enjoy the quiet."

"Once they go to school, it will be quiet at every hour. Will it not be wonderful? Peter has made inquiries, and Petey will be accepted early."

Nausea stirred in Gemma's stomach. "But he is so young."

"You indulge the children so, but you are not a parent. You do not understand what is in their best interests."

Gemma rose, willing herself to composure. She dragged her gaze over the floral wallpaper, the unlit sconces and the landscape of Verity Hill hanging over the mantel. Then, when she had calmed, she stared at her sister-in-law.

"Petey and Eddie are not my children. Nevertheless, I disagree with you. Sending Petey away at such a tender age will do naught but harm him."

Cristobel's eyes flashed. "I did not ask your opinion."

"No, but I pray you will consider it." Gemma tipped her head. "If you have no need of me, I shall take a constitutional."

Cristobel waved her hand.

In her bedchamber, Gemma leaned against the window, glancing out at the familiar scene. Gray skies shrouded the soggy grass and thinning oak branches, their yellowing leaves laden with mist. The cold windowpane nipped her fingertips, so she donned her heaviest cloak. She hadn't worn it in months, not since spring.

She could wear it again. No one would mistake her for a smuggler today.

The cherry wool smelled of lavender, but within moments, Gemma's nostrils filled with the scents of damp earth and decaying leaves as she hiked to the edge of the New Forest. Mud sucked at her boots and a pleasant ache strained the muscles in her legs. Soon, she emerged from the trees and mounted the slope of Verity Hill.

She had not walked this way since the Sovereign. But now it felt right, as if the Lord held her hand and walked beside her.

At length, she stood at the crest. Gusts of cool wind caressed her cheeks and ruffled the folds of her red cloak. A thrill of excitement shot through her that didn't fade while she stayed atop, enjoying the view, before slowly marching back down the hill.

Reaching the grassy park surrounding Verity House, she stomped her feet so as not to trail mud through the house—

"Aunt Gemma!"

At Petey's shout, her gaze shot to the drive. Both boys jumped up and down beside a blood bay held by one of Peter's grooms. A yellow landau pulled by four matched grays turned onto the drive. Gemma frowned, unable to recognize the conveyance.

Cristobel would take her to task, greeting guests with a dew-soaked hem. She brushed a clump of mud from her cloak.

But no one exited the carriage. The driver paused, spoke with their groom and drove the carriage around the side of the house toward the outbuildings.

Had Peter purchased a new landau? It was a fine one. The horses were high steppers, too, and would make a grand addition to his stable.

"Aunt Gemma!" Petey called again. "Hurry!"

The front doors opened. Peter exited the house alongside a broad-shouldered gentleman donned in a bottle-green coat and fawn pantaloons. Gemma's breath caught in her throat. If only Peter's guest wore black, he would look just like—

"Mr. Knox!" Eddie screamed, no doubt giving Cristobel a headache. "Mr. Knox has come!"

After all this time. And wearing *green*.

"Did you hear us?" Eddie ran toward her. "Mr. Knox says we may ride Raghnall."

"Has he now?" Her voice was breathy, though not from her hike. Tavin walked toward her.

"As soon as Raghnall is rested." Eddie grinned.

"Me first. I am the oldest." Petey puffed out his chest.

"Unfair." Eddie screwed up his fists and then caught Gemma's eye. His gaze lowered to his tiny boots. "We will take turns like gentlemen."

"Well done." Gemma laid her hands on the boys' heads. Her precious boys. Would they be devastated when Tavin left again?

She would be.

He stopped before her, his dimple deep as he smiled.

The green of his coat flattered his coloring. Sweeping his beaver hat from his earth-colored curls, he bowed low. "Good afternoon."

She dipped her knees. "Good afternoon."

Eddie bounced around him. "We've waited for you. Forever and ever."

It certainly seemed just that.

"I am glad I came at this minute, especially now that I see what your aunt is wearing." His smile for the boys widened when it landed on Gemma. "You did not burn the cloak."

"Of course not. It is a perfectly good garment."

"And becoming." His eyes twinkled. "Like a charming... tomato."

The boys giggled. Gemma's brows lifted in mock horror. "Why not a rose? Or a cherry?"

"I am not a man of poetry, you may recall."

She recalled everything.

Tavin laid a hand on the boys' heads and ruffled their fair hair. "Your father has invited me to stay for a time. I hope that is satisfactory."

"Huzzah!" Eddie bounced higher.

"We will ride Raghnall later." Tavin smiled. "And I wish to learn everything you have done since you returned home."

"We found toads—"

"And brought them in to Nellie."

"—and they gave her the fright of her frail li'l life, she said."

"They hopped all over the nursery. Took us almost an hour to find the last."

"Aunt Gem found it. She puckered her lips like this." Petey pulled a face.

Tavin laughed. "Did she?"

She sighed. "I do not care for toads."

"You were brave to pick it up, then." His eyes smoldered, sending shivers down her limbs. "Boys, I must speak to your aunt. I've heard Cook prepared that cake you like."

They ran for the house. Peter had gone, and so had the groom and Raghnall.

"Is that your landau?" Heat flushed her cheeks. She had not seen him in months, and she asked him *that*?

"Yes. I rode ahead on Raghnall, but I have need of a carriage for where I am going next."

Gemma stared at his gleaming Hessians, formed of soft brown leather instead of black. His entire wardrobe shone with rich color. What else had changed?

Not his beguiling smile. "May I walk with you? Or would you rather sit, since you've been out?"

"Why not both? To the garden?"

"To the garden." He offered his arm. She laid her hand on his sleeve and joined in the familiar rhythm of walking on his arm. He smelled of horse and travel and wood, comforting and stirring at the same time.

All the garden blooms had begun to fade, but the greenery was neat and trimmed, creating an inviting retreat. Not that Tavin seemed to notice. His gaze fixed on hers as he led her to a bench among Mama's rosebushes and sat beside her.

"I suppose you heard, but Garner's trial was swift, and his justice equally so." With an absent motion, he adjusted his neck cloth. "His followers were routed. Beauchamp will be transported to Australia."

Gemma had heard as much from Peter. "Is that why you came? To assure us Garner is no danger to us or the Crown anymore?"

"Yes. No. I mean to say, I wanted to tell you about Garner. But that is not all." His Adam's apple jerked against his precise neck cloth. "You know why I left."

"You had a task to finish." *You did not love me.*

"There was much to do at the Board of Customs. I ceased being a clandestine agent and transitioned into a more visible, and vocal, role." He smiled. "However, the Royal Navy's blockades have quelled smuggling ships with great success. Free traders still do their work, but it has grown more difficult for them."

He had come all this way to tell her *that*? He might instead have sent a clipping from the newspaper. "I have prayed your work will not be as burdensome as before."

"I have almost worked myself out of a job." His eyes twinkled. "So I have changed positions again. I am now a consultant for the Customs Office."

"Congratulations." Was that the correct thing to say?

"Instead, congratulate me on my recent purchases. The landau. And a herd of Highland cattle. Beautiful, furry beasts. Red. One of my favorite colors."

"Cattle?" Surely he jested. "You did no such thing."

"I did. They roam the land I purchased in Perthshire." He took her hand in both of his and breathed deeply. "I may be a consultant, but I will no longer draw pay or serve in London. I am going home. To Scotland. It is time I try to reconcile with my brother."

She squeezed his hand. "I think it wise. Even if Hamish will not see you, you will have tried."

"Thanks to you." He removed his gloves and took her chin in his thumb and forefinger. His fingers were warm on her face. "It is all thanks to you. Even my coat. I donned myself in mourning clothes for six years. I grieved my behavior, my sins, my past, and I wanted my mourning apparent to the world. I did not deserve to be free from my past, or so I thought. You reminded me I was set free.

You taught me to forgive myself. So here I am, with a new heart, wearing a new coat."

"It is fetching." Did he read the joy in her eyes?

"You like it?"

"I do." *I do, I do.*

His gaze fixed on her lips even as his hand fell from her cheek. "Since leaving you, I thought of you and the boys at first light and midnight and every minute in between. You helped set my heart free, Gemma. And now I am free from the things that bound me to London."

Her breath caught in her throat.

"From the first moment I saw you, I thought you too good for that dandy Beauchamp. Actually, I wanted to boot him from your brother's house. And when I saw you with the boys, my heart broke for all I had lacked and all the love in your heart. I was concerned for you, maddened by you, beguiled by you. But I could not begin to think of you as a part of my life." His gaze bored into hers. "Somewhere along the muddy way, though, I knew panic. Fear. I was more concerned with your well-being than finding the Sovereign. Something awoke in me, which frightened me. And I knew I had started to love you."

Her stomach swooped. He— "You did?"

"You would not have guessed from my terrible proposal, would you?" He shook his head. "I was petrified. I could not tell you how much I loved you. I emphasized Wyling's insistence that I propose because of the servants, which—"

He broke off, his brows furrowing. "Has there been trouble for you in that regard? Talk of me in your chamber that night?"

"No. Amy bade the housekeeper set them straight and there was naught a word, but…you didn't propose out of duty?"

His head shook. "But how could I tell you that, when

you deserved so much better than me? When you needed stability for the boys' sake? They are a part of you. I would never ask you to change that. Although I had come to care for you, I could not give you what you and the boys needed. Nor could I change what I did for the Crown. All I could do was offer my name and protection, since I couldn't yet offer you my heart."

Gemma's stomach swooped. "Yet?"

"I am here because I love you, Gemma."

She hadn't known she'd started smiling. Grinning, like an idiot. "But why didn't you tell me during the fire? When we thought all was lost?"

"Had I told you then, you would not have left, would you?"

Her head dipped. "I did not leave, anyway."

His hand touched her face again. His thumb brushed her lips, sending a surge of joy trembling through her. "You did not leave, because you love me, too."

"With all my heart, I love you, Tavin."

His arm went around her. Drew her close. Slowly, slowly, he bent toward her. His lips touched her jaw. Then lifted to her cheekbone. Then the corner of her mouth. At last his lips met hers.

So *this* was what it was like.

It was nothing like the boys' soft, wet kisses. Nor was it like the slimy force of Mr. Scarcliff's lips. Neither was it like Tavin's previous kiss, which had been brief. This kiss of Tavin's did not stop.

His lips molded hers with intoxicating, gentle pressure as his hand cradled her face. Good thing she was seated. Her knees melted like wax.

He kissed her until she had no breath, until the wind rippled her cherry cloak about her ankles. Then, after pressing one last, lingering kiss on her lips, he pulled back.

"Please marry me, Gemma. These last few months have been wretched. We do not have to stay in Scotland after I make amends with Hamish, not if you don't wish to. I will go anywhere with you. This past three-quarters of an hour I've spoken with Peter, and I do not think he will retract his permission as long as we make haste before Cristobel bemoans her fate."

"You asked Peter?" Gemma's heart ratcheted.

"Of course. I asked Wyling, too. I will even ask the boys."

"The boys." Her smile fell. "Oh, Tavin. I cannot leave them."

"That is the best part." He stroked her cheek and smiled. "Peter thinks it a capital idea for the boys to join us in Scotland—as part of their education, and far less expensive than boarding school. And I offered to hire the finest tutor available and promised to see they're molded into fine gentlemen. I have a feeling their stay with us will be quite extensive."

"You asked for the boys?" Tears streamed down her cheeks and onto her smiling lips. "For me?"

"For me, too. I love the lads."

"Yes. Oh, yes!" Gemma popped up and kissed him.

Much later, when their hands and cheeks were chapped from the autumn wind, Tavin took her hand and led her to the house.

"I forgot to tell you of a *second*-best part."

"Better than the boys? Would could it be?"

"We will need to do some building on the land I purchased."

"There is no house?"

"Oh, there is a house. A cozy one, too. But I wish to rebuild the castle."

Her boots became rooted to the flagstone. "Castle?"

"Castle." He tucked a stray tendril of hair behind her ear. "Most of it is in ruins, but one can still climb the northern turret. I thought reconstructing it might be an enjoyable project for us and the boys. What do you say?"

She leaned into his blue-coated chest and grinned. She had tried to construct her future for so long, just as Tavin had tried to earn redemption from his past. God had something better in mind for both of them—a present where He could be relied upon to work out His will.

"A husband, my nephews *and* a castle. Oh, let us be married at once."

"Tomorrow wouldn't be too soon." His brow arched, and a hot blush burned her cheeks.

She kissed his chin. And then his jaw. And then he claimed her lips and kissed her until the light changed and a soft rain dampened their colorful cloaks.

"Shall we tell the boys?" he asked, his voice breathless.

"Oh, yes." Nothing else would have made her move from this spot.

Hand in hand, they entered the warm house, eager to begin the most wondrous adventure of all.

Epilogue

Perthshire, Scotland
November, 1817

That little rapscallion!

Gemma Knox curved her hand around her mouth to shout. "Petey Lyfeld, get down from that wall this instant! 'Tis far too high."

Her call carried over the upended blocks of the castle ruins and stopped her nephew short. The stone wall on which he clambered was higher than the height of a man. Petey spun on his toe and scrambled back to the shorter section, and with a gap-toothed grin, he leaped onto the grassy remains of the castle keep.

"Me next." Eddie hurried to climb the shorter wall, his smiling cheeks gleaming rose like ripe apples.

"That's as high as you may climb, boys." But Gemma couldn't blame them for their enthusiasm. Since arriving in Perth last night, they'd been eager to explore the castle ruins on the property. Gemma wouldn't have dared deny them the opportunity today, despite the bitter autumn wind biting her cheeks and whipping her red cloak about her legs. Not even the presence of guests deterred them, especially when their visitors were as eager to explore the castle ruins as Petey and Eddie were.

Tavin's five-year-old nephew, Flora and Hamish's son, Archie, beckoned Petey to the wall. "Let's leap together, cousin!"

Two more tiny ginger-haired tots pulled Eddie's arms with cries of "this way, cousin!"

Gemma's hands clasped over her heart. Petey and Eddie had *cousins* now. Not just Wyling and Amy's tiny son, David, whose early but safe delivery in Portugal had been met with great rejoicing among the Knox family when they learned of it before starting their trip north. Now Petey and Eddie had Flora and Hamish's three bairns as "cousins," too. Perhaps not by blood, but the children didn't concern themselves with such matters. Petey and Eddie had taken quickly to little Archie, Mary and Augusta.

The children's swift acceptance of one another helped thaw things betwixt Tavin and Hamish, too. The reunion of the Knox brothers an hour ago in the drawing room of the cozy home down the hill was awkward at first, but both Tavin and Hamish addressed one another with humility. And then, embraces and apologies.

The pretty, ginger-headed woman beside Gemma, Hamish's wife, Flora, nudged her shoulder, looking past the children over the gorse-covered green. "If anyone is more excited about the ruins than the children, it is our husbands. Look at them."

She couldn't *stop* looking at Tavin, despite having been married to the man for four weeks. Handsome in a dark blue coat and fawn pantaloons, he and fair-haired Hamish stood several yards distant, their heads bent over plans for the new castle hall. It would be a grand room in a grand castle, as rich in modern conveniences as it would be in historic charm. A place where they could return after sharing adventures.

Lifting his head from the plans, Tavin looked up at her. A saucy grin split his features.

A blush heated Gemma's cheeks. What was he thinking, looking at her like that in front of everyone—

"Archie and Mary, there is room enough for two on that stone." With an apologetic look, Flora strode to the children bickering over a block.

Tavin ambled to Gemma's side, grinning. "You are blushing as red as your cloak, my love."

"You're incorrigible, Tavin."

"So I have been told." The wind whipped the cherry-red tails of her bonnet ribbons into her cheek, and he brushed them aside, letting his fingers trail the length of the ribbons in a manner that bespoke a promise. "Are you having a good day?"

"How could I not? This is our new home. You and Hamish are not only speaking, but friendly. Flora is lovely, and the children are ecstatic." While Peter's and Cristobel's lack of interest in their sons still grieved Gemma, her primary emotion was relief, tempered with gratitude that Peter and Cristobel had relinquished the boys into their care for the foreseeable future. "Peter and Cristobel think we do them a favor by keeping the boys, but it is I who am blessed."

"I still cannot fathom it. They are ours." Tavin shook his head. "And you are mine."

"Have I told you of late that you are the best of husbands?"

"You may like me even better when I tell you that this spring we may venture to Tuscany."

She must have looked astonished, because he frowned. "Or Athens. Anywhere you'd like to go. I want to give you adventures."

"I do not need to go anywhere else. I have more adventure than I ever dreamed, right here in Perthshire."

It was true. She had new family. Castle ruins to rebuild, and the deep green loch and high tor in the distance that reminded her of Verity Hill. A cozy manor house down the hill with a nursery large enough for Petey, Eddie and a baby or two, when and if God chose to bless her and Tavin. And, of course, Tavin himself, who looked at her now with such tenderness it was all she could do not to kiss him here and now, in front of the children.

She peeked. They were all busy. Even Flora and Hamish were occupied, studying Tavin's plans for the castle. So Gemma hopped to her toes and kissed her husband's cheek. "I have all I need, Tavin. But if you want to go to Tuscany, or Athens—"

"I want to be wherever you and the boys are." He kissed her cold nose. "You are my heart, and I'll spend my life proving to you how happy you've made me."

Eddie barreled into them, inserting his body between theirs. "I want cake."

"Me, too." Petey patted her leg. "Did you bring some in the hamper, Aunt Gem? Oh, I say, is something in your eye? You are tearing."

She swiped her eyes and smiled down at them. "Sometimes, one sheds a tear or two when one is so happy."

"That makes no sense." Eddie shook his head.

Tavin lifted the boys and spun them in turn, and Gemma breathed a prayer of thanks.

"Come, family," her husband said. "Let us share cake with our cousins and celebrate."

"Celebrate what?" Petey scrunched his brow.

"Our blessings and the adventures of the coming years," Gemma said, smiling up at her husband. "I cannot wait to see where God leads us."

* * * * *

*If you enjoyed this Regency romance, look for
A PRACTICAL PARTNERSHIP by Lily George
and A HASTY BETROTHAL by Jessica Nelson
from Love Inspired Historical.*

Dear Reader,

Thank you for choosing *The Reluctant Guardian*. I hope you enjoyed spending time with Tavin and Gemma in Regency-era Britain.

There is no record of the Board of Customs ever employing undercover operatives like Tavin (although you and I know the truth!), but the "Lady in Red" mentioned in the story was a real person. In the early 1800s, a young woman named Lovey Warne assisted her family's illegal smuggling endeavors by climbing Vereley Hill in Hampshire to look out for revenue men. If she saw any, she'd signal her brothers below to stay away by donning a red cloak.

It's hard to believe smugglers were so bold as to carry out their illicit trade in broad daylight, but the historical account of a fellow named Warner claims a caravan of over twenty wagons hauled smuggled goods from Christchurch into the New Forest during the day, guarded by over two hundred horsemen! A solitary revenue agent on patrol stood no chance against such an army, day or night.

Should you pass through Hampshire today, you can visit Vereley Hill (quite similar to Gemma's Verity Hill) and stand in Lovey Warne's footsteps. Perhaps you can even imagine Gemma in her red cloak, arm in arm with Tavin, as they enjoy the view and keep a careful eye on Petey and Eddie, who are getting into all kinds of mischief.

I love hearing from readers, and if you'd like to say hello, please drop by my website, www.susannedietze.com, or my Facebook page, SusanneDietzeBooks.

May the Lord bless you and keep you!
Susanne

COMING NEXT MONTH FROM
Love Inspired® Historical

Available March 7, 2017

PONY EXPRESS MAIL-ORDER BRIDE
Saddles and Spurs • by Rhonda Gibson

Needing a home and a husband to help her raise her orphaned nephews, Bella Wilson heads to Wyoming in response to a mail-order bride ad. But when she discovers that Philip Young, her pony express rider groom-to-be, didn't place the ad, she must convince him to marry her for the sake of the children.

A TEMPORARY FAMILY
Prairie Courtships • by Sherri Shackelford

Stagecoach-stop station agent Nolan West's best chance to protect Tilly Hargreaves and her three nieces from the outlaws threatening his town is by pretending Tilly is his wife. And soon his temporary family is chipping away at his guarded heart.

HER MOTHERHOOD WISH
by Keli Gwyn

When Callie Hunt and Chip Evans discover two orphans and become their caregivers, neither is ready for a relationship. But can the children draw Callie and Chip together and convince them to put their plans aside and become a family?

FRONTIER AGREEMENT
by Shannon Farrington

When she goes to live with her Native American mother's tribe after her father's death, Claire Manette is told she must find a husband, but she wishes to marry for love. Is there a chance she can find it in the marriage of convenience Lewis and Clark Expedition member Pierre Lafayette offers?

LOOK FOR THESE AND OTHER LOVE INSPIRED BOOKS WHEREVER BOOKS ARE SOLD, INCLUDING MOST BOOKSTORES, SUPERMARKETS, DISCOUNT STORES AND DRUGSTORES.

LIHCNM0217

SPECIAL EXCERPT FROM

Love Inspired HISTORICAL

Needing a home and a husband to help her raise her orphaned nephews, Bella Wilson heads to Wyoming in response to a mail-order-bride ad. But when she discovers that Philip Young, her pony express rider groom-to-be, didn't place the ad, she must convince him to marry her for the sake of the children.

Read on for a sneak preview of
PONY EXPRESS MAIL-ORDER BRIDE,
by *Rhonda Gibson*,
available March 2017 from Love Inspired Historical!

"I'm your mail-order bride."

"What?" Philip wished he could cover the shock in his voice, but he couldn't.

"I answered your advertisement for a mail-order bride." Bella's cheeks flushed and her gaze darted to the little boys on the couch.

Philip didn't know what to think. She didn't appear to be lying, but he hadn't placed an ad for marriage in any newspaper. "I have no idea what you are talking about. I didn't place a mail-order-bride ad in any newspaper."

She frowned and stood. "Hold on a moment." Bella dug in her bag and handed him a small piece of newspaper.

His gaze fell upon the writing.

November 1860

Wanted: Wife as soon as possible. Must be willing to live at a pony express relay station. Must be between the ages of eighteen to twenty-five. Looks are not important. Write to: Philip Young, Dove Creek, Wyoming, Pony Express Relay Station.

Philip looked up at her. He hadn't placed the ad, but he had a sinking feeling he knew who did. "Did you send a letter to this address?"

Bella shook her head. "No, I didn't have the extra money to spare for postage. I just hoped I'd make it to Dove Creek before another woman. I did, didn't I?"

"Well, since this is the first I've heard of the advertisement—" he shook the paper in his hand "—I'd say your chances of being first are good. But this is dated back in November and it is now January so I'm curious as to what took you so long to get here."

"Well, I didn't actually see the advertisement until a few weeks ago. My sister and her husband had recently passed and I was going through their belongings when I stumbled upon the paper. Your ad leaped out at me as if it was from God." Once more she looked to the two boys playing on the couch.

Philip's gaze moved to the boys, too. "Are they your boys?"

"They are now."

Sadness flooded her eyes. Since she'd just mentioned her sister's death, Philip didn't think it was too much of a stretch to assume that the boys had belonged to Bella's sister. "They are your nephews?"

"Yes. I'm all the family they have left. The oldest boy is Caleb and the younger Mark." Her soulful eyes met his. "And you are our last hope to stay together."

Don't miss
PONY EXPRESS MAIL-ORDER BRIDE
by Rhonda Gibson, available March 2017 wherever
Love Inspired® Historical books
and ebooks are sold.

www.LoveInspired.com

Copyright © 2017 by Rhonda Gibson